## "They'll be back, won't they?"

"Right about now," Simon said as he gently urged her behind a bush.

Merry thought that if she survived this trip to the nation's capital and anyone asked her what sights she'd seen, she'd at least be able to describe the bushes quite well.

She could feel her companion's breath on her neck, warm and comforting, as they both peered into the darkness beyond the streetlight. Whenever he was by her side, the danger seemed less frightening. She was beginning to think that in all the world he was the one person she trusted totally with her life.

Internal musings were immediately eclipsed by external reality. Merry's heart began to race as she caught sight of two figures stealthily moving toward them from across the street. They had already searched her apartment. Now they were coming back for her....

## ABOUT THE AUTHOR

M. J. Rodgers believes a romantic intrigue is for the intelligent reader who enjoys finding out how sensitive and brave heroines triumph over evil as they find their special someone. She thinks Harlequin Intrigue is especially appealing to those readers who are themselves sensitive and brave, living in a world where not all the villains have been vanquished. M.J. lives in the Pacific Northwest.

## Books by M. J. Rodgers

HARLEQUIN INTRIGUE
102–FOR LOVE OR MONEY
128–A TASTE OF DEATH

Don't miss any of our special offers. Write to us at the following address for information on our newest releases.

Harlequin Reader Service
901 Fuhrmann Blvd., P.O. Box 1397, Buffalo, NY 14240
Canadian address: P.O. Box 603,
Fort Erie, Ont. L2A 5X3

# Bloodstone

## M. J. Rodgers

*Harlequin Books*

TORONTO • NEW YORK • LONDON
AMSTERDAM • PARIS • SYDNEY • HAMBURG
STOCKHOLM • ATHENS • TOKYO • MILAN

To Great Aunt Elisabeth,
a lovely, spirited heroine
in her own right.

Harlequin Intrigue edition published June 1990

ISBN 0-373-22140-1

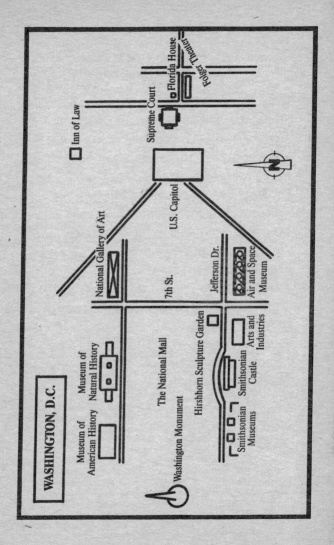

# CAST OF CHARACTERS

*Meredith Anders*—She came to the nation's capital looking for justice. She found murder.

*Simon Temple*—He rescued Merry but if he was a real hero, why wouldn't he talk to the police?

*Karen Richfield*—Merry's law clerk friend... but what wasn't she telling Merry?

*Mike Calder*—He was the police sergeant on the case. Why wouldn't he believe Merry's story?

*Joseph Freedman*—Even Merry's client held back some truths.

*James Tritten*—He was the security guard at the Smithsonian, but why was he so friendly to one of Merry's abductors?

*Laura Osbourne*—Did this senior partner send her younger colleague to Washington for an undisclosed motive?

# *Prologue*

Fire Mountain roared in magnificent, primitive fury, spitting smoke and hot, glowing lava a hundred feet into the air. Its erupting anger soon transformed the December night sky into a daylight brilliance and churned the waters in the Mozambique Channel bloodred.

Simon Temple stared transfixed at the new volcano through the small, ash-cloaked window of his clinic outside the rural coastal town of Massinga, Africa, situated dead center on the Tropic of Capricorn. He could not deny nature's latest offspring was a breathtaking sight, and even after two months of watching it spew up the bowels of the earth, he was still fascinated at its spectacular thunder and force.

Yet Fire Mountain irritated him, too. He hadn't come to Mozambique for the same reason the earth scientists and news reporters from all over the world had so recently invaded its shores. He was a medical research scientist, an epidemic intelligence service officer for the Centers for Disease Control in Atlanta, participating in a medical exchange program with the Mozambique government. His concerns were controlling malaria and rampant TB among the agricultural villages.

However, those other scientists and reporters were making his work very difficult.

First there was the French scientist who brought with him an infectious case of mumps. Nearly a quarter of the villagers had come down with it. The small clinic had been instantly overcrowded with makeshift beds to accommodate the infected. He and Mabunda, a Mozambique doctor, were up day and night for nearly two weeks nursing the sick back to health.

But their troubles had just started. Two Japanese news photographers had gotten too close to the hot rocks of the flowing
lava and had received some very painful second-degree burns
on their feet. No sooner had they been treated, bandaged and
sent home than a German scientist collapsed from a severe
heart attack. For two days Simon had fought to keep him alive
as arrangements were made to send him back to Germany for
open-heart surgery.

And now this latest victim had staggered into the clinic that
evening, an English geologist suffering from a high fever,
vomiting and delirium. His wallet identified him as David
Carmichael, a forty-year-old Londoner. His thinning hair and
emaciated state made him look more like sixty.

Mabunda had drawn a blood sample from Carmichael and
driven into the city to get it analyzed. Simon had stayed behind with the patient, giving him frequent sponge baths with
cool water to keep his temperature down and even trying some
chloramphenicol in case his disease turned out to be typhoid.
As the hours pressed on, however, Simon could see the man was
losing his battle with the mysterious illness he had contracted.
A taste of helplessness was on Simon's tongue as he leaned over
the cot, studying the bright burning head lying back against the
pale pillow case.

The fevered glaze clouding the sick man's eyes seemed to
clear for a moment as he looked up at Simon. David Carmichael's forehead puckered in a frown and he reached his hand
quickly to his side, exhaling in some relief to apparently find
whatever it was he was looking for there.

He stared at Simon, his voice a breathy croak. "Where am
I?"

"A clinic on the outskirts of Massinga. You stumbled in here
about three hours ago. I'm Dr. Simon Temple. How do you
feel?"

Carmichael was having difficulty keeping his weak and wa-
tery eyes focused. "Bloody awful."

"How long have you been ill?"

Carmichael coughed and then gasped for air as though his
lungs were overburdened. "Two, three weeks, I think. It came
on gradually at first, a creeping kind of weakness and nausea,
and then the vomiting and diarrhea started. Flu, of course. Had

a spot of it few years ago in London. Thought I'd be right as rain in a week or so, but I can't seem to shake it. Guess I should've popped in here sooner.''

His talking brought on more coughing. Simon handed him some tissues to wipe away the spots of blood. It was the only moisture left in his fever-racked body. The man stared in horror at the red flecks. Then for the first time he saw the other used, blood-stained tissues in a paper sack on the floor next to his cot.

Carmichael stiffened and turned fear-filled eyes back to Simon. ''I'm not going to make it, am I, old chap?''

Simon tried to keep his voice encouraging as he laid probing fingers on Carmichael's neck. ''Of course you will. As you said, probably just got a bad case of flu. How long have you been in Mozambique?''

''A bit over a month.''

''Have you noticed your lymph nodes this swollen the whole time?''

''Can't remember.''

''Where exactly have you been in Mozambique?''

''Mostly at a pitched tent on the beach near the Fire Mountain volcano. I've been collecting samples of new lava flow to take back to London for further analysis.''

''Have you come in contact with anyone who was sick?'' Simon asked.

Carmichael shook his head.

''Do you feel pain when you cough?''

''And when I don't cough. My hair's coming out in clumps. Feel so damn weak. What kind of a bloody flu is this?''

Carmichael went into another coughing fit as Simon replaced the covers around his patient. ''Honestly, I don't know. I've sent a sample of your blood to the lab for analysis. We should have the results by morning.''

Carmichael's face looked very much like the erupting Fire Mountain—lava red with the black shadows of death on its periphery. ''Might'n it be too late by morning?'' he asked.

Simon knew he could not let the man give up. He grasped his hand firmly. ''As soon as we know what kind of a bug or virus you've caught, we'll be able to treat it. All you have to do is hang on. You're a scientist so you can't be a quitter. Surely you're curious enough to want to stay around to find out?''

Carmichael's smile was weak. "Good show, doc, but it's no use. I think I'd better say my peace while I still have the breath. You seem like a decent sort, the kind who would do a dying chap a favor.''

Simon saw the pleading look in his patient's weak eyes and nodded. "If I can, of course I will.''

Carmichael stared at Simon's face for a moment and then he reached into a hidden pocket inside his shirt, the same place he had checked immediately upon wakening, and pulled out a small, shiny black metal box. It seemed to take all his strength to open it and take a large, white stone from its dark interior. He held the stone up to Simon with a shaking hand.

The white stone's edges were opaque and rough, but one small surface had been worn smooth and flat. As Simon looked into it he saw a beautiful burst of white light with a glow of dazzling red at its center. His breath caught at the hauntingly spectacular heart of what otherwise looked like an ordinary chunk of rock.

"It's a diamond?'' he asked.

Carmichael's colorless lips drew into a smile as his strength gave way and his hand and the stone dropped to his side. It took a moment for him to get enough breath to speak again. His words came out strained.

"The most fabulous diamond of all time, as yet unrecorded by the history books, formed in the Precambrian rocks beneath Fire Mountain, thrown up from the bowels of the earth to land at my feet. I found it while gathering fresh lava the second day I was here. Still warm to the touch it was.''

Carmichael was interrupted by a new bout of coughing, but Simon saw the determined fight the man was making to regain his breath. He was eager to tell his story now that he had started. His fingers fumbled to replace the diamond in its protective, shiny black box. He lay back, exhausted.

"I have no family. My whole life has been spent in pursuit of some momentous geological find that would put my name in the history books. All folly, of course. All I've been is a nobody. Until I found this diamond.

"I knew right away that it would be my legacy to the world. The money it could bring is unimportant, you understand. I'm not one of those men mad for wealth. But I do want the credit for having found this beauty, even if I don't live to read about it in the journals. Will you take the diamond? Will you see that my name shows as its discoverer?"

Simon nodded as he dipped a fresh towel into a chipped ceramic basin of cool water and bathed Carmichael's burning face. "I'll do as you ask if it becomes necessary, but rest easy now and concentrate on getting well. You can do it. Just think about how good you will feel when you stand before your colleagues as the proud finder and owner of this spectacular diamond."

Carmichael's eyelids had closed. His voice was barely audible. "Jolly good, that," he said before drifting once more into unconsciousness.

Simon took his patient's pulse and blood pressure and as he recorded them on the man's chart, a small noise caught his attention. He looked up to see Mabunda standing in the doorway, his large dark eyes locked in an intense stare.

"I didn't hear you come in. Will the lab be able to send a car around tomorrow with the results of Carmichael's tests?"

Mabunda nodded his dark head. "Yes," he said, but Simon could see that the blood-test results were now of no interest to his colleague. He wondered briefly how long Mabunda had been standing in the doorway and how much he had overheard.

"You get some rest, Simon," Mabunda said. "I will watch the patient through the night."

Simon nodded and got to his feet, taking a moment to stretch his cramped muscles. "We'll take turns. No reason for you to lose all the sleep. Wake me in about four hours."

Mabunda mumbled something and Simon left for his small sleeping tent, adjacent to the clinic's thick, mud-packed walls. Fire Mountain grumbled and glowed on the eastern horizon of the hot, muggy night as Simon adjusted his makeshift mosquito net and eased his weary bones onto his hard cot. After a succession of many long days and short nights, he was exhausted.

Sleep came soon, too quickly. He would ask himself many times in the years following what would have changed had he stayed awake on that fateful night beneath the fabulous Fire Mountain volcano.

# Chapter One

Meredith Anders stood transfixed before the spectacular new Fire Diamond display at the Smithsonian Museum of Natural History in the nation's capital. Out of the corner of her eye, she saw the shape of a man come to lean up against the display case next to her, but her real attention was focused directly ahead on the fabulous Fire Diamond.

"One of the fairest stars in all the heaven," she said, taking license with the words of Shakespeare's Romeo.

The man said nothing. Merry reminded herself that few people understood or even recognized Shakespeare anymore. She decided she'd best share her enthusiasm with more colloquial expressions.

"It's so fantastic, it doesn't even look real." The man still did not reply. Merry thought she understood. Sometimes looking at such beauty took even her breath away. Of course, nothing ever kept her quiet for long.

"I can see why some experts want to establish a new color classification for it. Look how it glows red in contrast to the set of Master Stones they've placed around it. It says here that those are carefully selected stones from each official color grade. See how they lose their sparkle when compared to this red diamond? It's certainly like nothing I've ever seen before—so many surfaces, facets, reflections."

The man next to Merry seemed to move a little closer, but still said nothing. She was sure of his interest, however, and had no qualms about carrying the conversation for the both of them.

"When the experts examined its color, they graded its outward edges Exceptional White, a standard high-grade color, while its inner heart is brilliant red, an extremely rare color in a diamond. The more I study it, the more I realize why it's called the Fire Diamond. Looking into this fabulous gem is like looking into liquid red fire dancing in the light. Don't you think so?'' she said as she finally turned toward him.

All visions of the diamond faded as Merry was immediately struck by the odd look on the man's heavy, beet-red face. His dark eyes bulged from the pink rims around their sockets. She could see his thick lips were open, as though he was trying to say something, but no sounds were coming out, only a drippy stream of saliva. Then his eyes rolled back into his head and, with a forward lunge, he collapsed against Merry.

It all happened so fast that she had no time to think, no time to move away. She let out a cry as they went down together in a heap, the strap of her purse falling away from her shoulder. The shock of her back suddenly coming into contact with the thick, hard carpet forced the breath from her body.

Blackness flashed before her eyes. For an instant, she felt no pain, just a smothering nothingness. Then, as though the shutter had reopened on a camera lens, consciousness returned.

Consciousness, but not sight. She was blind! In astonishment and horror, Merry realized she was pinned to the floor beneath the large man's unconscious weight. His dark coat jacket was draped over her face, blocking out all light and air. His clothing reeked of cigarette smoke.

She felt herself choking from the stale tobacco odor; however, she knew she had even worse things to worry about.

She couldn't get her head out from under the suffocating blanket of his body and clothes. His uncompromising weight pressed her into the rough carpet, scratchy threads of which were already pricking the back of her neck and digging into the sensitive skin of her cheek.

A growing panic shot through her body as wild thoughts jumped inside her head. If she didn't do something soon, she might suffocate, die beneath this man! She strove hard to steady her thoughts, to concentrate on her options. Did she have any?

She strained to find any physical mobility. The large bulk of the man on top of her was substantial and covered most of her much smaller frame. As she tried diligently to move arms and legs, she found her right arm was unencumbered from the elbow to her hand.

Some hope pumped her into action as she used her free arm to pull and tug at his body, trying to push him off her. After a moment or two of struggle she knew it was no use. His weight on the upper portion of her arm robbed her of both leverage and strength and her exertion seemed to have freed the precious little breath that hadn't already been squeezed from her caved-in lungs.

Panic returned.

"Help! Somebody help!" The volume in her breathless voice could only have qualified her for auditions as Minnie Mouse.

"Check the pockets, quick!" a muffled voice said somewhere to Merry's right.

A voice? People were there! She was going to be freed!

The man on top of her was jostled around. Merry felt one of the bones in her neck crack as the weight above her was shifted. The scratchy carpet dug farther into her cheek. What did these people think they were doing? Couldn't they see she was under the man?

"Under here! Help!" she said. At least she thought the words. Had they been audible?

"It's no use," a voice said from somewhere. "Maybe the purse?"

"No, I checked already. Someone can come in any minute. We've got to get out of here. Get the woman."

Get the woman? What were these people talking about? Merry didn't have much time for conjecture. In indescribable relief, she suddenly felt the terrible weight rolled off her. Light and air rushed at her face. She drank them in greedily, thinking she now knew what it was like to be dough under a rolling pin.

She opened her eyes and concentrated on breathing deeply. Before she had time to do much of anything else, strong hands clasped her on both arms and dragged her to her feet. Pain was registering somewhere in her brain, but she was so happy to be free, she ignored it.

She looked at the two men in business suits who flanked her sides. One was quite short, round and dark, the other tall, very muscular and blond. Her next words gushed out to them between several quick breaths.

"Thank you. You have no idea how awful that was! I couldn't move! I couldn't breathe! That poor man! He collapsed right before my eyes! We'll need to get an ambulance right away."

However, Merry's words were not being heeded. The strong hands gripping both of her arms had begun to lead her forcibly through the snaking corridor toward the exit of the Gem and Mineral Room.

Something was wrong. Very wrong. She looked at the faces of the men on either side of her. Their expressions were anxious, determined, even angry. She couldn't understand what was driving their actions, why they helped her only to treat her so roughly.

"Who are you? Where are you taking me? What is going on? If this is *Candid Camera*, I'm *not* smiling!" she said.

"Shut up, lady. You'll live longer." It was the short, dark, man on her right who had given the warning. Nothing remotely helpful or friendly projected in his raspy voice.

A flash of fear jolted Merry. She tried to turn, to yank her arms away from the men, but she was held fast. They kept close to her sides, walking quickly and determinedly.

She looked around desperately for help, but saw no one. She had rushed into the Museum of National History when the doors had opened at ten. The other visitors obviously hadn't made it up to the second-floor gem display. At the moment she was on her own.

She looked again at the two men who had quickly turned from saviors to captors. She was becoming afraid, and when Merry was afraid, she talked.

"I demand to know who you are and what this is all about! What can you possibly think you're doing? You're supposed to be helping that man back there. He may be dying! You have no right to be treating me this way. Are you crazy? Let go of me!"

Her comments were mostly directed to the tall man on her left, as though she hoped for a better response from him than his companion had shown. But his thick, heavy jaw clenched shut; his small, light eyes continued to stare straight ahead. The other man dug his hands into Merry's arm and the pain shot up her shoulder. Any doubts she had about the intentions of the two people who had her in tow vanished. They meant her harm. She had to get away.

She stopped walking and became an instant dead weight. She screamed and began recklessly to kick at the heels of the two men on either side. Her determined attempts to hit ankle bone elicited a smattering of cursing. But the damage apparently wasn't enough because the pace of the two men picked up again as they resorted to dragging her uncooperative body along.

"Quick. Get her into the elevator," the shorter one said.

She screamed again, as loudly as she could, hoping to pierce their nearby eardrums, if nothing else. When a hand came up to her mouth to silence her, she sunk her teeth into the leathery palm as far as she could. It was quickly ripped out of her mouth with a loud curse. For a moment, Merry thought her two front teeth might have followed. But the sudden pain stabbing through them assured her they remained in her gums. She screamed again and kicked out.

Miraculously, one of them suddenly let her arm go. She didn't further question her good fortune, but immediately faced the other who still held onto her left arm. She kicked and scratched, aiming the nails of her free hand at his face and screaming as loudly as she could into his ear.

He howled back as her nails dug into the flesh of his cheek. Then, something pushed her body hard from behind. She paused in her assault to turn to see her other assailant wrestling with a third man. Someone had come to her aid!

Her relief was short-lived. The stocky man had recovered from her recent assault. She looked back to see his left arm poised to hit her. Ducking just in time, she went on the attack with renewed vigor, kicking and scratching and screaming furiously.

She was losing, of course. He grabbed hold of both her hands and concentrated on pulling her toward him. In the panic of a cornered animal, she screamed again and kicked out as hard as she could.

The force of her kick caused her to lose her balance and fall. The next thing she knew, she had landed fanny first on the floor, her legs crisscrossed beneath her. For once she felt thankful that that particular end of her anatomy was amply padded. But how could she have fallen while the man had been pulling her toward him? It took her a second more to realize that incredibly, her attacker had let her go.

He was standing in front of her now, staring over her head, a look of disbelief on his pinched face. From the corner of her eye, Merry could see the taller blond man running away, toward a back staircase.

She followed her captor's stare, turning to see the man who had come to her aid. He was thirtyish, at least six three and muscularly built, his dark hair and tan contrasting sharply with the white in his long-sleeve pullover shirt. Everything about his well-built frame stood powerful and threatening. Her rescuer's large fists were raised menacingly.

A primitive jolt of excitement shot through Merry as she looked up at this powerful ally. Any normal civilized aloofness vanished as she felt instantly and intimately bonded to this handsome stranger, her protector against these men of evil intent.

The stranger's very blue eyes flickered toward her and then back to the short man. Facing his adversary, the stranger's look froze into a stare so fierce and cold that Merry was doubly happy he was on her side. When she turned back to look at her remaining assailant, he had already turned and was running away.

Still not quite believing her miraculous rescue, she followed his movements as he darted down the back staircase his companion had taken a moment before.

Almost instantly, Merry heard a slight noise to her right and turned to see the uniformed figure of a guard coming quickly forward from another passageway. She waved. He nodded at her as he walked up, reaching a hand out to help her to her feet. She took his offered hand and slowly raised herself, trying to detect if she had anything broken. Apparently everything was intact, although her muscles felt somewhat battered and numb.

"What's going on here? Were you the one screaming?" he asked.

"Yes. Thank you for helping me up."

Merry had tried to keep her voice civil, despite the guard's snarling tone and the deep scowl that seemed to employ all the muscles in his small face. He was looking her over as though he wasn't impressed with her appearance, either.

"Well, lady? What's going on? You look like you've been in a fight."

Merry looked down at her beige blouse. She had lost a couple of buttons and the thin belt of her matching slacks had been severed. It hung loosely through the only still-intact belt loop at her waist.

She could imagine how her hair must look. A couple of unruly, blond curls were bobbing in front of her nose. She raised an unsteady hand to smooth them back into place as she nodded in response to the guard's question.

"A fight? Yes, I'll say. I was being attacked. Two men were trying to take me forcibly out of the museum."

The guard's face wore a startled expression. "Attacked? Two men? What two men?" He looked quickly around.

"It's no use looking for them. They ran off down those stairs. This man fought them, scared them away," Merry said as she turned to point behind her. But as she did, she noticed to her surprise that no one was there. She stared in disbelief.

"What man?" the guard said.

"He was here just a moment ago. I don't know where he went, maybe back to the display case in front of the Fire Diamond. Another man is back there. He collapsed on top of me. I think he's badly hurt or sick or maybe even... Come, you must see."

Merry led the way back to the Fire Diamond. When she and the guard arrived, however, just the large man who had collapsed on her was there. The man who had come to her rescue was nowhere to be seen.

The guard bent over the fallen man as Merry stood watching. He put his ear on the man's chest. Merry looked away toward the adjoining corridor that led into the Fine China area. Where had her rescuer gone?

"I can't hear a heartbeat. He's not breathing."

Without hesitation, the guard performed what to Merry looked like a creditable attempt at cardiopulmonary resuscitation. But after several minutes, the guard gave up on trying to revive the man and shook his head.

"No response. He's a goner."

"Dead?" Merry said as she leaned unsteadily against the display case. She swallowed down her queasiness and closed her eyes against a wave of cold that seemed to be washing over her. She heard the guard saying something and opened her eyes to see him talking into the radio-transmitter unit he had unclipped from his belt.

Then the guard came to stand in front of her. He was a short, square man, with excessive dishwater-blond hair and slanted gray eyes. His long nose and chin seemed to be heading for a collision course. His colorless lips parted suspiciously.

"Perhaps you'd best give me your name and explain what's going on here."

Before Merry could respond, she heard a voice from behind her echo the guard's words. "What's going on here?"

She turned, hoping she would see her rescuer again, but looking at yet another new face.

"Who are you?" the guard beside her said to the man walking up.

The newcomer moved with the assurance of a predator, a predator who had the good grooming and dress to have just walked off the cover of *Gentleman's Quarterly*.

She guessed him to be somewhere in his thirties, maybe six one. He was impeccably dressed in a light blue suit, impeccable except for his tie chain. Curiously, a link had been severed and the broken end lay limply against his starched shirt. Merry was staring at it as though fascinated by this out-of-place imperfection when he reached into his coat pocket and flashed a badge in front of the guard and her.

"Detective Sergeant Mike Calder, Metropolitan Police Department. A man just halted my car outside saying there was a disturbance in here. Something about a screaming woman. What's this all about?"

"That man is dead," Merry said, pointing to the body on the floor.

Sergeant Calder seemed to become aware of the body in front of the display case for the first time. Merry wondered at the placid expression in his dark brown eyes. How did someone become so used to death? He dipped his compactly-built frame down on one knee, as though he was trying to be careful not to crease his trousers, and felt for a pulse in the stricken man's neck.

"I tried to revive him. It was a no-go," the guard said.

When Sergeant Calder stood up again, he flipped his head back to disengage a dark curl that almost appeared to have purposely been combed onto his forehead. He was a physically attractive man and everything about him said he knew it.

"You guards are well trained in CPR," he said. "I'm sure you did your best."

His arm made an elaborate sweep as he reached into his pocket for what appeared to be a pen and notebook.

"I have a call in for an ambulance," the security guard said.

Sergeant Calder did not look up from his notebook. "Good. Who was the man?" he asked.

"I don't know," Merry said.

Sergeant Calder's eyes moved inquiringly to those of the guard.

The guard shook his head. "I was just about to ask this woman, Sergeant. I heard someone screaming. I found this woman sitting on the floor, around the corner, in front of the Gem and Mineral Room corridor. She told me she had been attacked and then brought me to this man here."

Sergeant Calder's eyes rested on Merry. "If you don't know who he is, how did you know to bring the guard here?"

Merry felt as though somewhere along the line, she had been placed on the defensive. She hurried to explain. After all, as soon as she told them what happened, they would both see she was an innocent victim. She gestured with her hands as she spoke.

"I was looking at the Fire Diamond over there when this man came to stand beside me. I said something to him about how beautiful the diamond was and when he didn't answer me, I turned to look at him. That's when he collapsed on top of me."

"This dead man fell on you?" Sergeant Calder said.

"Right on top of me. I was never so astonished in my entire life. I—"

"Was he still alive?"

"Well, yes, I think he had to have been. Then. He was moving. At first his eyes were open and he seemed to be trying to tell me something. The expression on his face was—"

"Did he say anything to you?"

"No. He didn't speak any words, but there was a kind of desperation in the way—"

"There wasn't anyone else around?"

"No one I saw. Not then at least. However, soon afterward—"

"So this man collapsed against you?" Sergeant Calder said.

Merry nodded, getting used to the Sergeant's interruptions. "I would have gotten out of the way if I had known what was coming, but everything was happening so fast. One moment I was looking at the diamond and the next this man was falling on me."

Sergeant Calder looked down again at the large-boned, heavyset corpse with the round face and sparse head of brown hair. Merry followed his eyes and could almost hear the questions coming into the detective's mind.

"He looks to be over six feet to me. Maybe two hundred pounds. You worked your way out from under him after he fell on top of you?" Sergeant Calder said.

Merry shook her head. "I tried for several minutes, but it was impossible. As you can see, he was a big man and his weight held me down. I thought I was going to suffocate. I tried to yell for help, but my lungs felt caved in. Then I heard two men talking. They seemed to be checking the man's body and then they rolled him off me. Before I could find out what was going on, they tried to drag me out of the building."

"Two men tried to drag you out of the building? Who were they?"

"I had never seen them before in my life."

"Then why were they dragging you?"

"I hate to keep saying this, but I don't know. This has been the strangest thing that's ever happened to me. I heard one of them say something like 'get the woman,' and suddenly there I was being dragged out," Merry said.

"Where are these two men?" Sergeant Calder said.

"They were fought off," Merry said.

An eyebrow, which looked like it had been brushed into place that morning, raised slightly on the Sergeant's forehead.

"Fought off?" he said.

Merry nodded, not missing the doubt in the man's voice.

"At first, I was trying to fight them by myself. I wasn't much of a match for them, of course, but I was kicking and scratching and screaming as best I could under the circumstances. Then suddenly, one of them was being knocked around by a stranger who came to my rescue."

"A stranger? What stranger?" Sergeant Calder asked.

"I don't know who he was! I tell you he was a stranger!"

Merry had begun to feel an uncustomary exasperation. She was used to being believed. Yet the sergeant's voice seemed to be laced with doubt.

"All right. What happened then?" he asked.

"Well, as I said before, this stranger came to my aid. Of course, I was still fighting, but I know it was his presence that upset their plans of taking me out of the building. They ran off."

Suspicion was written all over the sergeant's face. Merry inhaled deeply, as though more air might help her to rise above the frustration of not being believed. She moved her hand almost unconsciously to her right cheek. It had begun to burn.

"Look, no matter what you think, I didn't make this up. It happened exactly as I've told you," she said.

Merry looked over at the security guard noting that after her explanation, his expression seemed more accepting than before. But when she looked back at Sergeant Calder, she was sure he wouldn't be surprised if the men in white suddenly came racing up with the straitjacket for her.

"What's your name?" Calder said.

"Meredith Anders."

"Well, Ms. Anders, I'm going to have to go back out to my car and call this report in." He looked around at the people who were beginning to enter the Mineral portion of the Gem and Mineral Room. He turned to the security guard. "Your name?"

"Tritten, sir. James Tritten."

"Okay, Tritten, I think you'd best get those people out of here and rope off this room until the crime-scene group can have a look."

"Crime scene?" Merry said.

Sergeant Calder turned back to her. "The cause of death for this man is undetermined. Your appearance suggests that at least a struggle did take place here. Until we know for sure what happened, I don't want any evidence disturbed."

He turned back to the security guard. "Close up shop, Tritten. I'll be taking Ms. Anders back to the office with me to get her complete statement. I'll tell my people I've left you in charge. After they've finished, I'd appreciate your coming down to the station to give your statement."

"Yes sir."

The pointed chin of the security guard went heavenward as he stood in front of the much taller police sergeant. Being placed "in charge" had obviously gone to his head. He seemed to grow a couple of inches.

"Are you ready, Ms. Anders?"

Sergeant Calder wasn't really asking her and Merry knew it. She leaned down to pick up her shoulder bag where it had been knocked to the floor. As she swung the strap over her shoulder, she glanced at the fabulous Fire Diamond, splashing out its brilliance beneath the fluorescent lights.

It seemed to suddenly glow brighter, blinking at her as if it were a warning light, flashing danger. She turned away with an effort, trying to shake off the mesmerizing strength of its message. Attempting to display a calm she didn't feel, she followed the sergeant down the corridor she had been dragged only moments before.

SIMON TEMPLE WATCHED the blond woman exit the Smithsonian Museum of Natural History with the man in the blue suit. He didn't know who either of them were, yet, but he was determined to find out. Unfortunately, he had lost track of the two men who had tried to abduct the woman from in front of the Fire Diamond. They had escaped as he had run after them, the tall one into a dark blue Cadillac and the short one into a green-and-gray Subaru.

He was sure he recognized the green-and-gray Subaru and the car being driven by the short man might be his most important find today. If only he hadn't lost it! Well, he wouldn't lose the blond woman.

She was going willingly with this man, so he might be a friend. Simon would follow and see.

This was not the way he had planned to spend his morning, but events had once again intervened to determine his fate. Simon knew he would have to learn the identity of the dead man and how he died. He also had to find out how well the woman knew the man whose corpse she had been pinned beneath. If the man died the way Simon suspected, the danger was great for them all.

Despite the gravity of the situation, Simon smiled as he remembered the warm look in the translucent-brown eyes of the blond woman as she stared at him from where she had fallen on the floor of the Museum of Natural History.

There was something alert and vibrant about her that enhanced her natural attractiveness. Her fierce struggle with her much larger and stronger would-be abductors showed a zest and fight for freedom that appealed to him. He had followed death so long, her contrasting exuberance for life was enticing.

Still, her fate might be sealed now that she had become involved with the Bloodstone. Was she to be its next victim?

## Chapter Two

Sergeant Calder drove Merry to the station in his unmarked, dark maroon, Ford. It smelled of his cologne. Merry didn't find the odor itself unpleasant, but it seemed to be a bit overpowering in the closed vehicle.

It was going to be a muggy day. She wasn't used to the humidity that folded over her skin like a light blanket. Fortunately, it must have been getting to the sergeant, too, because he turned on the air conditioning.

"Thank you," she said. He didn't answer.

As she looked down at her hands resting on the vinyl seat, she realized she was shaking. Reaction, no doubt. Having a dead man fall on her wasn't exactly a daily occurrence and neither was fighting off abductors. Although far from cold, she felt a sudden shiver.

She clutched the seat, as though the action might help her to get a grip on herself. Then, she reverted to her old standby of circumventing fear and uncertainty and nearly everything else. She talked.

"This is a wonderful city, so much to see and do. Everywhere there's something incredible to experience. I was at the Lincoln Memorial this morning watching the sunrise. Its columns were like rainbows shimmering in the early-morning light. When I think of all the famous people who have stood there before me, well it's almost intoxicating. It must be wonderful living amidst the excitement of history makers, both past and present."

Sergeant Calder hadn't said anything in response to her comment. Still, even if her companion didn't feel much like talking, she did. Talking always helped her to relieve tension.

"There's so much to do here. Even if I had a month to spend on sight-seeing, I don't think I'd be able to take it all in."

"When did you get here?" Sergeant Calder asked.

"Early this morning. I took the red-eye last night from Seattle. Hardly slept on the plane, so I suppose I should be tired, but this is such an invigorating city, I haven't wanted to miss things by going to sleep on my first day here. When you're not at work, you must find yourself in all the great museums."

Sergeant Calder frowned. "Not on your life. I wouldn't dream of going into one of those musty and damp old relics. They're always filled with you tourists."

His tone wasn't particularly pleasant. For all his impeccable appearance, Merry was getting the feeling he wasn't much of a gentleman.

"But they're so close. How could you miss even one opportunity to see what's happening at the White House, the Capitol, the Smithsonian Museums?"

"They're not so close. My apartment is in Rockville, Maryland. When my work day is up, the first thing I think of is getting out of this congested mess and back to the sanity of the suburbs. Only time you'll ever find me hanging around one of the tourist traps is when I get an official call, like now."

The sergeant looked at Merry as if she were a criminal. It seemed so ludicrous, she smiled back. "I wasn't after the Hope Diamond—or the Fire Diamond, for that matter. I haven't even robbed a bank this week."

Merry's attempt at levity was met with a scowl. She shrugged off his ungracious response. Before she could think of another way to try to approach this difficult man, he pulled the car diagonally into a parking space in front of a large, concrete building with an etched sign proclaiming it to be the Municipal Center with the number three hundred beneath it. She wasn't sure what street she was on, but it had been a short trip.

They got out of the car and walked up the wide, concrete steps. As the tension returned, so did her voice. "Have you been a policeman long?"

Calder looked at her as though she was passing him a silent message. He almost smiled. "Nine years."

He opened the glass door on the right-hand side to the entry and preceded her into the building. A uniformed guard on their immediate right nodded in recognition at Sergeant Calder as they walked up to the bank of elevators. They stepped through and he pressed the third floor button.

"Do you enjoy your work?" Merry asked.

The sergeant looked at her as though he was a hawk watching a white field mouse trying to hide behind a brown bush. "Don't try to come on to me with this feigned interest approach. I've been at this business too long to be taken in."

Merry couldn't believe her ears. "Come on to you?"

"The innocent act doesn't wash with me, either. I spent a couple of years in vice and learned all the tricks. In case you've forgotten, I'm the policeman here and you're the suspect. I'll ask the questions and you'll provide the answers."

Merry bit down the answer she wanted to provide to Sergeant Calder at that moment. It took all of her restraint to keep her voice calm.

"You're calling me a suspect? A suspect in what?"

"A suspect in an unexplained death," Calder said.

Merry was having trouble taking this unpleasant sergeant's last comment calmly. "Well, it won't be unexplained soon," Merry said. "The man obviously died of some kind of a heart attack. I'll never forget the awful look on his deep-red face. He was obviously in pain, having a terrible time breathing."

The elevator had stopped and Sergeant Calder led the way out and to the right between the polished stone that partially lined the walls of a long hallway. Merry almost reached a hand out to touch the sandy-colored marble. It looked so cool and reflective above the softly-waxed, granite-colored floor.

Sergeant Calder's tone dripped with disparaging amusement. "So the guy died of a heart attack? What do you think you are, some kind of doctor?"

He straightened his already straight tie and seemed to notice for the first time that his tie chain was broken. That brought an instant scowl to his face.

Merry tried to remind herself that truly confident people did not have to go around defending their opinions. Reasonable opinions spoke for themselves. Unfortunately, she just could never give up an opportunity to speak her mind.

She heard the defensive tone of her voice. "I don't have to have a medical degree to see when someone is having trouble breathing."

"No, just an overactive imagination," Calder said.

His dismissal of her words felt like a slap. She was having trouble understanding why he was treating her so discourteously. Did he really think she might have caused the man's death in the Smithsonian?

They turned right down another hallway and Merry looked up in some shock at the word Homicide on the plaque over Room 3032 as the Sergeant entered. She stopped and stared, the sudden weightiness of her involvement in an unexplained death registering like a swallowed but undigested elephant inside her.

Calder looked over his shoulder at where she hesitated in the hallway. "Waiting for a formal invitation?"

Merry tried to hide her uneasiness. The last thing she wanted to do was to let this insensitive man know how uncomfortable and off-balanced she felt by her recent experience. She lifted her head and marched past him, trying to bluff a confidence she did not feel at all.

She stopped at the front desk. The crowded office was filled with small, littered tables and a noisy air-conditioning unit rumbling away beneath the partially-raised venetian blinds at the window. A tired-looking desk sergeant was speaking on an old, black, multi-button phone. He put one caller on hold as another line rang through.

She surrendered her purse to the desk sergeant and while waiting for a receipt, glanced at the Metropolitan Police Department's bulletin board, which announced that year-to-date, two hundred and forty-six homicides had been committed and only one hundred and twenty-seven of them had been solved. Somehow she wasn't comforted by the fact that one hundred and nineteen murderers were still apparently on the loose.

Sergeant Calder led her to a back room. It was a tiny soundproofed area with just enough space for a small metal desk with a simulated woodgrain Formica top, a manual typewriter and two uncomfortable-looking chairs. Calder pointed to the orange-vinyl seat of the metal chair beside the desk.

"Take a seat. I have some telephoning and checking to do. I'll be back in a couple of minutes."

He left, closing the door. Merry was glad she wasn't claustrophobic. She had seen closets bigger than this interview room. Time passed slowly. Her right cheek was still feeling sore, but at least the burning sensation had ceased.

She concentrated on looking at the abstract painting that hung on the narrow wall. Could it possibly be some kind of fruit?

Finally the door opened and Calder came in. He sat down and put a multi-carboned form in the manual typewriter. Merry caught a quick look at the heading: Metropolitan Police Department—Washington, D.C.—Complaint/Witness Statement.

She was a witness in an unexplained death. Strange how, despite her innocence, she still felt a guilty nervousness. It was as though being involved in an unexplained death, no matter how innocently, had somehow cast aspersions on her character. She tried to refocus her mind to allow her thoughts to rebalance.

She noticed Sergeant Calder had removed his broken tie chain and replaced it with a small, gold tie clip. He was obviously very conscious of his appearance. Too bad he didn't spend as much time on improving his personality. His cologne began to permeate the small amount of air. She knew that it wouldn't be long before it became unpleasant.

"Full name?" he asked.

"Meredith Jean Anders."

Calder's fingers approached the typewriter keys in what Merry had always called the Bible method—Seek and Ye Shall Find.

"Address?"

"Here or home?" Merry asked.

The Sergeant looked irritated. Merry thought she certainly had the more cause for irritation, but for once she kept her thoughts to herself. She just wanted to get this unpleasantness over with and get on with her life.

"Let's start with here," he said.

"Best Western Downtown Corp Hill Inn. It's on Third Street. Room 306."

"Telephone?"

"I don't know. The Yellow Pages should have it."

Sergeant Calder swatted the manual metal carriage return irritably to skip that space on his form. He seemed easily upset. "And where's home?" he asked.

"Washington State. 3401 Seaview Lane. Bainbridge Island."

"And you're vacationing in D.C.?"

"I'm arguing a case before the Supreme Court on Monday."

Sergeant Calder looked up from his typewriter keys. Disbelief grew in his eyes as he surveyed her. Merry sat up straighter on the uncomfortable vinyl seat, which had begun to stick to her slacks. She tried to imagine what Calder was seeing as he looked at her. Unconsciously, she smoothed back the still-unruly blond curls that she hadn't had an opportunity to reposition beneath the barrette at the back of her head.

Even at five foot seven, she knew her small bones, her casual clothes and her disheveled appearance couldn't be presenting a very imposing figure. Calder's look confirmed her assessment.

"I suppose you can prove this?" he said.

Merry exhaled, only realizing at that moment that she had been holding her breath. "If you check in my bag, you'll find a number of business cards embossed with the name of my law office and address on Bainbridge Island."

Calder frowned as he continued to stare at her. Merry felt the need to elaborate.

"I'm a junior partner in the firm of Osbourne and Anders. Our case before the Supreme Court is being made on behalf of the Freedman Diamond Company. You can check the Court document for the case number. It will be under *Freedman Diamonds* versus *The State of Washington*. It's slated as the second case Monday."

"You represent a diamond company? What is this case about?"

"The firm I represent is being taxed unfairly on the sale of its diamonds within Washington State. Freedman Diamonds has no office or personnel in Washington, but when it makes a sale to a resident of the state, an authorized representative of the company naturally flies out to deliver the jewel."

"Naturally?"

"These are very expensive diamonds, Sergeant. You can hardly send them by UPS. Washington State claims the delivery of a diamond by a company representative constitutes a physical presence for tax purposes. We believe Washington State Law is in violation of the Equal Protection Law of the U.S. Constitution because it discriminates against out-of-state diamond businesses in favor of local businesses."

The Sergeant's look was disappointed. Apparently he had to believe her, even though it was obvious he still didn't want to. "So why are you here two days beforehand?"

"To sight-see, just like any tourist. This is my first time in the nation's capital."

"What drew you to the Natural History Museum?"

"The diamond collection. Specifically, the one called the Fire Diamond. I've always had a fascination for diamonds. I heard about the controversy over the classification of the new red gem that was donated recently and I wanted to see it."

Calder was somehow disturbed by her explanation. He hadn't typed anything additional on his form for several minutes. Was he still disbelieving her story? He shook his head irritably.

"All right. Start from the moment you entered the museum and tell me everything that happened," he said.

Merry launched into her story without hesitation. Calder stopped her on several occasions to caution her to slow down. Still, he seemed to be typing out only one of her every fifty spoken words. He asked no additional questions about the physical appearance of her two attackers, but he did seem inquisitive about the stranger who had come to her aid. Perhaps it was because she had not volunteered his description.

"How old was he?"

"Somewhere between thirty and thirty-five."

"How tall?"

"Six foot two or three I think. Muscular build."

"Hair?"

"Dark. Straight. Well cut. His complexion seemed more tanned than naturally dark."

"Eyes?"

"Very blue."

"Very blue? What does that mean?" Calder said.

"Well, some people have blue eyes, but you have to look twice to really be able to tell, because as you know, light eyes can sometimes be shades of gray or green. But this man's eyes, well, you didn't have to look twice to tell they were blue."

Calder shrugged. "Clothing?"

"Dark slacks. White pullover cotton shirt. Frankly, I don't see why you need this kind of detail on the stranger. After all, he wasn't one of the men who attacked me."

Calder's dark eyes refocused on her face as he leaned his arms over the typewriter carriage. "You could have gotten roughed up by wrestling with the dead man. If you struggled with him, you could have been the cause of his death."

Neither Merry's voice nor look wavered. "I could have, but I didn't and I wasn't."

Sergeant Calder was the first to look away. He shrugged. "If your story is true, if there really were two men trying to abduct you, what makes you so sure this third man was coming to your aid?"

Merry looked at Sergeant Calder as though he was some escapee from an institution. "I don't understand your statement. I told you. He fought with my abductors, causing them both to run away. His intervention saved me from being physically dragged from the museum."

Calder seemed to be enjoying Merry's unhidden agitation. "Perhaps his only interest was in revenge against the two men. Perhaps he killed the dead man and the other men were the dead man's friends."

"The dead man was killed?" Merry said.

Calder's wooden chair creaked as he rebalanced his weight.

"We don't know yet. I spoke to the crime-scene people a few minutes ago. They found no outward signs of violence. We'll have to wait for the medical examiner to perform an autopsy. But if it's murder, then I think you'll agree the motives of this stranger will have to be more closely examined."

Merry shook her head, refusing to accept Calder's suspicion. She wanted to believe the stranger had come to her aid. She wanted to believe that men still existed who would put themselves on the line for another human being in trouble.

The sergeant's negative attitude and the cologne-saturated air were making Merry queasy. She longed to be on her way. "Is there anything else you need from me?"

Sergeant Calder made an elaborate business of disengaging the official report form from the tenacious jaws of the manual typewriter's black rollers. "Read and sign this," he said.

Merry picked up the typed statement, finding only a skeleton description of what she had told the sergeant. She tried to tell herself that she was being too critical, that the legalese she was used to dealing with had corrupted her into being only truly satisfied with thorough redundancies. Her argument with herself was interrupted by Sergeant Calder's next statement.

"NCIC has nothing on you, but the computers are down this weekend in Seattle."

Merry wondered what language this law officer had begun to speak. "What is NCIC? And what does computers being down in Seattle have to do with me?"

Calder looked irritated again. "Don't tell me you're a lawyer and you don't know that NCIC is the FBI's computer network? You can't think I'm that naive."

Merry gripped the metal arms of her uncomfortable chair. "Naive, no, but presumptuous, yes. My field is corporate law, Sergeant. I represent companies, not individuals. In my line, I don't get involved with public-enemy-number-one."

Calder smirked. "How do you know?"

Merry thought she'd best let that one pass. "If these Seattle computers represent another criminal identification network, what have they got to do with me?"

"Standard procedure, Ms. Anders. They'll tell me if you're wanted for anything in Washington State. What did you think I was checking? To see if you had won the state lottery?"

Merry quickly signed the incomplete statement Calder had typed and stood up. She decided she had had enough of this particular policeman for a lifetime. "If you'll excuse me, Sergeant, I have some sight-seeing still to do."

Merry stepped to the door and turned the knob. Sergeant Calder's hand came out of nowhere to press against the door, keeping her from opening it. His voice cut into her ear like a slippery butter knife.

"One day autopsies will be done by computer and we'll get them in an hour instead of a day. Since the law only gives me three hours in which to either charge or release you, I have no choice but to let you go. But don't go far, Ms. Anders. I want to know if your local address or number changes. Is that clear?"

It was no longer just the smell of the man's cologne that made Merry sick. She wondered fleetingly what the charge would be for throwing up all over a detective sergeant. She was almost ready to risk it, except reason reminded her that the act would only prolong the time she would have to spend around the man. It was enough to restrain her.

Her next words came out through clenched teeth. "What is clear is your complete lack of intelligence or manners, Sergeant. Now remove your hand from this door so I may leave."

Calder leaned away from the door and she yanked it open. "I'll escort you to the front desk where you can pick up your purse, Ms. Anders. If you don't want a ride back to the Smithsonian, you can take a cab. It won't hurt my feelings."

Merry stepped out into the comparatively clean-smelling air of the larger room. She inhaled thankfully, trying to will away the unnatural flush making its way beneath her skin.

Sergeant Calder was obviously as glad to get rid of her as she was to go. The officer at the desk downstairs called a taxi at her request and fortunately it arrived in just a few minutes. As she proceeded down the front steps to reach it, however, she paused and turned. She had the funny feeling she was being watched.

The only person in sight was a man standing near a large, concrete planter to the right. His back was to her, his pantleg resting against the circular rim of the planter as his dark head bent into the pages of a newspaper. She thought there was something familiar about him, but she couldn't be sure because of the considerable distance between them and his averted face.

She got into the taxi and directed the driver to take her to her hotel. She had walked to the monuments and Smithsonian that morning. They were only a few blocks from where she was staying, and, with the difficult parking situation in D.C., she hadn't wanted to be fettered with a vehicle.

As the taxi passed the street names on the corner, she realized she could have even walked to her hotel from the police station. It was probably better to take the taxi. Her legs were definitely feeling a little wobbly.

She sat back into the cushions of the cab seat and reached into her purse for her compact. Its mirror showed the reason for the continuing discomfort of her cheek. A circular patch of scraped skin glowed red like raw meat. Her small, first-aid travel kit back at the hotel had an antiseptic cream. She just hoped she had enough makeup to cover the wound until it healed.

While she was still looking into the compact's mirror, she suddenly caught a reflection of a man carrying a newspaper and hurrying to get into an older gray Mercedes parked in front of the police station. A couple of blocks later, Merry became sure of her suspicion. She was being followed. A shot of fear squirted inside her. Who could it be?

"I'll give you a ten-dollar tip if you speed up and lose that gray Mercedes following us," she said to the large lady who was her driver.

The driver's dark eyes filled the rearview mirror. "Ten dollar tip? Fare's only gonna be a few bucks."

Merry looked behind her again to see the gray Mercedes turn the corner. Her hands had begun to shake unreasonably. "Please. I don't want him following me to my hotel."

The driver's lips disappeared in back of a big, toothy smile. "You having man problems, honey? Not to worry. I knows all the angles. You see, the trick ain't to try to outrun these men folk. That gray Mercedes back there can catch this ole crate any day. But we can outfox him."

"How?" Merry asked.

"Well, we're gonna pretend to do what he expects. Pretend, mind you, cause just when he thinks he's got you, we're gonna pitch that batter a curve."

The driver's voice was warm and assured. It was extremely comforting to Merry's nervous state.

"I'm in your hands," she said. "What do I do?"

"He's expecting you to make for a hotel, ain't he?"

"Yes. I guess."

"Then, we'll go to a hotel, all right, but one where you ain't staying. One with those circular-type, drive-in entries where he ain't gonna be able to see you getting out. I knows just the place."

"Is it close by?" Merry said.

Her driver shook her large head. "Nope, several blocks in the other direction. Which is okay on account you don't want that rascal anywhere you are really going. And we're gonna drive nice and slow so he don't know we even suspect he's behind us."

"I see. I won't really be getting out at this circular drive hotel?"

The driver nodded, sending her short dark curls bouncing.

"That's the play, honey. Now, when I tell you, you slump down back there and stay low. I'll drive round the circle, stop, then drive out like I've let you off. And when I'm sure he ain't following, I'm gonna take you where you really want to go."

It was so simple, Merry thought it just might work. They drove along at a decorous pace, as though oblivious to the car matching every move behind them. Merry stared straight ahead, not daring to look back. She was just about to ask her driver when they would be there, when she volunteered the information.

"This one is where we stop. I'm turning in. Get ready."

A busload of tourists had gathered along the curved driveway of the hotel the cab driver had selected, further blocking the view of anyone trying to see the entrance from a distance. The taxi pulled in front of the bus and stopped.

"Now get down!" her driver said.

Merry hunched down on the floor of the back seat without additional prompting. She was crouched there when suddenly the door to the taxi was opened by a red-uniformed doorman of the hotel. He stared down at Merry in stone-faced astonishment.

Merry looked up, her smile a bit sheepish. "Sorry," she said. "I've changed my mind. Too many, uh, tourists here."

"Yes, madam," the doorman said. "Few residents of the city seem to require the use of our facilities." His face didn't crack a smile nor did he move away from his very dignified stance in front of the car door.

Merry couldn't restrain the chuckle gurgling in her throat.

"We gotta be moving along," Merry's driver said.

Merry crawled over to the still open door being held by the nonplussed doorman and leaned over to catch the handle with her outstretched fingers. Still trying to smile her apology, she slammed the door shut again.

"Okay, let's go!" she said as she resumed her resting spot on the floor. As they drove off, Merry couldn't help but think that she'd like to go back to that hotel someday just to meet that doorman again. People undaunted by life's madness always fascinated her.

After several blocks, Merry's driver announced they had lost the gray Mercedes. Merry got up thankfully and sat back on the seat, stretching her legs out of their cramped position. She smiled at her driver's face in the rearview mirror.

"You're great! Have you been doing this kind of work long?"

"If you means dodging men folk, I's been doing that my whole life long! But if you mean driving a cab, just about a year. We're here at your hotel, honey."

Merry got out and handed her driver twenty dollars over the recorded fare on her meter. "I'm Merry Anders," she said holding out her hand.

Her driver smiled broadly as one of her warm, chubby hands shook Merry's energetically. "Jackie Thomas. Who was that man scaring you so?"

Merry shook her head. "I'm not really sure. But I didn't think this was the time for us to get acquainted."

Jackie Thomas chuckled. "You take care now, honey. Be seeing you."

Merry smiled as she watched the taxi drive away. But she frowned as she entered her hotel, wondering at Jackie's very pertinent question. Who was the man in the gray Mercedes? Had Sergeant Calder arranged for her to be followed? Or had her follower been one of the two men who grabbed her in the Smithsonian?

SIMON TEMPLE PICKED UP the telephone book in the battered and soiled booth, irritated with himself for having lost the blond woman. The desk clerk at the hotel had sworn no one by her description had checked in, despite the cab's stop there. He was going to have to check with the cab company's dispatcher for the real destination. It was fortunate he had taken down the cab's number.

He mustn't lose track of her. He also had to find time to get over to the medical examiner's office and try to talk his way in to examine the corpse. The sooner he found out the cause of death, the sooner he'd know whether she was in danger or not. He'd have to also follow up on the two men, of course. But right now the woman concerned him most. She had had the closest contact.

He tried to put the disturbing thought of her contagion out of his mind. He had no time for personal feelings. He had a mission beyond the significance of any single life, despite what anyone said or who ended up firing him.

Still, as he remembered the look in her eyes and the sunny cast to her hair, picturing her dying the way the others had was becoming more and more unthinkable.

## Chapter Three

Sergeant Calder walked past the prominently displayed lettering, Office of the Chief Medical Examiner, and through the glass doors of the salmon-colored building.

Several hallway turns later and he was standing in front of a short, round man whose inability to grow hair on his absolutely bald head seemed to be more than compensated for by the bushy black-and-gray beard completely covering his jaw and chin.

"So, you're taking a personal interest in this one, Mike?" the medical examiner asked.

"Not exactly, Don," Calder said. "But it looks as though my prime witness isn't expecting to stay in town long. I'd like to know if I really have a murder on my hands. You've done the autopsy?"

Don was nodding his head as he removed the surgical gloves from his hands. "It's murder all right. Although, this is the first time in my twenty-five years I've seen the likes of this kind of weapon. Wait a minute. Let me show you."

Don walked away to retrieve something from a tray and returned to the waiting sergeant.

"Put out your hand, palm up," Don said.

Sergeant Calder complied and felt something heavy drop into his palm. He looked down at the shimmering stone, sparks of red and white exploding under the fluorescent light.

"This killed him?" Calder asked.

Don nodded. "Don't be afraid to handle it. I gave it a thorough washing after I got all the tissue samples off. That red you see isn't blood. It's some kind of natural phosphorescence in the diamond. Although, of course, it did have a lot of blood on it. You see, somebody forced that beautiful stone down your John Doe's throat, choking him to death.''

Calder moved the diamond over to the natural light from the window. He took a moment to draw the drapes and open the venetian blinds. Then he repositioned the stone to study it carefully under the full glare of the late-afternoon sun.

"Well, Mike? Is it a real diamond?'' Don asked.

Calder shook his head, turning back toward the room. "Beats me. A gem expert is going to have to have a look. Do me a favor.''

"Like what?'' Don asked.

"Like call the Smithsonian and arrange for a gemologist to examine this stone. I've got to trace this John Doe's finger-prints. Now that I'm sure it's murder, I've got to move fast be-fore my suspect packs her bags and leaves town.''

"*Her* bags?'' Don said as he looked down to undo his stained smock. "I doubt it, Mike. The strength it would have taken to force that stone down the throat of a man the size of your John Doe would have been considerably more than that possessed of the average woman. So unless your woman suspect is close to six feet tall and at least one hundred and seventy-five pounds...''

Calder shook his head as he held up his hands in surrender.

"Okay, okay, I get the picture. Too bad, though. She made a dandy murderer. Oh, well, at least now I can look at the jewel-thief file, that is if you find out this is real,'' Calder said as he handed the red stone back to the medical examiner.

Don turned the beautiful gem over in his hand almost lov-ingly. "I don't know, Mike. If I do find out this baby is real, you might just never see me again.''

Calder's voice was playful. "Hey, careful, Don. I'm a cop, remember?''

"So, I'll cut you in for half,'' the medical examiner said, chuckling at his trip into fantasy. "Neither of our pensions are worth a pittance of what this beauty would fetch. Of course, we'd have to become exiles on some South Sea island with dozens of beautiful women... Hey, maybe that's where the lady comes in.'' The medical examiner's voice had become thoughtful.

"Lady?" Calder asked.

"Yeah. Your lady who can't be the murderer. You might get lucky. She might have been the murderer's accomplice."

Sergeant Calder smiled. "Now there's an angle I hadn't thought of. Thanks, Don."


SIMON PACED OUTSIDE the salmon-colored building, fuming over his boss's refusal to verify his credentials when the medical examiner's office called. For months now, his boss, the chief of medical epidemiology at the CDC, had threatened to have him fired if he didn't stop his "fanatical obsession."

Simon had tried to explain, time and time again, but his boss wouldn't listen. He resented Simon's impromptu vacations that corresponded to new information concerning deaths his boss contended had nothing whatsoever to do with an epidemic. No doubt his boss was smiling now that he had squelched Simon's latest attempt to use his position to get into the autopsy room.

Simon exhaled his frustration as he tried to decide what to do next when he saw the man in the blue suit come out of the glass doors of the office of the chief medical examiner. He crouched behind the gray Mercedes as Calder walked over to the dark maroon Ford and got in.

He recognized Calder as the same man who had taken the blond woman to the police station. Simon had gotten his name from the desk officer after following them there. He wished he could approach the detective, tell him the story and get his help, but he knew he couldn't.

He'd never forget the nightmare of a week he had spent in a Mozambique jail or the two very uncomfortable nights he had paced in a European jail before the authorities reluctantly let him go. Now the metropolitan police homicide department wanted him for questioning regarding the death of the multi-millionaire. And if they picked him up, they might never let him go.

No, he couldn't go to the police. What he had to do, he had to do by himself. It wasn't a particularly comforting thought, but he had become accustomed to it over the last couple of years. As he watched the detective drive away, he rose to his feet refreshing his resolve. He would go pick up his own car and return the loaner and then he would go to the woman's hotel and watch her. At the moment she was his best lead.

MERRY ENTERED Blackstone's Restaurant, located on the first floor of her hotel, and surveyed the people sitting at the pink-and-black decorated tables. Her eyes finally alighted on the bent head of a young woman sitting along a side wall, reading some legal-sized papers. Merry's face broke into a smile as she walked toward her.

"Well if it isn't my favorite ex-sister-in-law!"

Karen Richfield immediately turned in her chair at Merry's unconventional greeting and stood up to embrace her. The smile on her face was wide. "I'm so glad Jack hasn't married anyone you like better yet! God, it's good to see you! It's been almost a year!"

Merry held the thin woman gently, almost as though she was afraid of hurting her. Karen's clothes felt like they were stuffed with feathers. When she leaned back from hugging her, Merry was smiling brightly.

"Here, let's sit down, Karen. You're such a tiny thing I'm always expecting you to faint away. My client should be joining us shortly. Let's get you a big dinner and fatten you up a bit." Merry sat down, waved for the waiter and kept talking.

"I can't tell you enough how much I appreciate your help in preparing the Freedman Diamond case for submission. Your considerable knowledge of the Supreme Court process has made all the difference. But you've obviously been working too hard on it. When you told me you couldn't get here until eight, I got a severe stab of conscience."

Karen shook her head. "It wasn't your case, Merry. Justice Stone had other work—"

"Oh, yes, Stone. The justice you work for. I've heard he's a real taskmaster for you law clerks. Did you even get a vacation after June when the Court supposedly took its break? I doubt it. You've probably been locked up all summer in the Court's law library getting ready for this session.

"Now put your face up to the light. Just what I thought. You're as pale as the white wall in back of you. Maybe you should take up jogging. It'll put a red glow in your cheeks.

"And, speaking of a red glow, I can't wait to tell you what happened today. I had the craziest experience. Visiting museums in this city of yours is not at all safe. Perhaps the Washington, D.C., Chamber of Commerce should put a caution on its literature for tourists. You know, like the one they have on cigarette packages? Something like, 'Warning: Sightseeing in this City May Be Hazardous to Your Health!' "

Merry stopped when she realized her friend was laughing.

"Okay, Ms. Karen Richfield. What's so funny?"

Karen wiped the moisture from her eyes with her dinner napkin. "It's just that you haven't changed a bit. You still talk at sixty-miles-an-hour nonstop. Only one I ever knew who could keep up with you was Jack."

Merry watched Karen's face when she mentioned Jack's name. In some relief, she saw no pain or discomfort. Merry's brother, Jack, and Karen had had a short, intense marriage six years before.

Jack had been married and divorced in a similarly quick fashion four more times since. Merry knew Jack had come through unscathed from each of his marriages, but she had always worried about the first casualty of his flippancy, Karen. Merry's quiet ex-sister-in-law had always been a lot more difficult to read than Merry's outgoing, flamboyant brother.

"Have you heard from him?" Merry asked as she took the menus from the waiter who had just come to the table.

"No," Karen said. "Not since his card announcing his latest divorce. Can you imagine him having special cards made up? He sent me ones for the other three divorces, too. They always arrived just a few months after the wedding invitations."

Merry couldn't help but laugh at the predictable absurdity of her younger brother's actions. Karen joined in.

"I've given up trying to understand or explain him, Karen. All I can say is that Jack believes in progressive polygamy."

Karen's laugh was easy. Merry decided she was in the proper frame of mind to be approached. "I noted the change of address on your letters. Has some handsome man come into your life?"

Karen's laughter died on her lips. Her dark eyes looked enormous in her thin face. "You know I would have told you about a man. Who have you been talking to?"

Merry didn't hesitate. The direct approach had always been her preferred way. "Your stepmother wrote me and said you had moved out of your family's home in Georgetown. She said you were uncommunicative since your father's death. She knew we had stayed in touch when you and Jack divorced. She thought I could tell her what had happened. Of course, I couldn't."

Karen shrugged. "It's no real secret. As soon as Dad died, she took it upon herself to start giving away his things. You understand, Merry, she didn't even ask me! She's too insensitive to even talk to. We can't get along. Let's leave it at that."

Merry shrugged. "Seems simple enough. If you don't like someone, avoid them. That's always been my motto."

Karen looked relieved. "Ever the logical one, huh, Merry? That's what I've admired most about you, I think. You never let your emotions gain the upper hand."

Merry's smile was small. "Don't kid yourself, my friend. Some of my days feel like emotional blood baths full of sound and fury and signifying nothing of redeeming logical value."

Karen smiled. "I see you're still misquoting Shakespeare. Sounded kind of clever, though. And that 'redeeming logical value' part is like the 'redeeming social value' phrase from that famous Supreme Court case on obscenity?"

Merry's nod was eager. "You'll never know how great it is to talk with someone who recognizes both Shakespeare and the law. You're a good friend, Karen. I've missed our conversations. Most of the men I meet can't even tell who I'm misquoting."

Karen laughed easily now. She seemed to have come completely out of her earlier upset over the mention of her stepmother. Merry had hoped her words would have that effect, but she was surprised at Karen's next question.

"You asked me a moment ago about my love life. What's happening to yours these days?"

Merry looked down at the elegant folds of her pale pink table napkin. Her fingers caressed its harsh linen fibers as she spoke. "Nothing to brag about and a sore subject since my birthday a couple of weeks ago."

"Why? Does your age bother you?" Karen asked.

Merry shrugged. "I'd be less than honest if I said it didn't. You see, even Jack at thirty, with all his flippancy and fickleness, has at least found five people he has loved, for however short a period of time. Here I am at thirty-two, and not only haven't I met anyone I really care for, but my list of requirements keeps getting longer—sensitive, intelligent, attractive, logical . . ."

"What about that attractive guy you introduced me to about a year ago? The attorney from California you met jogging? Greg was his name, I think?"

"Yes, Greg. Well, he was logical. He planned our dates only on the weekends he didn't spend with his wife and kids."

Karen looked startled. "Married? You didn't know?"

"Not until he slipped up and used his credit card to buy some theater tickets for us. His wife got curious and hired a private detective. The private detective discovered me."

Merry had paused to take a sip of water.

"What happened?" Karen said, on the edge of her seat.

"Oh, I got a call from his wife one day, must be about nine months ago now. She explained who she was, quite nicely really, all things considered. And I think after a while she even believed me when I said I hadn't known Greg was married."

"Merry! My God, how awful! Were you in love with him?" Karen said. Her tone was tentative, as though she was afraid of opening a wound.

Merry shook her head and smiled. "Not for a minute. And don't look so glum, my friend. The story has a happy ending. When he got home that night and was getting into the shower, his wife whacked him with a vase and sent the bum to the emergency room for twenty-two stitches."

"She did? How did you find out?"

Merry had begun to laugh in remembrance. "Because he called me from the hospital room before the anesthetic took hold. He was mad as hell because he thought I had found out about his duplicity and told her. He kept yelling about how it was my fault he wasn't going to be able to sit down for a week!"

"Oh, so that's where the vase hit him!" Karen said, laughing at the thought.

Merry smiled. "Yes, I guess you could say he got it in the end." Merry's expression sobered. "Still, it was an experience that has added a couple of more requirements to my ever-expanding list for the right man. Forthrightness and honesty are now definite musts. Without them, none of the rest seems to matter.''

Karen nodded in understanding and then seemed to be distracted as her eyes focused in on something behind Merry.

''Isn't that Joseph Freedman, the president of the diamond company you're representing, the one who brought me the legal references to your case brief a week ago?''

Merry looked around to see Joseph Freedman walking toward them. He was a tall, nice-looking, medium-built man in his early forties with light brown hair and eyes, fine features and thin-rimmed glasses. He always walked hesitantly, as though he had to watch out for people waiting to trip him up.

For the president of a major diamond chain, Merry had always thought him to be abnormally withdrawn and shy. He had never been married, his natural shyness and overwhelming concentration on business probably the reason. She waved for him to join them.

''I'm glad you were able to make it, Mr. Freedman,'' Merry said as the man approached. ''You remember Ms. Richfield?''

Joseph Freedman nodded briefly as he adjusted his glasses farther back on the bridge of his perfectly straight nose and sat down in the chair opposite them.

''I do apologize for being late. I was on a very important call and felt it would be awkward to terminate it prematurely.''

Merry smiled at him. ''This is going to work out just fine. We haven't ordered yet and here comes the waiter.''

After their order was taken, Merry once again turned to Karen. ''I need to call my partner, Laura Osbourne, back in Washington tonight. I've held off until we could talk. What does Justice Stone think about our case's chances?''

Karen sipped a bit of her water and picked up a breadstick before answering. Her forehead creased into a slight frown.

''I know this seems like it should be a pretty clear case of whether Mr. Freedman's company is being unjustly treated under Washington State law, but in reality it's become a question of states' rights.''

''You mean the Supreme Court decided to hear the case so it could make some other point?'' Merry said.

Karen shook her head slightly. "No. A possible violation of the Equal Protection Clause was enough to get the case on the calendar. But since the Court has gained so many new conservative members, Justice Stone thinks they may vote against your petition in order to expand the interpretation of states' rights."

"Even when those rights border on the infringement of Federal rights granted by the Constitution?" Merry asked.

Karen sighed. "By focusing on certain elements in your case, the Court may just decide that Federal rights are not violated. It's another step that Stone thinks this new conservative coalition would like to have in the record to strengthen precedent on the states'-rights issue."

Joseph Freedman looked confused. "I don't understand."

Merry turned toward him fully. "What Karen is saying is that there is more here than just a question of whether your company is being unfairly taxed by the State of Washington. Certain members of the Supreme Court want to use your case to make a point of their own, a point that states can make certain laws that conflict with Federal laws and that the Supreme Court of the land will not oppose their doing so."

Freedman sat back in his chair as though it was extremely uncomfortable. "Then, we don't have a chance?" he asked.

Merry smiled at him. "Of course we do. Hidden agenda or not, these Supreme Court justices will listen to what I have to say on your behalf. Don't worry. They've agreed to hear the case and that's a good sign. All I've got to do is sway them to our way of thinking on Monday."

Merry turned to Karen. "Has the news media discussed this states'-rights issue?"

"No. None of the justices on the Court have officially said anything and the *Washington Post* hasn't carried any editorial conjectures in that direction."

Unaware of her own action, Merry shook her head. Karen watched her uneasily.

"I know it's a tough one, Merry. So many of these new justices want controversial issues handled by state law. In their minds, many previous Court interpretations have been too liberal. Their fervor to swing the pendulum back is spilling over into the corporate arena."

Merry smiled at Joseph Freedman. "Don't worry. We'll have our day in court. I'll get through to them."

Karen spoke up with more encouragement than conviction. "I'll be in your rooting section. Monday should be an eventful morning. You've always been good to watch in action."

Her words triggered Merry's memory. "Which reminds me of what I was going to tell you earlier," Merry said. "I had one most eventful morning already in this extraordinary city of yours."

"You mean today?" Joseph Freedman asked.

Merry nodded. "You heard about the new red diamond on display at the Smithsonian, the one called the Fire Diamond? Well, I got intrigued about the controversy over whether it can be classified under an existing color-grading system or be given a new classification of red, so I went to see it this morning."

Merry looked at her companions, expecting their interest and attention but finding herself surprised at their averted heads. Had she been talking too much?

"Look, I'm sorry. I'm cursed with this talkative nature as you both know. You just have to speak up when I start to go overboard or you'll be stuck with the boring consequences."

Karen's face turned back to Merry's, a slight frown fading from her forehead. "Merry, you know it's nothing like that."

When Karen didn't go on to explain further, however, Merry felt a sudden unease she attempted to fill with a little levity. "Then it must have been my soap that failed? Or my roll-on? My mouthwash?"

Karen and Joseph Freedman chuckled politely at Merry's suggestions as the waiter arrived with their salads.

Joseph Freedman finally offered a late and somewhat plausible explanation. "Sorry, Ms. Anders. My mind wandered. Please continue with what you were about to say."

During the commotion of moving the dishes about, Merry decided that maybe it had just been simple attention span that had faltered in her two dinner companions. She plunged forward eagerly.

"Both of you are probably not going to believe what I'm about to tell you, but..."

Between bites of spinach salad, Merry went on to tell her companions of going to see the Fire Diamond, the dead man knocking her down, the attempted abduction, her rescue by the mysterious stranger and the discourteous treatment by Sergeant Mike Calder of the Metropolitan Police.

Joseph Freedman was the first to interrupt with a question. His sounded confused. "Why did this policeman treat you like a criminal?"

Merry raised her hands palms up, as though to assure her listeners the answer was not held in them. "I don't know. All I can think of is he didn't believe my story. I suppose it does sound a little like previews for the *ABC Saturday Mystery*."

"Still, it was obvious you had been hurt," Freedman said. "A real man, a gentleman, would have seen to your injuries."

It had been a nice thing to say. At least, Merry felt good about Joseph Freedman saying it because she had often thought the definition of a real man should include a long paragraph on consideration. But Karen was shaking her head. Merry asked her what was wrong.

"He doesn't sound like much of a law officer to me," Karen said. "You told him you had scratched this guy's face. He should have had a forensic technician remove the skin cells from underneath your nails and have them DNA coded. Then they could have been matched later when he found a suspect."

Both Merry and Joseph turned to the law clerk. Merry was the first one to speak. "Why didn't I think of that?"

Karen's dark eyes shone like two polished coffee beans. "Because your field is corporate law, of course. Had you had to research the criminal side recently as I have for another case on the Supreme Court calendar, you would have suggested it immediately to the doubting Sergeant Calder."

Merry tried to shake away the burden of a lost opportunity. "Well, it's too late now. I took a bath when I got back to the hotel. Unfortunately, all the evidence is now washed away."

It was at that moment that she happened to glance at the man who had just gotten up from a table on the other side of the room. A jolt of sudden recognition propelled her to her feet.

"Correction," she said to her dinner companions. "Not all the evidence has been washed away!" Not taking time to explain, Merry dug into her purse for her American Express card and literally threw it onto the table in her sudden rush.

"What are you doing?" Karen asked.

"I've got to go. Sorry to leave this way. I'll call you later," she said, and was off and running after the fast-disappearing man. She almost collided with the waiter bringing their dinners. A sniff at the broiled salmon made her moan, but she quickly turned away from temptation and dashed after her quarry. She had a bigger fish to catch. She caught up with him at the front door of the restaurant.

"Hey! Wait a minute!"

He stopped and turned abruptly at her call, giving her just enough time to reach him. "I'm so glad I've run into you. I want to thank you for your help this morning."

Merry reached for the man's hand. It felt warm and strong. Contact with that strength brought forth once again that exhilarating feeling she had gotten that morning when she realized this very capable fighter had been on her side. She pumped his hand gingerly.

"If you hadn't come along...well I'm sure you saved my life and I'll be forever grateful. But it was awkward when you took off like you did, because the police—"

Simon removed his hand from Merry's grasp and put it up as if to stop the steady stream of one-way conversation coming from her direction.

"Excuse me, miss, but I'm afraid you've mistaken me for someone else." He turned away from Merry and opened the door to leave the restaurant by the parking lot side.

For an instant Merry stood perfectly still in temporary shock at the message in his words. Could she possibly be wrong? She discounted that absurdity immediately.

"Nonsense, you must remember," she said as she followed him determinedly out the door and down the well-lit concrete steps, flanked by solid, red-brick banisters.

"It was at the Smithsonian's Museum of Natural History this morning, a little after ten. You pulled those two men off me just in front of the Gem and Mineral Room on the second floor. You must remember. I can't imagine it's something you do every day."

Simon turned slightly toward her as he reached the edge of the parking lot. A small accent light barely illuminated his frowning features in the dark, muggy night. Thirsty clouds stretched in the sky overhead like sponges collecting water.

"Look, miss, I don't wish to be rude, but I do have to be on my way. I hope you find your friend. Please excuse me."

Once again Simon turned from Merry and walked quickly away.

As stunned as Merry felt by his continuing denial, she couldn't let him just leave. Not without an explanation. She pushed her shoulders back in determination and readjusted the strap of her purse over the shoulder sleeve of her white cotton dress. Then she hurried to catch up, calling loudly after his retreating figure.

"Now look here. I don't know what the problem is, but I don't intend to let you just walk away from me denying who you are. We both know what you did this morning and your denying it all night isn't going to change the facts. So you might as well stop alleging ignorance and start explaining what's going on."

They had reached Simon's car, a black 928 Porsche. Merry stopped abruptly, bumping into him when he paused to bend over to unlock the door. After he opened the driver's side, he turned to her, his face barely discernible in the deepening shadow.

"What do I have to do to satisfy you? Do you want me to claim to be some guy you met this morning? Will that end this conversation in a pleasant way? Okay, I'm the obliging sort. I'm some guy you met this morning. Now, may I go in peace?"

Merry's jaw locked in unshakable determination. She didn't like being told someone was only humoring her.

"Look, I know I owe you a lot, but what point is there in your pretending not to have helped me? You might as well face it. Technically, you have witnessed a crime. Now all I want is for you to drive down to the police station with me to—"

Merry never got a chance to finish her sentence. Something whizzed by her ear and the next thing she knew the stranger had grabbed her shoulders with both his hands and shoved her through the open driver's door into the Porsche. She landed headfirst in the passenger's seat, her legs sprawled across the gear shift.

"For God's sake! I'm not in this big a hurry! Damn, I realize men seldom open car doors for women anymore, but this is ridiculous!"

"Sorry. No time for formalities," Simon said.

By the time Merry lifted her head, he was behind the wheel and she heard the roar of the engine turning over. She scrambled to get her legs untangled from the gear shift.

"What is it? What are you doing? What's happening?" she asked as she battled to reposition her extremities into the arrangement nature had intended for them.

"We're being shot at," Simon said as he gunned the car into a roaring start and rushed forward at a speed that kept Merry pinned to the back of her bucket seat.

"Shot at? You've got to be kidding!"

At that very moment a bullet shattered the back window of the Porsche as the car made a sharp, left turn onto Third Street, going the wrong way on a one-way street.

"Oh, God, you're not kidding!" Merry said as she fell back into the leather bucket seat, hanging on for dear life.

# Chapter Four

It was going to take a lot more than the sudden acceleration of the Porsche to take Merry's breath away.

"What do you think you're doing?" she said as she edged forward in the seat to get a better look.

Simon's tone was proud. "Zero to sixty in 5.7 seconds."

Surprised, Merry looked at his face to see a small smile. Was there some good news here she had missed? His eyes never left the road as he took another sharp turn to the left.

"I'm going to try to get out of range. Hold on tight."

It was a needless directive. Merry was already clutching the bucket seat with all the strength in her suddenly aching arms. What a time for her exertions of that morning to start being felt! She looked longingly at the dangling edge of the lap and shoulder belts, but there was no way she could let go of her grip on the seat to take time to fasten them.

"Who's shooting at us?" she said through chattering teeth.

"Your playmates of this morning. They had just pulled into the parking lot when they spotted us and started shooting. Since there wasn't any nearby cover, I thought the car would be the best means of escape."

"My playmates of this morning? You mean my abductors?"

"Yes."

"So I take it you're now admitting you were the man who helped me this morning?"

Before Simon could answer, Merry was distracted by a blazing horn. She looked up to see they were again going the wrong way on a one-way street. Her fingers dug into the leather seat.

"For God's sake, you'll get us killed!" she said.

Her companion whizzed around another car in an incredibly tight maneuver, barely avoiding a head-on collision.

"I thought coming this way might discourage the car following us," he said. "They're still back there, though."

Merry risked turning her head to look back between the bucket seats. The rear glass was a spiderweb of cracks.

"How can you see a thing out the back?" she said.

"I just have to look for two headlights. This is a one-way street, remember? Besides I already got a look at their car back at the restaurant. It was a dark blue Cadillac."

Merry struggled to keep calm. "How did they find me?"

Simon didn't take his eyes off the road. "Good question."

Merry licked her dry lips. "A gray Mercedes followed me from the police station today. I thought I had lost him."

Simon's voice was matter-of-fact. "You did."

Surprised at his words, Merry turned to look at her companion's face. "Are you saying what I think you are?"

He nodded. "That was me. My Porsche was in the shop, so they gave me that old gray Mercedes to drive. You pulled a fast one at the hotel, didn't you?"

Merry nodded, unable to mask her surprise that this man was freely admitting to following her. She had the sudden feeling that she had stumbled into a game in which everyone knew the rules but her. "Who are you? What's going on?"

Simon exhaled as he made another quick turn. "Detailed explanations will have to come later. Right now we've got to get away from those two behind us. This should be fun."

Simon made two more screeching left turns, lodging her heart in her throat and sending her stomach into somersaults.

But when she looked over at her driver, she saw him smiling proudly. "That should have helped. What I need are some twisting roads to outrun them. That's what this baby is made for." He quickly patted the dashboard.

Merry shook her head over her companion's lighthearted tone. "Men will always be a mystery to me. Give them peace and intellectual pursuit and all they seem to do is yawn. But give them guns and hot car pursuits and they act as though they're in seventh heaven."

Simon chuckled, his smile becoming broader. "I suppose it's all part of the need for adventure."

"The need for adventure?" Merry looked heavenward. "Oh, dear God, why didn't you make men second after you had had some practice?"

Her companion laughed deeply. "I knew I was going to like you," he said.

Merry tried not to feel so pleased. They were racing for their lives, after all. She concentrated on putting a sober tone into her voice. "Do you know the city well? Can you find these twisting roads?"

"Sure. But we've got a few straight ones to be concerned with first. H Street should give us some maneuvering room."

Merry wasn't that familiar with Washington, D.C.'s streets. H Street didn't ring a bell. Her only alternative, however, seemed to be to open the door and jump from the car. She held on and tried to put her trust in the man next to her, hoping she was making the right choice. After a sharp right turn less than a minute later, she was already questioning her decision.

"What is this street? It's a mess!"

"This is H Street, of course."

Merry blinked, hoping the chaos before her might vanish. It didn't. "For God's sake, three of the right lanes are closed for construction! There's only one lane left and the traffic is piling up! I thought you came here for maneuverability? This is a nightmare. They'll catch us for sure!"

Her companion shrugged. "I admit I forgot about the construction. Makes it a bit more of a sporting proposition."

His quick hands twisted the wheel to pass the car in front of him through an absolutely impossible small space. Merry melted into her seat as he pounced on the accelerator.

"Sporting proposition? Are you mad?" she said.

Merry glanced back at her driver to see yet another smile spreading his lips. "More than likely," he said.

She shook her head and looked away from that smile, out the windshield, then braced herself anew in sudden terror. She was sure they were about to hit the Pinto just in front of them. She remembered reading how those cars could explode on impact because of the placement of their gas tanks. She didn't want to scream, but she was finding she was doing it anyway.

"Oh, no! Not a Pinto!"

She closed her eyes tightly. Her teeth clenched as her face squinted in anticipation. She felt the Porsche bouncing back and forth as she waited for the final ending smash and explosion into flames. But it didn't come. Seconds crept by. She finally ventured one eye open and regretted it immediately. The Pinto was gone, but they were heading smack into a large truck!

"Help! A truck!"

Her companion's voice seemed uncommonly mild. "I do appreciate your pointing out these obstacles, but I have twenty-twenty vision."

"It's not your vision I'm concerned about. It's your sanity! Watch out for that limo up ahead," she said as they missed the truck by some sort of magical maneuver she didn't follow at all.

He chuckled. "Are you always so, uh, helpful to the drivers of cars you're in?"

Merry knew her companion was finding amusement in her frequent outbursts. She had to admit he was an excellent driver and obviously had faith in his own reflexes, but this wild ride had her nerves on edge.

"Look, I don't know how you handle fear, but I find talking helps. It serves to keep my mind employed while my emotions— Don't hit it! Don't hit it!"

A last-second swerve and the Porsche scooped up the dirt on the almost nonexistent shoulder, barreling past the limousine.

Simon's voice was irritatingly calm. "You were saying?"

"You did that on purpose!" Merry's voice was accusing, even though when she thought about it, she realized her companion had maneuvered the car at precisely the right moment.

Simon deliberately pretended to misunderstand her. "Yes, you're right. I missed it on purpose. Foolish me, I thought that's what you wanted me to do. Just point out the next car you want hit and I'll oblige you in whatever way I can."

Simon was coming up fast on the flashing brake lights of an old VW bug. His mood was too playful and he had already admitted he was crazy. Merry decided she couldn't chance remaining quiet. "No! Don't do it!"

"You don't want to hit anything?" His voice was almost sad with feigned disappointment.

"Yes, damn it! A certain driver I'm with!"

Her companion chuckled as he once again took refuge on the sidewalk to circumvent the VW bug and several other cars, which had stopped for a red light in front of him. When the Porsche leaped the curb and began to fly across the intersection, the rough jarring proved too much for the shattered back window. It suddenly broke away from its frame and crashed with an ear-shattering noise onto the pavement behind them.

"The back window's gone! There's glass all over the street!" she said.

"Good," Simon said.

Merry couldn't believe her ears. "Good? Look at that mess back there!"

Prudently, her driver didn't take his eyes off the road when he answered, but his grin remained broad as he swerved off the sidewalk, wildly careening past the flashing yellow caution lights fixed to the construction barriers.

"The broken glass might get in our pursuer's tires and cause a blowout. Our rear vision has just been improved substantially. I'd say the only problem is the cost of replacing that window."

Merry grabbed the dashboard to keep her head from sailing through the windshield as Simon again drove onto the sidewalk.

"Dear, sweet heaven! We have been shot at and are being chased at breakneck speed by two gunmen obviously out to fill us full of holes and you're worried about replacing a window?"

He jackknifed back onto H Street, missing the three-foot concrete partition by less than a whisper.

"Well, it's the only thing broken so far. You are still in one piece, aren't you?"

His tone was inquiring but not overly concerned. Merry felt the lighthearted gurgle in her throat. Her next words were said with a small laugh, much to her own surprise.

"If I survive this, I may end up killing you!"

He chuckled. "You're not exactly giving me a whole lot of incentive to do my best."

The swift intensity of his action belied the easy banter of his conversation as the Porsche shot around what ended up being the last car in its path on the now infamous H Street.

Merry looked in front of her in some amazement. Her voice rose excitedly. "The construction zone has stopped! The street's back to four lanes!"

The Porsche tore along, but Simon said nothing. Concerned, Merry looked at him only to notice that his recent ready smile had been replaced by a slight frown.

"What's wrong? I thought this was the time for rejoicing?"

Simon's eyes darted to the rearview mirror. "Take a look back there."

Merry leaned left to look between the bucket seats and through what used to be the back window. The shattered glass had broken clean away leaving a large black hole to let in the dark night. Less than a block away, two headlights beamed.

"How could they have kept up with us?" she said as she turned back to her companion.

"We blazed the trail and they just had to follow it. Not only that, but there's no traffic to speak of in this four-lane expanse. They'll catch us if we're here too long. I've got to keep well enough ahead of them until we reach Washington Circle. We'll be jogging onto Pennsylvania Avenue any minute now."

It was no sooner said than done. Merry was getting to be a veteran of the jostling. She hardly noticed it.

"What are you going to do when we reach Washington Circle?"

The tone of his voice was almost nonchalant. "I'm not sure yet, but I'll think of something."

Merry felt her blood pressure rise along with a sense of the absurd for his easy-going manner at a time when a normal human being should be sweating blood.

"You'll think of something? Here we are madly dashing for a specific place for no better reason than you'll think of something when we get there?"

"I'm open to any suggestions," he said.

"Well, I realize this might be a phenomenally new and shocking idea, but what's wrong with finding a police station and stopping to get some help and protection?"

"You want to go to the cops?" he said, running a red light.

Merry wasn't sure what the tone of his voice was conveying. Was it surprise or dismay?

"The last time I heard," she said, "they were the ones getting paid for protecting the public. We are public, aren't we? Why don't we let them earn their money?"

"It's too late," he said. "Here's Washington Circle."

Simon slowed down and paced his speed carefully as he approached the roadway around the circular green space, looking out the rearview mirror almost as often as he did the front windshield. Merry wasn't sure why reaching Washington Circle now prohibited them from seeking out police protection. But a sudden curiosity about what this unpredictable man might come up with to lose their pursuers kept her from pressing the point.

Nothing spectacular seemed to be happening, however. Simon just kept tightly cornering the Porsche in a repeating circle around the center greenery. Merry's sides were aching from the constant strain and she was also beginning to feel dizzy. Finally, she couldn't stand it any longer.

"What are you doing?" she asked.

"Driving around in circles," Simon said.

Merry's tone was exasperated. "That much I could figure out. I meant why are we driving around in circles? They're still behind us, aren't they?"

"Yes. But I'm keeping exactly one-hundred-and-eighty degrees ahead of them. They're on the other side of the circle."

Merry waited, expecting him to go on to explain. When he didn't, her exasperation continued with her next question.

"Please forgive me for being confused, but I don't remember my geometry class containing a theorem covering this one-hundred-and-eighty-degree maneuver."

As always, he was undaunted by the challenging sarcasm of her words. The smile was back on his lips. "That's because this situation is covered by a postulate. You see, every so often I let them get a glance at us, let them think that we're going in as tight a turn as we can. That way they think if we pull off into a side street, they'll come around the curve in time to see us and follow."

"I hate to keep repeating myself, but I still don't understand what you're gaining by this," Merry said.

"Well, the secret is that I'm not making as tight a turn as I can. Now when the time's right, I'm going to speed up and pull off onto one of the streets leading away from here. But I'll be doing it a lot faster than they expect or can duplicate.''

"So we'll be out of sight and they won't see us turn off?''

"Go to the head of the class!'' he said.

Her companion's exuberance was getting catchy. Merry tried to fight becoming overly infected. "When will you be ready?''

"Right . . . NOW!''

Merry felt her left hip suddenly digging into her chest as the Porsche hugged the center divider in a much tighter circle and then lurched ahead down another street. Just when she thought she could straighten up, the car suddenly veered to the right and stopped dead, the lights and engine cutting off simultaneously.

"Get down!'' her companion said.

Merry peeled her body off the dashboard, dropping to the floor in front of the passenger's seat. Simon was spread over the gearshift, his head resting on the seat she just vacated.

They both lay still as a couple of very long seconds passed. In her cramped position, Merry could barely breathe, much less move. Her companion's face was hidden by the darkness of the night. No street lamps illuminated their quickly chosen parking space. She was sure that's why he had selected it.

Was he waiting for their pursuers to drive by? What if they weren't fooled by the ruse? What if they were parking right at this moment, ready to approach the Porsche with guns drawn?

She could clearly hear her own heartbeat. She caught the cool, light scent of soap coming off her rescuer's skin. It was pleasant and natural.

"How much longer do we have to lie in this position?'' she said in a voice barely over a whisper.

"Not too much longer. Why were you sighing just now?''

"I was sighing?'' she asked.

There seemed to be real concern in his disembodied voice this time. "Yes, you were sighing. Are you in some pain?''

Merry hurried to correct his misunderstanding. "No, I feel okay. I was sighing because I was so glad you don't smell bad.''

Merry was at first surprised at her companion's muffled laughter. When she finally heard in her own mind the words she had said, she quickly hurried to explain.

"No, you don't understand. I didn't say that quite right. I mean, I have this great nose..."

More peals of laughter, audible this time. Merry shook her head. "Oh, God, that's not it. I mean I smell real good."

Even Merry started to spurt laughter as she heard her own words and watched her companion starting to roll on the seat in an agony of mirth.

"Now, you must know that's not what I mean. Oh, no, how am I ever going to say this right? I know, I can distinctly detect the subtleties of odor passing in the air..."

It was too late. Her companion had gone from spasms to convulsions. Merry decided she'd better stop talking before she became the cause of his mirthful death. One dead man falling on her a day was all she could take. As it was, she was having a hard time keeping her own laughter stifled.

Suddenly, a pair of bright headlights sobered them both up in an instant. As the laughter withered on Merry's lips, she could almost feel her nearby companion stiffen. Fortunately, the sound of the car engine roared past them.

Simon inched up to watch the retreating vehicle. "That was them. After chasing their tail a few times, they finally figured we had driven off. I hope it was just luck that made them take this street. We'd better get out of here."

In one fluid moment he was back in the driver's seat and had started the engine.

"Wait, please," Merry said. "This time I want my seat belt on before we make like entries in the Indy 500."

He waited until he heard the click of her seat belt and then pulled the car out of the parking space only to stop dead. He put the gear in reverse and backed up at full speed.

"What do you think you're doing?" Merry said. "This is a one-way street. You can't go backward!"

"Why not? I have a reverse gear."

Merry shook her head. This was an absolutely crazy man she was with and she might as well accept it. And in truth, she thought he was rather a lot of fun. So she just held her breath as he backed into Washington Circle amidst the blaring horns of the oncoming traffic. Somehow they emerged unscathed, and her crazy driver drove around to another street, which headed them in the opposite direction from their pursuers.

"Are we safe yet?" she asked.

"If you consider riding in the same car with me safe," he said with his ready smile.

She leaned back in her seat and looked at him then. She couldn't clearly make out all of his features in the semidarkness of the car interior. But her mind's eye remembered the high forehead and cheekbones, the expressive eyebrows and quick-to-smile mouth. And those very blue eyes.

She reached out her right hand to him. "I'm Meredith Anders. My friends call me Merry."

He took her hand. "Simon Temple."

His touch was warm and steady. It gave Merry a comforting feeling. "All right, Simple Temple, why were you following me?"

He exhaled heavily. "It's hard to know where to begin to answer that question. Maybe we'd best find a place we can talk."

"We're not going to drive to the police?" Merry asked.

Simon shook his head. "Not me."

"But those two men were shooting at us!"

"That fact hadn't slipped my mind," Simon said. "If it's all right with you, I'd like to drive over to the Lincoln Memorial and walk around the Reflecting Pool for a while. I think keeping off the streets for the next hour or so should ensure those two don't pick up our trail again."

Merry looked at Simon's purposely averted face, still perplexed as to why they were not heading for the police, but sensing his obvious reluctance to do so. Her curiosity over what he might tell her quieted the urgings she had to approach the proper authorities. She found herself agreeing.

They soon were among many strollers admiring the beautiful lights sparkling through the still waters in the warm evening air. On the steps of the Lincoln Memorial a young man softly strummed the chords of a ballad on his guitar. Merry looked over at the man walking so silently beside her. His look told her he was far away from the serenity that surrounded them.

She felt the same close bonding with him that had come over her when she first saw him that morning facing her attackers, fighting on her behalf. Tonight he had proved their worthy mental opponent, outfoxing their determined pursuit. She admired the mental gymnastics he had used and his skill behind the wheel. A primitive part of her, something she hadn't realized she possessed, was aroused at such abilities. She shook off the disturbing images, reminding herself she knew next to nothing about this stranger. She sought to discipline her thoughts before she spoke.

"Well, Simon Temple, how about some answers?"

He turned to her then, his eyes refocusing on her face. "All right, I'll answer your questions, but first you must answer a few for me. Do we have a deal?"

Merry looked up into his eyes and felt an agreeable warmth climbing up the back of her spine. She purposely looked away. "All right. What do you want to know?"

"What were you doing in the Smithsonian this morning?"

"I came to look at the diamond exhibits."

"How did you get positioned underneath that dead man?"

"I turned to say something to him and he fell on me."

"You knew him?"

"No. When I saw him out of the corner of my eye, I thought he was a fellow admirer of diamonds. I had no idea something was wrong with him until I turned to face him. The first thing I noticed was that he was beet red, like he was unable to breathe. Then he collapsed on me."

"And you're sure you had never seen him before?"

"Never. What's this all about? How did you know that man fell on me?"

Simon was quiet for a few minutes as he gazed out over the Reflecting Pool, almost as though he was trying to decide something. Then he turned his eyes back to Merry.

"Yes, you have a right to know the story, at least my side of it. But first I have to tell you that I just happened by this morning when I saw those two men pull you out from under the dead man. I don't have any idea who that man was who fell on you or who the men were who tried to take you from the museum. But you're welcome to what I do know. It all began nearly two years ago in Mozambique, Africa. You see, I'm an epidemic intelligence service officer, a sort of medical detective for the Centers for Disease Control in Atlanta."

"Centers? There's more than one?" Merry asked.

"Yes, since 1980 when everything was reorganized into separate centers for health, education and prevention services. My job is in their infectious-diseases branch."

"You treat infectious diseases?" Merry asked.

Simon shrugged. "In a way. I'm the guy who gets the call in the middle of the night from the CDC duty officer telling him to fly across the country to discover the cause, transmission and host factors of some unidentified outbreak."

"You mean like Legionnaire's Disease?" Merry asked.

"Yes," Simon said. "The CDC was called in on that case. A bit before my time, of course. Well, anyway..."

They continued to walk around the Reflecting Pool as Simon explained his position at the CDC and his special exchange assignment with the Mozambique government almost two years before. He described the events following the eruption of the Fire Mountain volcano and the appearance at the clinic of the very sick geologist, David Carmichael, and of the huge diamond he had found.

Simon paused at the point when he went to sleep on his cot that night. Merry felt the tension of his tale tightening her nerves. "What happened to the Englishman?" she asked.

Simon exhaled heavily. "Mabunda, my Mozambique colleague, never came to get me for my second watch that night. When I finally awoke the next day, my passport and visa were missing from my tent. I walked into the clinic to find David Carmichael dead, his body covered in gasoline and deliberately burned by fire that had spread to wipe out most of the clinic's beds and supplies. Mabunda was gone."

"And the diamond?"

Simon shook his head. "It was gone, too, and so was the black box that held it. I immediately called the local authorities, told them the truth. They didn't believe me. Mozambique is under a Marxist regime that is very suspicious of foreigners. As I think back on it, I realize they needed someone to blame to satisfy their superiors, and since Mabunda couldn't be found, I was the most likely scapegoat. I spent quite a while in a Mozambique jail before the CDC worked with the State Department to get me released back to the States."

Merry was totally engrossed in her companion's tale. "Simon, how awful for you. Thank goodness you were freed. I suppose you never heard from Mabunda?"

"Not exactly, but I did eventually trace him."

Merry felt surprised. "You traced him? You went back to Mozambique?"

Simon shook his head. "No, I'm no longer welcome in that country, as you can imagine. Actually, Mabunda turned up in Amsterdam just over a month later. He had been the victim of a mugging, received a severe blow to the head and ended up a D.O.A. at a local hospital. They found my altered passport on him—my name and address, his picture. He'd obviously used it to get out of Mozambique and into Europe. Anyway Amsterdam notified the State Department and they in turn notified me."

Merry thought she was beginning to see the light. "Isn't Amsterdam known for diamond sales? Couldn't Mabunda have gone there to sell Carmichael's huge rough diamond?"

Simon nodded. "That's what I believe."

Merry was trying to think of the possibilities. "Do you think the muggers killed Mabunda to steal the stone?"

Simon shook his head. "The muggers didn't kill Mabunda. According to the paramedics who brought him in, Mabunda was already deathly ill. The blow to his head wasn't fatal. His illness was. He had the same symptoms as Carmichael."

Merry was trying to think through the implications of what Simon was saying. "He had caught Carmichael's disease?"

Simon nodded. "The high fever, the vomiting, the diarrhea, the weak pulse—the paramedics recorded it all."

"But you didn't catch the disease?"

Simon nodded. "And I don't know why."

Merry frowned in thought. "Maybe Mabunda was with Carmichael longer. What did the autopsy on him reveal?"

Simon shook his head. "There wasn't one. His death was attributed to injuries sustained from the mugging by a busy and unconcerned doctor. The body was shipped back to Mozambique when the authorities finally identified him. I arrived in Amsterdam too late to intercept it. If I hadn't gotten lucky and located the paramedics, I wouldn't have even found out about the similar symptoms. Losing the body after suspecting what really killed him was a tremendous disappointment.''

"What were you hoping to find?" Merry asked.

"What I have been on the trail of since that fateful December night—the disease that killed the English geologist.''

"You never got the analysis of Carmichael's blood back from the lab in Mozambique?"

"No, I was arrested as soon as I called the authorities that morning. Still, I didn't believe it was coincidence that both Carmichael and Mabunda had the same symptoms. The next deaths made me certain I was right.''

Merry's stomach began to feel queasy. "The next deaths?"

Simon nodded. "They happened a few months after Mabunda's and followed the trail of the spectacular diamond Carmichael had shown me in the clinic in Mozambique. Two somewhat shady European gem cutters, both rumored to have worked on cutting a large red-centered diamond, died within four months. A third died six months later.''

"So you think Mabunda took the diamond and the street muggers took it from him and somehow it ended up in the hands of these gem cutters and each in turn contracted this killing flu?"

"Yes. It began with Carmichael and the contagion is still going strong. Wherever I've tracked Carmichael's red diamond, I've found death.''

Merry tried to shake away the sudden chill that had slithered up her spine. "Do you know how the gem cutters died?"

Simon shrugged his shoulders. "The rumors were vague and concentrated mostly on the stone, but in all cases a strange weakness followed by a deadly flu killed the men.''

"Could you determine whether the rumors about the red diamond were correct?" Merry asked.

Simon nodded. "They must have been. Last spring a freelance broker announced the sale of an enormous, flawless red diamond, a 525.5-carat brilliant-cut stone. It was on the open market, outside the hands of the De Beers Company.''

"The De Beers Company?" Merry asked.

Simon nodded. "It's an English company that markets about eighty-five percent of the world's gem diamonds, but they didn't have this one. Rumor had it that the flawless stone was the largest finished diamond from the original, rough red-and-white stone. Its unusual properties dictated its name. It was advertised as the Fire Diamond.''

Merry's eyes grew quite large. "You mean the Smithsonian's spectacular jewel is Carmichael's diamond? *The* Fire Diamond?''

Simon's mouth twisted. "Actually, I've begun to think of it more as the Bloodstone.''

# Chapter Five

Merry was remembering the almost liquid-red glow of the fabulous Fire Diamond as she and Simon continued to walk beside the Reflecting Pool. She had thought the diamond looked like dancing fire. Now she was beginning to visualize it as flowing blood. The image sent a chill up her spine.

"You've traced the stone to the museum?" she asked.

Simon nodded. "Yes. It changed hands in Europe several times. Then it was sold at auction for an undisclosed amount to an unidentified American multimillionaire. Within days of the transfer of the diamond, the auctioneer who sold it was dead."

Merry shook her head. "Don't tell me. The same deadly un-identified flu?"

Simon nodded. "Only this time I got to Antwerp, the site of the auction, in time to get a blood sample from the dying man. He had the same symptoms as Carmichael, and when I exam-ined his blood, I found an abnormally low white-cell count. I identified no known virus, no foreign bacteria, but it was as though his immune system had ceased to function."

"What could cause that?" Merry asked.

"I don't know of any communicable disease that could have lowered the white blood cell count without leaving traces of it-self in the blood. Too late I realized I needed a tissue sample and other bodily fluids. But by then the auctioneer had died and his family, not understanding the possible gravity of the situation, refused any further tests to be run on his body."

"But why would they do that?" Merry asked.

"The auctioneer had never owned the diamond. He had only handled its sale for an unnamed diamond broker. There was a lot of secrecy surrounding the transaction since the real owner had paid him to keep quiet. His family was jumpy that a stranger like myself was poking around."

"But surely with your position at the CDC, you could have insisted on the body being thoroughly examined?"

Simon shook his head sadly. "I was in a foreign country. The CDC doesn't have any clout there. Besides, everything I'm doing I'm doing on my own. My superiors at the CDC don't believe a deadly infectious disease is out there."

"Even though people are dying?" Merry said.

"Yes, even though they're dying. I've been unable to identify an infectious agent, you see, or even identify a significant sample of people suffering from the same symptoms. For the three hours I sat next to Carmichael bathing his feverish body, I came into contact with his exhaled air, his expelled blood and his perspiration and I wasn't infected. The auctioneer's wife and family, keeping even closer contact with him during his illness, never came down with the flu. The question remains, how is it being transmitted?"

"What's the answer?" Merry asked.

Simon shook his head almost wearily. "I don't know. It's possible those who get it may have some inherited predisposition that makes them susceptible. Finding that predisposition might be more important than the carrier vehicle."

"What type of predisposition?" Merry asked.

"Good question. You see, everyone who's died from this mysterious flu has been operating on the periphery of the law. They're not the type of people to tell a doctor the truth on how they have contracted an illness. Their clandestine involvement with the Fire Diamond has made a normal tracking of contagion and symptoms impossible. Unless I'm able to study the host factors in several victims, I may never know."

"The host factors?"

"Yes," Simon said. "The things such as sex, age, overall health, habits, that sort of thing. I've made a chart and filled in as much as I can about the known victims, but there are still too many blank spots. I don't know what vehicle transmitted the illness to Mabunda and after him the others. And I don't know why I can't find evidence of the agent in the blood sample."

Merry could hear the frustration in Simon's voice. Nothing of his earlier levity remained. "You ran every test?"

He nodded. "Serological testing proved negative for all known influenza viruses. It was not AIDS. The blood smear was negative for malaria parasites. I even had the lab run the tests for viral hemorrhagic fever. It's rare, but it's deadly and has been known to come from Africa. The results were negative. Whatever the bug, it wasn't in the blood."

"Are you saying it had invaded the body through some other means?" Merry asked.

"I don't know. I desperately need tissue samples from an infected person in order to be able to diagnose the illness. Without them, I have no hope of convincing my boss that I'm not just on some wild-goose chase."

Merry was frowning. "There haven't been a whole lot of deaths from this strange flu. You've admitted some people in close contact haven't proved susceptible. Is it possible—"

"That I am on a wild-goose chase?" Simon finished for her.

Merry shrunk from the sudden disappointment in his voice. "I only meant—"

Simon exhaled heavily. "I know what you meant. But what you and my boss have forgotten is that the deaths I've mentioned are the only ones I'm aware of. Those who handled the Fire Diamond did not want their identities known for the most part. There could be many more people dying from what looks like a severe case of flu and is going unreported because flu appears to be the cause. Do you understand what I'm saying?"

Merry nodded. "Yes, I see. Many more could have been infected that you haven't heard about. What about the American multimillionaire who bought the diamond?"

Simon looked away from Merry out over the Reflecting Pool. He seemed all of a sudden withdrawn, his expression cloaked. When he finally spoke, his voice carried an underlying strain she had not noticed before. "I didn't find him in time."

"So your search has ended at the Smithsonian?"

Simon's eyes came back to her face. "Yes. It drew me to the man who collapsed on you in front of the Fire Diamond."

The import of Simon's words brought new anxiety to Merry. "You think he might have died of the mysterious disease?"

Simon shrugged. "It could be coincidence. But when I chased after those two men who tried to abduct you, one of them jumped into a green-and-gray Subaru to get away. I recognized the car as the one..." Simon's voice faded as he looked away.

"You recognized the car as the one what?" Merry asked.

Simon looked back at her. "I've seen that Subaru before in my pursuit of the Fire Diamond. The specifics don't matter. What does is that these two men are somehow involved with the Fire Diamond and with the man who dropped dead in front of the stone. All three men are now links in my investigation."

Merry nodded. "So you have to check them out. What have you learned so far?"

Simon sighed, running a large hand through his thick dark hair. "I haven't been able to get into the medical examiner's office to find out for sure. I know that's where they sent the body. I saw that sergeant who took you in for questioning come out of the building. But my boss wouldn't back up my request."

A thought occurred to Merry. She licked her suddenly dry lips. "If the dead man had this mysterious flu and I came in close contact with him, could I have caught it?"

Simon looked at her and nodded. "It's the reason I've been following you. I thought you might have known, even had a close relationship with the dead man. Forgive me, but I thought if you began to show signs of illness..." His voice trailed off.

Merry nodded. "It's all right. I think I understand. If you had come up to me right away and tried to tell me I may have been exposed to a deadly disease, I probably would have thought you unbalanced. Frankly, if my abductors hadn't tried to kidnap me and to shoot at us tonight, I doubt if I would be even listening to you now."

Simon looked puzzled. "You believe me because of them?"

Merry smiled into his questioning face. "Yes. You've protected me from them without knowing why they were after me or even who I am. That kind of natural chivalry could never spring from an unbalanced mind."

His small smile at her words seemed to be interfering with Merry's ability to inhale. She looked away from the warm look in his eyes to catch her breath.

"Would you mind if I drew some blood from your arm and had it tested?" he asked.

Merry fought the queasiness that had entered her stomach at the implication in his request, even though she knew she should have seen it coming. She concentrated on keeping her voice even. "You mean you want me to go to a lab?"

Simon shook his head. "That won't be necessary. I have my medical bag. I could draw some blood now, if you don't mind?"

"Well to tell you the truth, I do mind, but I mind the idea of having contracted a deadly disease even more. Whatever I've got to face, the sooner I know what it is, the better. So, okay. I'm your guinea pig. But I thought you said you needed tissue samples and other bodily fluids?"

Simon rested his hand on her shoulder for a brief moment. "Only if I were to find you infected. This is only precautionary. Remember, I have no evidence that this man had Carmichael's disease."

She found his assurance somewhat comforting. They made their way back to the Porsche and Simon sat her in the passenger's seat as he carefully and expertly filled three specimen tubes with her blood. Then he withdrew the needle. As she was pressing against the cotton to inhibit the bleeding from her arm, she watched him labeling the tubes with her name and tried to imagine him in a white doctor's smock. With that thick dark hair, deep tan and very blue eyes, she imagined the effect as devastating. He looked up at her then and she began to feel as though she was indeed catching a fever.

"Have you been in close contact with anyone today?"

Merry tried to think back. "I hugged a friend."

"Nothing else."

Merry shook her head. "Are you telling me I should quarantine myself?"

Simon looked at her and exhaled. "No. I don't see that at this point it would be of any use. Under true suspected epidemic conditions, everyone around you would be in protective cap, mask, gloves and gown and you'd be resting in an isolation ward. Now all I can tell you is try not to get too close to anyone."

Merry tried to push down her rising unease. "When will you have the results of the blood tests?"

Simon had finished putting away her samples in his medical bag. "Tomorrow morning. I'll put a rush on it. By the way, what happened with the police this morning?"

Merry sighed as she proceeded to describe her very uncomfortable interview with Detective Sergeant Mike Calder. "So you see, your not being available to corroborate my story has the police suspicious of me. That Sergeant Calder all but accused me of the man's murder."

"But from everything you've told me, there's no evidence the man was murdered," Simon said.

Merry nodded. "Still, you have to understand that is only a minor detail in the mind of the suspicious Sergeant Calder."

"But a major one needed before a charge is laid," Simon said.

Merry began to think of the possibilities. "What if the dead man was murdered?"

Simon shook his head, a twinkle finding its way into his eyes. "I wouldn't let it worry you. You'll be exonerated. And if not, be sure to let me know when visiting hours are."

Merry shook her head in mock gravity, secretly thankful for his ready humor. "Always on hand to spread a cheerful word, I see. What are you going to do next?"

Simon closed his medical bag and shoved it onto the narrow back seat of the Porsche. "I'm going to take your blood sample to a lab and see how your white-cell count is doing."

"It was the white blood cells that were low in the infected man's blood, wasn't it?" Merry asked.

Simon nodded, not seeming to want to pursue the subject further. "I'll keep in touch about the blood-test results."

"Good," Merry said. "Then we can work together to find out who this dead man was and if he had your mysterious flu."

Simon looked at her in some surprise. "Work together?"

Merry heard the surprise in his voice but she pretended not to notice. "Sure, why not? You need to trace the spread of the illness and I need to find out why these men are after me. We can help each other. Since these men and the deadly flu all seem tied into the Fire Diamond, it's our common denominator, wouldn't you agree?''

Simon smiled over at her. "Yes, I guess it is.''

"Well, that's settled, then. And this way you'll be able to keep an eye on me to see if I start showing symptoms.''

She had said the words bravely, but inside the fear of possible infection by something undefined and deadly was very real.

Simon's next words seemed to pick up on her unspoken fear. "Merry, even if you have become infected, early detection puts all the odds on your side. Don't worry. I'll be with you all the way. Right now it's time to take you back to your hotel.''

Merry thought about his words as Simon circled the car and got in the driver's side, immediately buckling up.

She turned to him as she made sure her own seat belt was secure. "Aren't you forgetting we have to go to the police first? They must be told about tonight.''

Simon shook his head. "I'm not forgetting. A stop there is not on my itinerary.'' He started the Porsche's engine and began to pull away from the curb.

Merry sounded as perplexed as she looked. "I don't understand. Those men shot at us, could have killed us. Why won't you go to the police with me to report it?''

He looked at her with a frown on his face. "You must do what you feel is best, of course, but I'd appreciate it if you wouldn't mention my name.''

Merry couldn't believe her ears. "Not mention your name? I don't understand. Why not?''

Simon shrugged. "I have my reasons, and believe me they are important ones. Please don't give the police my name.''

Merry was disturbed by his response, but she could see the firm set to his jaw. A slew of unasked questions began to burn on her tongue. She found it hard to remain quiet.

"If you could just give me a general hint?''

Simon frowned, ignoring her half-asked question. "Getting you home safe might be tricky. Those men have spotted you there. They may go back and stake it out.''

Merry sighed out her mounting frustration. "I don't see I have a choice, since my move to go to the police station has been overruled. Besides, I can't wear this white sleeveless dress for the rest of my stay, and I can't do without my business papers."

Simon nodded as though he had agreed to something. "Okay, we'll head for there, but we'll have to be careful. What are these business papers? Are they the reason you're in D.C.?"

"Yes. I'm a lawyer from the State of Washington. My firm is representing a diamond company being unfairly taxed by a discriminatory interpretation of a state statute."

He seemed to digest the information for a moment. "I don't know a lot about law. What court is hearing your case?"

Merry smiled proudly. "The highest one in the land."

Simon's eyebrows rose. "The Supreme Court? Well, well. Will you be appearing personally before that august body?"

Merry smiled proudly. "That's the general idea."

"When?"

"Monday, the opening day of the new session. Ours is the second case on the calendar. I'd send out embossed invitations, but the gallery is seated on a first-come, first-served basis."

He smiled. "You're excited about it, aren't you?"

"It's right up there with hitching a ride on the space shuttle," Merry said. "To argue a case before the Supreme Court is a once-in-a-lifetime experience. And I have this faith that it's going to go well. I know our side is right, and somehow I know I'm going to be able to convince the justices of that fact."

He glanced over at her. "You believe strongly there's still a clear right and wrong that must be supported no matter what?"

"Well, of course. And you do, too, otherwise you wouldn't be putting so much effort into tracking this flulike disease," Merry said.

"'... For there is nothing either good or bad, but thinking makes it so...'"

Merry was surprised at Simon's words. "You just quoted from *Hamlet*!"

Simon smiled. "I should have thought up something by Portia from *The Merchant of Venice* considering your upcoming day in the Supreme Court. So you like the law, diamonds, Shakespeare and people who don't smell bad. Anything else?"

Merry chuckled at the returning light tone to his voice. "You're too perceptive. I'm going to have to try to keep a few secrets from you."

He shook his head. "I doubt it. You're a very open person. You speak easily about yourself, your feelings. You're not the type to hide who you are. I think that's one of the things that makes you comfortable to be around."

Merry felt pleased by his assessment of her character. But his next words didn't give her a chance to respond.

"We're coming to Third Street. Let's try to find a parking space and get out and walk the last block. We'll be better able to see if anyone is lurking about."

Merry shook her head. "I don't like thinking about the possibility that my hotel is being watched, but I guess I can't start pulling faint heart on you now. Besides, it's better to face rather than shrink away from whatever lies in wait."

Simon smiled. "Are you trying to convince me or yourself?"

Merry smiled back. "Both of us, of course."

Miraculously, they found an empty parking space and made good their intent. Simon had Merry walk several paces ahead of him so he could keep a close watch. By the time he caught up with her in front of the red awning entrance to the hotel, she felt relieved, until she heard his next comment.

"Well, you're home safe and somewhat sound. I'll say good night."

Merry quickly turned to face Simon, thinking only that she didn't want him to leave.

"Do you have to go right away? I mean, wouldn't you like to come up for a drink? I have to call room service for dinner and I hate to eat alone. Of course, you've already eaten, haven't you? Perhaps you're more in the mood for coffee and dessert?"

Merry watched somewhat fascinated as curtains opened and closed across Simon's face, each one revealing a different scene of what coming to her room for a drink might entail. She rushed to reassure and convince him at the same time.

"I'd at least like to buy you a drink. If you let me, perhaps I wouldn't feel so much in your debt. You saved my life this morning and again tonight. I owe you so much."

Simon's hands came up in denial. "You owe me nothing."

"I appreciate your saying that but it's not how I feel," she said. "Your allowing me to thank you would give me a lot of pleasure."

She paused. He still watched her face. She went on, determined to win her case.

"We could go to the bar if you don't think my hotel room seems quite appropriate. Although I personally see no problem with it, considering who you are and who I am, that is."

Merry shook her head. "I'm not sure what I meant by that last strange statement. I think I was trying to say I don't think either of us is the type of person to try to take advantage of the other, but somehow it didn't seem to come out right. For someone who is supposed to deal in the precision of word meanings, I've become amazingly incoherent in getting across some of the simplest of thoughts these last few hours."

The shifting curtains closed across Simon's face and his easy smile was back. "Perhaps that's because your mind is more fine-tuned to the complex?"

Merry sighed into a smile. "Your manners are excellent. My compliments to whoever was your teacher. Is it the bar, then?"

"Turn down the offer of a drink in an attractive woman's hotel room? That mother you have just complimented so kindly would disown me if I proved to be so foolish. Lead the way."

Merry felt good at his decision. She wanted this man to like her for the very simple reason that she liked him. And she was confident that they would work well together on discovering the mystery surrounding the deadly flu he tracked and the death of the man at the Smithsonian. She turned to go inside.

The Downtown Corp Hill Inn was small and had an old-fashioned, elegant feel. Merry appreciated the beautiful trim and fine detail of the well-kept walls and columns. They seemed so in keeping with the expected architecture of the nation's capital.

She and her companion took the elevator to the third floor, then walked the few feet to her door.

Merry had retrieved the key from her purse but soon saw she would have no need for it. She halted dead in her tracks as her body tensed in preparation for flight. A sliver of light sliced into the hallway carpet from the slightly ajar door to her room.

"Don't move," Simon's voice said behind her. His strong arms pulled her back, away from the door. "Stay here. If I'm not out in a minute, go get help."

The deep whisper of his voice sent a chill up Merry's spine. Was someone waiting in there for her?

Simon kicked the door inward and ran quickly past as it swung shut, disappearing behind its closing bulk. Merry stayed on the other side of the door, hearing only her heartbeat.

She was trying to judge the passing of a minute when common sense finally reminded her to look at her watch. But then she remembered her new digital watch didn't have an indicator for seconds. It flashed 10:15. How much of a minute had passed already?

Just as she was thinking the thought, the watch flashed 10:16. Fortunately, in spite of her momentary indecision, Simon also appeared at the door. She sighed in relief as he smiled and waved her inside, closing and locking the door behind them. But immediately inside the door, she stopped in dismay as she saw what was left of her room.

The once beautifully made bed was a shambles. Its white, chenille bedspread had been ripped and dumped in a heap by the torn drapes next to the window. Even the foam from the mattress stuffing had been ripped with what had to have been a sharp knife. The cushion of the chairs had suffered a similar fate.

Merry next turned to the beautiful mahogany wardrobe, now lying facedown on the carpet. Its back had been kicked in. The drawers of its matching dresser had been ripped out and thrown down beside the bed.

Her clothing was lying all over the floor and the mutilated furniture. She picked up her suit coat that was on the carpet near her feet. Examining it, she found the shoulder pads had been slashed, although it seemed intact otherwise. Across the room she could see that even her two pieces of luggage had been slashed and torn. She was horrified.

"My God! Someone has massacred this place!"

Simon put his arm around her for just a second, squeezing her shoulders in a gesture of comfort. Then he moved away from where she stood in the center of her room's chaos and gave her one of his small smiles.

"Well, I'm glad to hear you say it," he said, gently moving aside a pair of her cotton pajamas from the chair in which he was about to sit down. "I'd worried this might be the way you kept house."

She sighed as she heard the tease in his words, relieved that he knew so well how to relieve the tension that had begun to ball inside her stomach. She sat down on the other ripped chair and shook her head, truly thankful that both his presence and his smile were taking the sting out of this latest bit of barbarity.

"Simon, why would someone do this? There's no money here, no valuables. What were they looking for? It just doesn't make sense," she said.

"'Her house is sack'd, her quiet interrupted, her mansion batter'd by the enemy...'" he quoted.

"That's Shakespeare, too, isn't it? Although I can't specifically place it."

He smiled, but didn't acknowledge her recognition. "Is there something you haven't told me?" he asked.

Merry's expression showed her surprise at his question. "Like what?"

"This man who fell on you in front of the Fire Diamond display this morning. Did he say anything? Give you anything?"

Merry shook her head. "No. Nothing." Merry's eyes suddenly became large. "My God, you think this was done by those two men?"

Simon nodded. "Who else? A random burglary stretches my belief in coincidence after the attacks of this morning and tonight."

Merry nodded. "You're right, of course. But why?"

Simon's hand swept the room. "After seeing this mess I'd say it's pretty obvious they're looking for something."

"That's why you asked me if the dead man gave me anything," Merry said.

Simon nodded. "And despite the fact that he didn't, these men obviously think he did. Could be the sole reason they've been after you. Are you sure he didn't slip anything into your shoulder bag while you weren't looking?"

Merry shook her head. "I'm not sure of anything. But those two men searched my bag before they grabbed me. If he had—"

"They would have found it," Simon finished for her.

She reexamined the suit jacket over her arm, shaking her head at the slashed shoulder pads. "Whatever it is, it has to be something small for them to think I could have hidden it in a shoulder pad. What does that suggest to you?"

Simon took a moment to reflect on her question. "Hmm. We've already surmised they are tied in with the Fire Diamond."

"Correction," Merry interrupted. "*You've* surmised because of one of them driving a green-and-gray Subaru, whatever that means."

Simon had the grace to look a little uncomfortable for not having explained the particulars of that observation. However, his answer still didn't offer an explanation on the Subaru. "I think they were looking for jewels or money," he said.

"Why jewels or money?" Merry asked.

"Well since they were involved with the Fire Diamond, that tells me they are interested in jewels. Their behavior at the Smithsonian, particularly their treatment of you and their disappearance before the police arrived, tells me they are hardly reputable dealers in fine gems. My guess is that they had some sort of deal with the dead man that involved his handing something over to them. My further guess is that something was either a hot jewel or the money to pay for one."

Merry nodded. "That makes sense. Now let me go through this step-by-step. You think they had a rendezvous with the dead man. He gets sick and dies before they reach him. They search his body but don't find whatever it was he had promised them. And because he has collapsed on me, they jump to the conclusion that I have taken whatever it was the dead man had?"

Simon nodded. "It's just a possible explanation."

"And a logical one. Except since I don't have whatever it was the dead man was bringing them, where is it?"

Simon shrugged. "I have no answer to your very pertinent question, but I do have a suggestion. Go back to Washington State tonight. Have someone else plead your case on Monday.

I may not have all the answers, but I do know those men who grabbed you this morning, shot at us tonight and who did this to your room are not going to give up. They'll be back."

"But if I tell them I don't have whatever they're looking for, that their assumptions are mistaken, then won't they—"

"Leave you alone?" Simon offered. "Do you really think they'd believe you? Merry, do you understand the type of men these are?"

Merry sighed as she sunk against the back of her chair.

Simon studied her distraught face. He very much wanted to put his arms around her and assure her everything was going to be all right. Trouble was, he didn't really think everything was going to be all right.

"There's got to be an answer why the dead man did not have what these men want, Simon. All we have to do is find it."

Simon reached over to take ahold of her hand. "All you have to do is get on the next plane."

Merry glanced up to see the worried look in his eyes. "I appreciate your concern, but we're in this together. We'll find out about the flu and these men. I'm no quitter."

Simon pulled away, suddenly afraid her brave determination could easily get her killed and fearing he might not be able to prevent it. He stood up and began to pace about the room, trying to find the words that would convince her she must leave.

She sighed, misinterpreting his withdrawal and suddenly feeling guilty. "If it wasn't for me, you wouldn't be involved in any of this violence. Clearly your focus must be on the man who died. Clearly mine must be on calling the police. When they see what these men did to this place, surely they'll give me some protection until Monday."

She waited for a moment to hear any protest from Simon her words might elicit, but he spoke none. Only the worried look in his eyes changed as it suddenly became framed in sadness.

Not able to bear seeing it, she tore her eyes away to once again survey what was left of her room. "If I could just find the phone," she said.

"I think it might be over there," Simon said, pointing toward an area beside the slashed box-spring mattress.

She stood up and headed in the direction of his pointing finger, stepping as best as she could around the rubble. Simon's eyesight proved accurate. She found the phone where it had been knocked off the nightstand. Finding it still worked, she rang the front desk and quickly relayed the story of the break-in.

"We'll contact the police right away, Ms. Anders, and check the other rooms," the desk clerk said.

"Will you tell them that this break-in might be related to a case Sergeant Calder is working on?"

"Sergeant Calder? Of course. I'll tell them."

"Well, that's taken care of," Merry said as she hung up the phone and turned back to her companion. But the chair he was sitting in just a moment before was now empty.

"Simon?" She stepped over to look past the open door leading to the bathroom, but the area was empty. Merry then went to the door leading to the hallway and swung it open.

It was no use. No one was there. Her rescuer had vanished once again!

# Chapter Six

Simon had watched the entrance to the hotel until the police cars arrived. Then he drove to the Georgetown Hospital located near Georgetown University, where he had a friend at the lab who would test out Merry's blood sample. After dropping it off, he slowly drove back to his brother's house in Georgetown.

Every mile of the way he kept reminding himself that he had to leave Meredith Anders in the hands of the police, that she would be safe there, that if he had stayed he would only have succeeded in embroiling her in his troubles. But through every mile he could still see the sad look in her eyes when she had waited for but had not received the offer from him to stay and face the police with her.

He exhaled a growing irritation with the events that had brought him to this state as he pulled into his brother's small garage and hit the remote control to close the door behind him.

He sighed as he still clutched the steering wheel and tried to count his blessings. At least he had a place to stay where he was comparatively safe. His brother had gone with his family on an extended vacation in Europe. Simon had the run of the place for at least another two weeks. If he could just find what he was looking for in that time, maybe the madness of the last two years would finally come to an end.

Theo, his brother, had listened to an expurgated version of Simon's search for the deadly flu's origin and had told him he should forget it, get on with his life, move away from involvement in something that spanned continents and eluded bureaucratic bumblers.

But Theo was a businessman, not a doctor. Simon could never just sit back and wait when even one life was at stake. He had taken an oath to that effect and it was one he deeply felt. He had tried to explain that to his brother, but Theo had finally just thrown up his hands and given Simon the keys to the Georgetown place on his way out the door.

It had been his brother's way of trying to help. But Simon realized Theo might have had second thoughts about offering that help if he knew Simon was wanted for questioning in a month-old death by the Metropolitan Police.

Now, however, Meredith Anders had entered the picture, giving rise to more complications. He realized she had to go to the police and was glad she would be getting their protection. But if they put a protective guard on her, he would have difficulty seeing her and that made him concerned. He told himself he needed to keep an eye on her in case she began showing symptoms of the deadly flu. But another part of him knew that his interest in her wasn't just from a medical point of view.

He tried to put those thoughts aside. With all that was hanging over his head, he couldn't allow himself to become personally involved with the attractive lawyer. It wouldn't be fair to her.

It was a shame, really. The time they had spent together that evening he had found very enjoyable. He couldn't ever remember meeting anyone like her. She generated a special electric current all her own, one that seemed capable of recharging his low batteries and reaching past his worries to find and tickle his funny bone. And then there were those times she looked into his eyes. . . .

He shook his head, trying to regain his perspective. He could only hope she would honor his request and not divulge his name to the police. What she didn't realize was that if the police found out she knew him, their suspicions of her would double. And if she told them all she knew, they would surely find him and no doubt connect him with the Georgetown murder. His liberty was in her hands. She had promised him nothing. Would she give him away?

"SO, LET ME SEE if I got this straight, Ms. Anders," Sergeant Calder said. "The stranger with the very blue eyes who came to your rescue this morning just happened to be having dinner downstairs in Blackstone's. You noticed him when he was leaving, you followed him out of the restaurant by the parking-lot door and then someone started shooting at both of you."

Sergeant Calder paused to brush an imaginary piece of lint off his immaculate coat. When he resumed, it was in the same less-than-enthusiastic tone for his subject matter.

"Then, this stranger whisked you away in his car and you drove around the city until you lost your pursuers who were driving a blue Cadillac, model and year unknown. Then you came back here to find your room ransacked, you called the desk to send for the police and when you looked around, the stranger had disappeared. Is this correct?"

Everything in the perfectly-groomed man's posture, every nuance in his tone told Merry he didn't believe a word she had told him. She was hungry and tired and fed up with his mocking disbelief. It was after eleven and a lot more than lack of sleep was getting her down. But she reminded herself that her protection for the next couple of days lay in his hands. Which was why she inhaled deeply and simply said, "Yes."

"And how much alcohol have you had this evening?"

There was no missing the message in that question. She kept having to remind herself that she must answer any questions nicely and that she must cooperate. The muscles in her jaw had begun to tighten.

"None."

"What drugs have you taken?"

It was getting harder by the moment to keep a civil tongue in her head.

"None," she repeated through locked teeth.

Sergeant Calder shook his head as his hand swept in a large arc across the room.

"How can you sit in the middle of destruction like this and tell me such a story with a straight face without the help of some pretty heavy duty drugs?"

At that moment Merry decided, despite the fact that this man represented the protection she might need to stay alive, she was still going to have her say.

She inhaled deeply to give sufficient volume to her words. "Over-the-counter aspirin compounds are the strongest drugs I've ever used. But talking to you, Sergeant Calder, is like swallowing an entire plate-glass window. You're such a pain, I doubt even Excedrin could assign a number high enough to properly describe my headache!"

Sergeant Calder crossed his perfectly pressed pant legs and calmly stared at his face reflecting in the shine on his shoes.

"Don't pull that indignant act with me. You're the one talking about disappearing men and wild car chases through the city's streets. And in case you've forgotten, you're also the one who called in this fantasy and insisted on my being dragged into it. I'll ask whatever questions I deem appropriate. That's what I get paid for."

Merry's mounting anger had spilled over and drowned all her resolve to keep her thoughts to herself. She jumped to her feet and glowered over the still-seated detective.

"You're also paid to protect. This morning I was assaulted. This evening I was shot at and my room broken into, and all you've done is try to place the blame on me. Is this how you treat victims of crime in this city?"

Sergeant Calder seemed a little taken back by the anger of her tone and the threatening position of her body over his. Apparently he decided now was the time to fill her in on a few more facts. His voice rose in what was almost a sneer.

"Would it surprise you to know, Ms. Anders, that the man who fell on you in the Smithsonian this morning was murdered?"

Merry heard her own gasp as his message was able to deflate the angry wind in her sails. "What?"

"That's right, Ms. Anders, murdered. As in with intent to consciously deprive of one's life. You getting the message?"

Merry's next question came out in a gulp. "How?"

Sergeant Calder was smiling, as though he was enjoying telling her. "He was choked to death."

"Oh, my God! But how is that possible?"

"Why don't you tell me?" Calder said.

Merry ignored the implication in his question as she strove to regain her equilibrium. "Who was he?"

Calder shook his head. "Any other information concerning this case is confidential."

Merry's hands came up to rest on the sides of her head, as though they could help to hold together her jumbled thoughts. "But how could he have been choked? No one was near him when he collapsed against me."

Calder smiled, not very prettily. "Still, we only have your word about that part, don't we?"

Merry winced from the blow of his unfair accusation. Her anger at the impossibility of her position began to take over. "Damn it, I'm not a murderer! I'm a victim of assault and battery, for God's sake!"

Calder was still smiling. "By whom? A dead man?"

Merry's head was shaking violently. "Of course not! By the two men in suits who tried to drag me out of the museum! I was their victim!"

Calder's look and tone were smug as though he was thoroughly enjoying putting Merry on the defensive. "How do I know you were a victim? No one else saw these two men. And on both of these occasions you've reported being saved by some mysterious stranger, a man who vanishes when anyone else comes near!"

Merry turned to sit back down in her slashed chair, feeling worn and defeated. In relaying her story to Calder earlier, she intentionally hadn't mentioned Simon's name. He had asked her not to, and she felt it was the least she could do, considering all she owed him.

But life would certainly be easier if she could tell Calder who her companion was and get the annoying sergeant off her back. Simon's refusal to come forward to the police was bothering her, particularly since she had learned the dead man had been murdered. What was Simon hiding?

Calder was watching her face expectantly. "Well, Ms. Anders? Are you going to tell me who this mysterious stranger is?"

She sighed, knowing that no matter what Simon's reasons for avoiding the police, she could not give him away. He had saved her life and he was counting on her. She could not betray him. Her shoulders rose with the effort of her continuing struggle to be believed.

"All I can tell you is he's real and his total involvement in this mess came from his attempt to assist me in getting away from those two men."

Calder's face began to collect color. "Are you going to sit there and try to convince me you don't know the man's name?"

Merry shook her head. "I'm trying to convince you that his name is of no importance to your case. It's those two men who are threatening me. The one's who grabbed me at the Smithsonian, shot at me tonight and came back to destroy this room. You've got to believe me, Sergeant. I need protection from those two men."

Calder's voice reflected his growing irritation. "I don't have to believe anything, Ms. Anders. You're withholding evidence in a murder case. You know it. I know it. If you and this stranger are really innocent, then you'll give me his name so I can check out your story. Unless you do, you might just find yourself—"

"What are you doing to Merry?" a very angry and loud voice said suddenly from the door. Merry looked up to see Karen hurrying to where she sat in the chair.

"You look terrible!" Karen said. "What has this horrible man been doing to you?"

Sergeant Calder did not look at all happy. "Now, just a minute, Miss—"

Karen ignored him. "What happened to this place? Are you hurt? Should I call the senator and have him intercede?"

Merry smiled over into Karen's quick blink, at once understanding what her friend was doing.

"I don't think that will be necessary," she said. "Not just yet, anyway."

Karen put her arm under Merry's and made a big show of helping her to her feet. Merry rose with a groan, deciding that the spirit of the moment demanded it.

"Come on," Karen said. "You can tell me all about it tomorrow morning. You're coming home with me right now. We'll get you something to eat and then put you into bed. Perhaps I'd best call the doctor."

Merry was getting tickled at her friend's take-charge attitude. It had been a lot of years since she had been mothered.

From the defused look on the sergeant's face, however, Merry knew Karen was doing and saying exactly the right things.

"I've got to get my clothes," Merry said.

Karen didn't take her protest seriously. "You'll borrow some of my things tonight. We'll have one of the servants come back and pack this stuff up tomorrow."

To Karen's credit, Sergeant Calder made no protests as she led Merry quite determinedly to the door. It was only when they were about to pass through that he halted their progress.

"And what is your name, please?" he asked Karen.

His use of *please* was not lost on Merry. Karen's nose went farther into the air as she still refused to look at the sergeant, as though looking at him might place him on a higher status than he deserved.

"That is none of your business."

"I'll need Ms. Anders's new address and telephone number," the sergeant said. It was a request made humbly.

"Ms. Anders will be in touch tomorrow. Good night."

Karen had spoken those last words in much the same tone she would have used to dismiss a particularly displeasing servant. Then, with the haughtiness of royalty having to deal with peasants, Karen marched Merry out the door and toward the elevators.

Merry almost couldn't believe she had escaped. She kept looking back, expecting Sergeant Calder to follow them. The elevator was already on the third floor. They stepped in and remained quiet until they reached the first floor. Only when they emerged from the elevator into the lobby did Merry sigh in relief.

Karen was the first to speak. "Merry, what's going on?"

Merry's sigh was deep. "It's a long story going back to that man who collapsed on me this morning. I've just found out he was murdered."

"Murdered? How awful! And to think he collapsed on you. My God, you poor thing!"

Merry shrugged. "I'm really okay. How did you know I needed rescuing?"

Karen swung her arm through Merry's and smiled. "When they told me they couldn't put my call through to your room because the police were here, I rushed right over. As soon as the uniformed officer outside your room told me it was a Sergeant Calder questioning you, I thought the uppity approach might be the best way to extricate you from his clutches."

Merry smiled. "You mean those references to senatorial intervention and the servants, of course. I thought them inspired. Heaven knows they did the trick. Where did you dream up that stuff?"

Karen smiled as they started down the front steps to her silver BMW at the curb.

"Works great, doesn't it? This is a city of privilege. I think probably more than in any other place in the world, who you are here determines how you are treated. I learned that when my father was a senator from Florida and I really did have servants catering to my every wish. Just because those little details have altered, I see no reason to stop using a line that works."

Merry laughed. "Someday you're going to have to tell me who other than Sergeant Calder has been the victim of your 'uppity' approach."

"We'll make it an exchange," Karen said as she unlocked the passenger's side. "But you first. I have to know what happened to make you run away from the table tonight. By the way, I put your American Express Card in my dresser. Remind me to give it to you later. And I had the waiter put your broiled salmon in a doggie bag. It's in the refrigerator at home. We'll reheat it in the microwave."

"Karen, my friend, you are without equal. I think I'd kill for that salmon about now."

"Ssh! Not so loud. Sergeant Calder might be listening," Karen said with a lighthearted chuckle. "Besides, all I ask is that you answer some questions. And for a starter, who was that tall, dark and handsome man you chased out of the restaurant?"

"He was the man who rescued me from those hoodlums this morning," Merry said as she got into the passenger's seat of Karen's car.

"That handsome hunk? This gets better by the minute. Tell your favorite ex-sister-in-law all!"

"Lead me to food first or I may faint in the middle of my story. And after it, I've got to find something out. Your reminding me of the power of privilege has given me an idea. What are your contacts in this city? Could you call in a favor or two from one of your father's friends?''

Karen shook her head. ''Not really. In Florida, maybe, but not D.C. As a Supreme Court law clerk I've been too busy to cultivate many political contacts. And whereas Diane, my stepmother, probably knows a few people, I would be loathe to ask her any favors.''

Merry shrugged. ''Well, that means I'm really going to have to take time out to telephone my partner, Laura.''

''Is Laura well connected?''

''Very well connected. Her husband was a U.S. congressman from the State of Washington before his death, and Laura is still widely accepted in D.C.'s political society. I need her help.''

''All right, I'm third on the list behind food and Laura. But I warn you, Merry. No sleep tonight until I hear it all.''

LAURA OSBOURNE WOKE to the incessant shrill of the telephone demanding attention on the nightstand. She pushed her thick chestnut hair out of her eyes and tried unsuccessfully to read the out-of-focus clock.

She grabbed for her reading glasses that had fallen on the bed and shoved them impatiently onto her nose. The fuzzy red numerals grew instantly sharp. It was just after 9:00 p.m. She must have fallen asleep while reading. She could think of only one person who could be calling this late on this very special night. She reached for the phone eagerly.

''Darling, I thought you were going to call in the morning?'' she said, without the preamble of a hello.

There was a momentary silence on the other end of the line.

''Laura?'' a woman's voice asked.

Laura cursed herself silently for her exuberant foolishness. Now she realized she should have made sure who was calling before blabbing her head off. Nothing to do but to try to talk her way out of it. Fortunately, Merry was a believing soul.

''Yes, it's me, Merry. Sorry. I was talking gibberish there. You woke me out of a deep sleep. I guess I didn't sound like myself, did I?''

"Well, you had me wondering who 'darling' was. Were you dreaming of Ed?"

Laura realized instantly Merry had assumed all her thoughts waking and sleeping were still about Ed Osbourne, her late husband. She didn't like deceiving her junior partner, but under the circumstances she didn't think she had much choice.

"Yes. I was dreaming of Ed. Sorry."

"No, Laura. It's I who should be sorry for calling this late. However things got a little out of hand for me here today. You see, I've run into some trouble."

Laura's normally deep voice went up an octave. "Trouble? Joseph Freedman?"

"No, not with the diamond case," Merry said. "I've met with Mr. Freedman and will keep in contact with him as promised. And although arguing convincingly for our side is certainly not going to be easy, it's not the court appearance that's bothering me. The trouble is personal. I'm afraid I've gotten into a bit of a mess."

"What's wrong, Merry?"

"Well, as crazy as this seems, I was witness to a man's death. I don't want to go into all the details, but the police have been giving me a rather rotten time since."

Laura sat up straighter in the bed with every word she heard.

"But I don't understand? Why are they giving you a bad time?" Laura asked.

"Well, there's someone who's helped me, someone I trust. The police want to question him, but I'm trying not to involve him."

"Him? Is this somebody I know?"

"No, Laura, and like I said, I don't want to go into all the details now, but there is something I'd really appreciate your doing for me."

"Of course. Anything. Just name it."

"Well, I was wondering if you still keep in contact with some of Ed's and your influential friends here in D.C.?"

"Yes. Several. What is it you need?"

"I need to find out the identity of a man. He was murdered in the Smithsonian Museum of Natural History this morning around ten o'clock, my time, that is."

Laura heard the incredulity in her own voice. "The man was murdered?"

Merry sighed. "Yes. I think it's important I try to find out why. So I need not just his name, but who he really was. You know, profession, friends, associates and as much of his past as possible. I also need to find out the specifics of how he died. Can you do this for me?"

Laura was quiet for a minute thinking. "It shouldn't be a problem. I'll call first thing in the morning. But the police must be digging for this same information if the man was murdered. Won't they give it to you?"

"The police haven't been exactly cooperative. I feel more like a suspect than a witness."

"Dear God, they suspect you? The imbeciles!"

Merry's newest sigh sounded relieved. "Thank you, Laura. Your confidence in my innocence feels real good about now."

Laura started to feel a mounting concern. "Merry, you sound strange, almost beaten down. Do you need a criminal lawyer to deal with the police? There are some fine ones there. I could put you in contact with one first thing tomorrow."

"No, Laura. Thanks just the same. So far I've only been subjected to a bad-mannered police sergeant and charged with innuendoes. Thoughts of a lawyer are premature."

"Wash your mouth out, Merry Anders! As a lawyer you should never say such a thing!"

Merry laughed. "I am properly chastised, and you're right, thoughts of engaging a lawyer are never premature. But I see no clear and present danger of my being charged with a crime I didn't commit."

Laura relaxed at the renewed confidence in Merry's tone. "Okay. I trust your judgment. Shall I call you at your hotel when I get the information about the murdered man?"

Merry paused just a bit before answering. "Uh, no. I'm not there anymore. I'm staying with Karen Richfield, my law-clerk friend. The number is 555-555-1212."

"Okay, got it. But I may not have this information until late tomorrow, your tomorrow, that is."

"Whatever you can do, Laura. And thanks."

After Merry had hung up, Laura lay awake for a long time staring in the dark. One thought kept raking through her mind. He should have told her when he called. Why hadn't he?

## Chapter Seven

Merry walked into the beautifully appointed kitchen of Florida House, the oldest state residence in the nation's capital, and gave a start at the ringing of the telephone.

Karen was leaning against the counter, a piece of toast in her hand. "It's Sunday morning and I just refuse to answer. Maybe whoever it is will go away," she said, smiling.

She kept her resolve through several more shrill, electronic whines. Then with a shrug of her thin shoulders, Karen belied her brave words by picking up the receiver. Her conversation was short and from the expression on her face, disappointing.

"I knew I shouldn't have answered. I've got to go into work today," Karen said as soon as she had hung up.

"You can't even take Sunday off?" Merry asked.

Karen shook her head. "It seems Justice Stone is depending on his staff to have certain information ready for him when Court opens tomorrow morning. I've got to spend time in the library today. Here, I'll leave the numbers for the library and the justice's private chambers on this note pad by the phone, just in case."

"When do you have to leave?" Merry asked.

"Now," Karen said, picking up her briefcase and shoving the piece of dry toast into her mouth. She reached into her pocket and brought out a key. "Keep this in case you need to go in and out. It's an extra key to the front door."

"Thanks," Merry said, taking the key. "Well, at least now I know why you hardly weigh anything. You hardly have time to eat anything! You are going to be careful to not overtire yourself, to monitor yourself for any possible weakness or fever?"

Karen watched Merry's anxious face as she swallowed her bite of toast. "Yes, of course, although I agree with Joseph Freedman. Your warning to us both is appreciated, but from everything you said, the possibility of being infected by this mysterious flu seems pretty remote."

"I really believe it is remote, Karen. Frankly, I wasn't going to mention it to you or Mr. Freedman. But since even Simon doesn't know enough to judge who could become infected, I felt I had to tell you. If either of you were to become ill and I hadn't warned you to be alert to seek treatment right away—"

"Yes, I understand," Karen interrupted. "Informed is protected, and you'll be the first to know if I don't feel well. Actually, what I really feel is guilt because your first day in D.C. was rotten and now on your second, I'm deserting you."

Merry shook her head, determined not to let Karen feel that way. "Nonsense. I'm glad to get you out of the house. It will give me a chance to concentrate on my legal maneuvering for tomorrow. So, begone with you. Parting is not such sweet sorrow after all."

Karen laughed. "As long as you're back to misquoting Shakespeare, I know you're okay. I've laid out a pair of light brown cotton slacks and a matching top. Oh, and while you were in the shower, I called one of the Georgetown house servants. He'll pick up your things from the hotel and bring them here later this afternoon."

"So you really are going to have a servant gather everything up?" Merry asked.

Karen nodded. "After thinking over your second escape from those awful men, I decided, why not? You'll love him, too. His name is Charles, but we call him Mr. T., with good reason as you'll see when he comes by. His presence should keep Sergeant Calder guessing awhile longer. Now, I've got to run."

Merry walked Karen to the door. "Know when you'll be home?"

Karen frowned in thought. "Probably between five and six. I invited Joseph Freedman here to an early dinner at seven."

"When did you do that? There was nothing said in our telephone conversation with him this morning about dinner," Merry said.

"After you ran out on us at the restaurant last night, I invited him over. By the way, you should have seen his face when you took off like that. For a minute there, he looked so worried, I thought he was going to follow you."

"Really? Joseph Freedman was worried about me?"

"You sound surprised," Karen said.

"Yes, it's hard for me to ascribe more than surface emotion to him. He seems so controlled and withdrawn. But anyway, dinner does sound like a good idea. Shall I help cook?"

Karen's tone sounded incredulous. "Cook? Merry, please. Toast is the extent of my culinary talents. I'm having dinner catered and I'll be here before it arrives. Now don't open the door to anyone after I leave. Are you sure you're going to be okay alone?"

Merry nodded. "Go jump into your musty law books. You're wasting my thinking time."

But as soon as Karen had left and Merry had gotten dressed, she knew she didn't have any new logical rabbit she could pull out of her legal hat. The case was pretty clear-cut. She believed in it and she believed in herself. That had been the winning combination in the past, and she knew it was all she had to offer the men and woman of the Supreme Court.

It was time to call Sergeant Calder and leave her address and telephone number as Karen had promised the night before. Merry picked up the telephone wishing she was dialing almost anyone else's number. But her spirits brightened when the office told her he wasn't in. She left her name and Karen's name and address and quickly hung up, considering her duty done.

She wondered where Simon was today and if he had gotten the results of her blood test. It suddenly occurred to her that even if he had, he wouldn't know where to get in touch with her since she had not left a forwarding address with the hotel. Damn. She wished now she had had the presence of mind to get his local address or at least his telephone number last night.

She almost picked up the receiver again and dialed information for the telephone number of the Centers for Disease Control in Atlanta to track him down, but at the last minute she thought better of it. If Laura got her the information on the dead man as she promised, it wouldn't be coming through until the afternoon. Before making an effort to locate Simon, Merry wanted to have something she could share with him.

Maybe if she could find out some useful information, she would feel like more of a contributor to the solving of their respective mysteries. She really wanted to help him ever since she heard the awful frustration in his voice when he described all the dead ends he had run into on his investigation. He had helped her so much. She'd like to be able to respond in kind.

Of course that wasn't the only reason she wanted to work with him. He was an extremely attractive, exciting man and she was finding she had few defenses against his engaging charm.

She leaned over to the wood-shuttered window and undid the latch to let in some natural light. Several multicolored fall leaves scooted onto the patch of grass near the curb, but most of the trees were still draped in their summer-green cloaks.

She drew back into the room feeling a deep ache from within her shoulders. Her body had begun to feel the abuse it had been put through the last day. She couldn't seem to locate one part of her anatomy that didn't have an ache pestering it. She stretched her muscles, feeling them cry out for movement. Then she suddenly knew what she could do next.

She'd walk to the Smithsonian to see what more she could find out about the Fire Diamond. After all, Simon had agreed the night before it was the connecting link between their two mysteries. The sudden decision sat well with her desire to be out in the air and sun. She placed the strap of her bag around her shoulder and headed out the door, down the red-brick steps to the street.

The temperature was somewhere in the sixties and the air was heavy with humidity, but she didn't find the day particularly unpleasant. The movement of her arms and legs already seemed to be helping her circulation.

However, when she reached the Museum of Natural History, she was disappointed to learn from the personnel at the information desk that not only wasn't the museum's curator for gems and minerals at work on a Sunday, but also that even if he had been, he did not make it a practice to meet with visitors.

She should have anticipated the difficulties. Explaining to the museum personnel she wasn't just a visitor to the museum but the woman who had been involved with the murdered man the day before would hardly supply her with impressive credentials. She decided the smart thing to do was to return to Florida House and wait for Laura's call. But before she did, she wanted to see the Fire Diamond just once more.

She took the elevator to the second floor and soon was standing before the sparkling red gem, again struck by the magnificent glow of its unusual color. It was mesmerizing, claiming her attention, drawing her into its dancing, fiery depths.

Suddenly, from the corner of her eye, Merry detected the presence of someone next to her. Startled, she turned in remembered horror of the man from the morning before.

"I'm sorry, miss. Didn't mean to scare you. But I thought I recognized you."

Merry was trying to will her racing heartbeat slower as she looked across to the gray eyes of the guard she had met the day before. He sounded a lot friendlier than his first greeting when he had come upon her on the floor outside the Gem and Mineral Room.

"Tritten's the name, isn't it?" she asked, recovering sufficiently to hold out her hand.

He gave it a limp shake. "Yes, James Tritten. And you're Meredith Anders. That was some experience you had yesterday. I see the police cleared you."

Merry nodded at his assumption, not feeling it necessary to mention she felt a lot less than cleared.

"Can't say I blame you for being jumpy," he said. "Radio news last night said that guy was murdered."

"You heard that on the news? When?" Merry asked.

"Oh, late. Ten or eleven, I expect."

"Did the report say who the man was or how he was killed?"

"Nope. Just that he was found dead in front of the diamond displays. Curious it should have happened here. But dead body or no, I can see the Fire Diamond has brought you back. There'll be flocks of people milling around soon. You should have seen the crowds we had to turn back yesterday because of the police investigation. It was after noon when they finally took the restraining yellow tape away. Gawkers were so thick after that, people could barely move."

"I can believe it," Merry said. "It's certainly the most beautiful diamond I've ever seen. From everything I've read, it's the only one that has that brilliant red shooting from its center. Some experts guess a form of phosphorescence, but no one seems to really know for certain what is causing it."

"Blood, more than likely," Tritten said.

The familiar word dripped stickily down her spine. She turned in surprise to see the guard's expression was quite serious. Perhaps he knew something that could be of help? She tried to keep her voice light and conversational.

"Blood? Whatever made you say that?"

"Well, because of the reason for the stone's donation to the museum, of course. Still, they don't like us to talk about that sort of thing. You know, bad publicity."

Merry could tell from the expression on James Tritten's face that despite any caution a superior may have given him, it was a subject he relished. She set about to coax him.

"I've read articles about the diamond in *The Gemletter* and *The Smithsonian*, but nothing was ever said about its owners or anything to do with blood."

Tritten nodded. "No, naturally not. You can't get the whole story from those official publications."

Tritten had said the word *official* as though it was synonymous with cover-up.

"What is the whole story, Mr. Tritten?"

The guard looked around, almost furtively. "Come with me," he said, taking Merry's arm.

He led Merry to the elevator and pressed the button for the third floor. When they stepped from its doors, he again looked around carefully. Satisfied no one was watching, he used a key to pass them through a door marked Staff Only. As they stepped through, it locked behind them.

Merry followed Tritten to the back of the room where he reached into a desk drawer and pulled out some papers. He handed them to Merry and pointed toward a chair beside the desk. The papers were photocopies of an article from a tabloid newspaper and had coffee spilled all over them. Merry could barely make out the date of publication as being two weeks before. She was just about to return the article to Tritten when the headline caused her to reconsider and sit down.

## MILLIONAIRE KILLED
## WIFE CLAIMS FIRE DIAMOND CAUSE

Merry looked over at Tritten. "The coffee stains make this difficult to read. What does it say?"

Tritten sat across from her, looking smug in his superior knowledge as he took the unreadable article back from her outstretched hand.

"Well, it seems that Fire Diamond was owned by this real wealthy guy who purchased it sort of quietlike, intending to keep it for his private collection. But in this article his wife says he only had the rock for a couple of months when he starts to get sick. Mesmerized by the blood in the stone, she says. Makes him sweaty and weak. Then one day after holding it a while, he walks out into the street, groggylike, and bang—a car hits him dead center. A doctor is even apparently right there on the scene, but he can't do anything for the guy. Dies in the street."

"From being hit by the car?" Merry asked.

"The police say so. They're still looking for the hit-and-run-driver. But the guy's wife tells them she knows it was the Fire Diamond that caused her husband's death. She unloads the rock real quick by donating it to the museum. Says its evil reached out to kill her husband."

Merry leaned back in her chair, feeling a little creepy. The description "sweaty and weak" sounded all too familiar. Was the previous owner of the Fire Diamond a victim of Carmichael's mysterious flu?

"Well, what do you say? You agree with the widow it's blood in the heart of that stone?" Tritten asked.

Merry stood up and tried to smile. "It's obvious she believed it. Does the article mention her name?"

Tritten shook his head. "No, those rich people don't like having their names in the newspapers. Pay to keep them out more than likely. Personally, I think this woman would have also paid the museum to get them to take that diamond. Scared, she was."

Merry didn't think she possessed enough of the facts to judge the truth of that statement. But she was thankful for the information. It was something she could tell Simon about when she saw him next.

She was sure she'd see him. Her nature just wouldn't let her be a defeatist. "Thank you for sharing the clipping with me," she told Tritten. "I'd like to look at the diamond again."

Tritten led the way out of the staff room without comment. It wasn't until they were going down the elevator to the second floor and the Gem Room that he spoke again.

"Sure is strange how that guy got it in front of the Fire Diamond. Kind of makes you wonder, doesn't it?"

Merry nodded out of politeness. Calder had told her that the man had choked to death. He hadn't died of the deadly flu that seemed to follow the Fire Diamond. Considering her close encounter with him, she was hoping the man hadn't had the disease.

Tritten left her at the Gem Room entrance. The museum had filled up considerably since she had arrived. It took her a few minutes to work her way back in front of the Fire Diamond through the stream of people wanting to see the spectacular jewel.

She couldn't help being struck anew with its beauty. She had always loved the sparkle of a diamond, and this red gem was a true miracle of nature. No crystals, no bubbles, no cracks, no featherlike fractures, no carbon spots or clouds—nothing to deter the passage of light through its beautifully faceted face. Just an internal red fire that enhanced its brilliance beyond all others.

How could something so incredibly beautiful possibly be linked with death?

SIMON THANKED the personnel at the information desk for their time and slipped the piece of paper containing the curator's name and office hours into his pocket.

He wasn't going to take a chance that the administrative personnel of the gem and mineral collection might check on his credentials like those at the medical examiner's office did. He just secured enough information to help him slip by their possible defenses when they returned to their offices the next day.

A desire to secure an appointment with the curator of the gem and mineral collection had been the reason he had come to the Smithsonian the day before and been on hand to witness the two men dragging Merry out. Perhaps it was just as well

other events had intervened. Now he was better prepared to
meet with the curator on Monday morning.

As he started toward the exit, a large influx of visitors coming through the doors of the museum caused Simon to step
back. He waited for them to pass, standing in front of the
stuffed, life-size, charging African elephant that dominated the
center of the first-floor rotunda.

A blond woman in their midst caught his eye as the shade of
her hair looked vaguely familiar. A second look convinced him
it wasn't Merry, however.

Thoughts of the vivacious lawyer brought a concerned frown
to his face. The morning's radio news said the dead man in the
Smithsonian had been murdered. Upon hearing that news, Simon had immediately tried to call her, but the hotel had informed him that she had checked out, leaving no forwarding
address.

He couldn't blame her for leaving the place and covering her
tracks. It was the sensible thing to do considering the fact that
her two pursuers had found her there. But it irked him that he
hadn't thought of that the night before and arranged to meet
her somewhere today. He just hadn't been thinking straight.

That seemed to be his general state of mind recently. He
should have figured the police would find her another hotel and
register her under an assumed name while they investigated her
story. He still couldn't be sure she hadn't told the police about
him, but if she had, at least they hadn't tracked him to his
brother's home. Yet.

The green-and-gray Subaru's presence lurked at the back of
his mind like a sinister shadow. Someone had used it to kill.
Had one of Merry's would-be abductors been the man who had
driven it on the day of the millionaire's death?

And what was causing this deadly illness that attacked the
body but didn't use the blood as its vehicle of systemic infection?

Questions without answers. His life had become riddled with
them ever since Carmichael had stumbled into that damn Mozambique clinic. But perhaps the question that bothered him
the most at the moment was whether he would ever again see
the warm look in a particular pair of translucent-brown eyes.

"Simon!"

Startled, Simon turned in the direction of the calling voice and blinked as though he was seeing things as Merry stepped off the elevator. He just stood as though in a trance as she walked through the crowd toward him, that warm, familiar look shining out of her eyes. He had the strange sensation he had just conjured her up from his thoughts of only a second before.

"You're here," he said, quite unnecessarily as she reached him. He was still finding her presence a little more than remarkable. It had been a long time since one of his wishes had come true.

The noise from the milling crowd caused Merry to raise her voice in response. "Yes, I came to find out more about the Fire Diamond. What luck running into you this way!"

Merry looked up into the full blue of Simon's eyes. Her eyes had been drawn to his instantly, despite the crowd. She was beginning to find new meaning to the phrase "magnetic personality."

Simon took ahold of Merry's arm and started to steer her toward the rear portion of the museum, away from the doors through which more and more people flooded every second.

He leaned down close to her ear. "Let's find a quieter place to talk. I think I saw a sign for a restaurant back here earlier. Since it's after eleven-thirty, they should be open. Are you hungry?"

Since she had eaten her warmed-up dinner late the night before, Merry hadn't wanted breakfast when she first arose. Now her stomach was beginning to protest its empty state. "Starved," she said into his ear.

He smiled at her enthusiasm, finding his own appetite suddenly stronger. There was something about the way she expressed her feelings that he found contagious. He led her down a hallway that was labeled the Associates Court Restaurant.

When the maitre d' asked for his membership card, he pulled it out of his wallet and they were shown to a table.

"Come here often, do you?" Merry asked after they were seated.

Simon smiled, realizing he had surprised her. "First time, actually. This is not that private a club. You see, anyone can be a member of the Smithsonian Associates by paying an annual dues. You get the *Smithsonian Monthly Magazine*, which is the primary reason I joined, and a few other perks, one of which is the right to eat in the Associates Court Restaurant when you come to town. Shall we sample the buffet?''

The food was good, plain American fare. Their full plates were quickly emptied. Simon sat back and watched Merry sipping her iced tea.

"I'd like to ask you if you've learned anything about the Fire Diamond, but I think it would only be fair to concentrate on a few other matters first. And number one is that I got the results of the blood test this morning and I want to assure you that there's nothing to worry about so far. Your white-cell count is right up there with the best of them."

Merry put her iced tea down and leaned back in her chair, a relieved smile on her lips. "Thank goodness. Well, at least that worry is over."

Simon shook his head. "Not entirely, Merry. I shouldn't have been so imprecise. What this means is that you aren't displaying any symptoms. That could mean either you're not infected or that you are, but it's too soon to observe the infection."

The air escaped from her pumped-up relief. "Oh."

Simon frowned, realizing he might be ready to give her more unsettling news. "Did you know the man who collapsed on you was murdered?"

She nodded. "Sergeant Calder was happy to inform me of that last night."

Simon detected the upset in her voice. "Happy to inform you? What's wrong? And why are you walking around unescorted? I thought you were going to ask for protection from the police last night?"

Merry sighed. "I tried, but Sergeant Calder just didn't believe my story of what happened. He acted like he thought I made up those two men. He seemed more interested in you than in them."

Simon studied her face. "You didn't give him my name?"

Merry looked at him with indignation. "Of course not. I'm not the kind of person who repays kindness with a betrayal. But I'm not going to pretend that I think you're doing the right thing. You should go to the police. Whatever is going on, they're the ones trained for straightening it out."

Simon cocked an eyebrow at her. "Like they've been straightening it out for you?"

Merry shrugged and smiled. "Okay, they haven't done such a wonderful job. But they might improve in attitude at least if you materialized before them in the flesh, so to speak. I know Sergeant Calder isn't convinced you're real."

Merry went on to relate as clearly as possible her very unsatisfactory conversation with the police sergeant, including his informing her of the dead man's murder by choking.

"That's when he really started drilling me about who you are," Merry said. "Frankly, I think he sees me as the primary suspect. Why is it that you don't want to talk to the police?"

Simon was saved from answering by the sudden appearance of the waiter to freshen their iced teas. By the time the waiter left, Simon was ready with a question of his own, which forestalled Merry's pursuit of the subject he was not ready to discuss.

"Did you learn anything new about the Fire Diamond?"

She looked at him for a moment, obviously disappointed. Then she sighed in resignation at his avoidance of her earlier question.

"Actually, I talked with James Tritten, the museum guard who came up to me after the fight with those two men yesterday morning," she said. "He told me some interesting background information about the Fire Diamond's last owners, that multimillionaire you mentioned."

"What did he say?" Simon asked.

Merry told Simon about the contents of the tabloid newspaper article. "Of course, considering the source, I'm not sure how much of the information, if any, is reliable. It was from one of those sensationalist tabloids. You know, the one in which the headlines occasionally claim things like extraterrestrial aliens have invaded the United States."

Simon nodded. "Yes. I seem to remember reading such headlines on the publications next to the junk candy while waiting in the check-out line at the supermarket."

"That's it," Merry said. "But I thought it was interesting that the widow was sure her husband had become ill after acquiring the stone and the words *weak* and *sweaty* seemed familiar symptoms from what you told me about the deadly flu.''

Simon was silently fingering his glass of iced tea, staring at the ice cubes but obviously seeing something else. Merry was about to ask what it was when he looked up at her.

"There weren't any specifics about the hit-and-run?"

Merry searched her memory. "Just what I told you. Something about how the guy had staggered into the path of the car and about him dying at the scene despite a doctor being there. The police were sure he died as a result of the hit-and-run. The widow claimed the Fire Diamond was responsible. Of course, this was all a pretty sensationalized account of whatever really happened."

Simon was quiet again and Merry frowned as the meaning of his previous question began to sink in. "There's something about the article that is bothering you, isn't there?"

He didn't respond, but Merry could tell from the look on his face that she had guessed right. "Simon, what is it?"

He remained quiet, still studying the glass of iced tea.

Merry was beginning to feel exasperated. "Simon, please tell me. You must realize that not knowing what is going on here is beginning to drive me crazy. If there's something you know that will help me to understand . . ." Her voice faded.

He exhaled a long breath before answering, finally looking up from the glass to meet her eyes. She watched him anxiously.

"The green-and-gray Subaru," Simon said. "The car one of your abductors drove away from the museum yesterday after his attack on you. It was the car involved in the hit-and-run of the millionaire who last possessed the Fire Diamond. That's why I said those two men were connected to the jewel."

Merry took another gulp of her iced tea, trying to swallow the surprising statement Simon had just made. "They were involved in the death of the millionaire?"

"The car was," Simon said. "I don't know who was driving it. Now I've told you what I know."

Despite his assurance, more questions immediately began to swim through Merry's head. "If you don't know who was driving it, how do you know about that car being the one involved?"

Simon shook his head. "I just know."

Merry felt Simon's reluctance to elaborate. She wondered uneasily what was preventing him. "Do the police know?" she asked.

Simon sighed. "Yes. They know everything I do. Now, please don't ask any more questions about the car, Merry."

Merry heard something sharp and unbending in Simon's voice that shocked her into an immediate quiet. Her teeth scraped across her tongue as she tried to curb the verbalization of a lot of flowing thoughts.

"All right," she said when she could keep quiet no longer. "At least now I know the men after me are tied into the death of the millionaire who last owned the Fire Diamond. Or, more precisely as you've pointed out, one of their cars is. Is there anything else you can tell me?"

"No. Nothing," Simon said.

Merry repositioned herself in her chair as though she was feeling uncomfortable with his response. "Still, wouldn't you say it's suspicious that a car owned by one of these men is the hit-and-run vehicle responsible for the death of the previous owner of the Fire Diamond? And then these two men show up at the scene of a second death, the choking of the man at the Smithsonian in front of that same Fire Diamond. Do you believe in that much coincidence?"

Simon was shaking his head. "No. Logic tells me those men must have been involved in the murder of the man at the Smithsonian. But unless we learn who these people are, I don't see much hope in our being able to figure out what's really going on here."

"Well, I may be getting some of those answers," Merry said.

Simon's voice sounded surprised. "From where?"

"My law partner back in Washington State. She's using her contacts here in the Capital to find out what she can about the guy who collapsed on me. As a matter of fact, she may be trying to reach me now. I should get back to Florida House and stay by the phone."

Simon nodded as he stood up to take Merry's chair. "You're staying at Florida House? I'll drive you there and we can wait together. My car is only parked a couple of blocks away."

Merry gladly agreed, but when, after walking a couple of blocks, they arrived at a dumpy-looking pea-green Toyota, she turned to him with a question on her face.

"The Porsche is in the shop. Back window, remember?" he said in answer to her unspoken question.

"What garage is open on a Sunday?" she asked.

Simon shrugged as he leaned down to open the passenger's side. "My brother's the owner, so the garage's manager gives me special treatment. Or at least he used to. When he handed me the keys to this baby, I began to wonder. Wait until you see inside."

Merry couldn't wait. She leaned down and peered through the window of the car at the faded and torn interior.

"For heaven's sake, it's red! Who in their right mind would order a red interior with a pea-green exterior?" she asked.

"Someone who didn't want their car stolen, maybe?"

Merry laughed. "I see your point."

Simon opened the passenger door for her and as she passed him to get in, she smelled the faint, clean soap scent that seemed so much a part of his skin. Smell had always been a powerful stimulator for her. She felt a warm rush spread through her body at his nearness.

She sat in the passenger's seat and, when he got in, found herself watching the well-developed muscles in his forearms flex as he positioned the key in the ignition and shifted the gears. Without thinking she picked up an old Publisher's Clearing House circular from the seat and began fanning herself with it.

Simon looked over at her, apparently misunderstanding her sudden warmth. "Sorry, no air conditioning. Once we get going there should be a breeze. Try opening your window."

Merry smiled as she complied with Simon's suggestion, aware it would take a bit more than a breeze to fan away the reason for her sudden warmth. But as she rolled the window down, she glanced into the outside mirror and saw a sight chilly enough to do the trick. A green-and-gray Subaru had just turned the corner and was coming up behind them!

# Chapter Eight

"Simon! Behind us!" Merry yelled.

"Yes. I see it. Don't panic. Believe it or not, I don't think it's after us. Look. The driver is pulling into the parking space we just vacated."

Merry's voice was a study in relieved disbelief. "He didn't see us?"

"I don't think so," Simon said. "My guess is he didn't expect to see us in anything but a black Porsche, so he didn't even give this Toyota a once over. We just got a lucky break."

"Is it possible it's not the same Subaru?" Merry asked.

Simon shook his head. "It's the same green-and-gray Subaru. That's a custom, two-tone job. Very distinctive. And I recognize the license. It's a Maryland plate that begins with the two letters, *SC*. Then the rest of the license is blotted out with dried mud. Look who's getting out."

Merry was looking. She recognized one of the men right away. He seemed to be alone this time. He took off toward the museum.

"Coming across the car this way is a stroke of real luck," Simon said. "Now I can find out what it is I need to know."

"What you need to know?" Merry repeated, turning in her seat toward him. "I don't understand."

"The rest of the license plate number, Merry. I'm going to drop you off at Florida House and come back to scrape off the mud and find out what it is."

Merry was shaking her head. "But, Simon, if he comes back unexpectedly or if the other man is around somewhere..."

Simon had already gunned the Toyota and was zipping around the corner. "Don't worry. They're not expecting me, remember?"

Unfortunately, after Simon dropped Merry off and drove back the few blocks to the museum, he couldn't find another place to park. The minutes ticked by as he drove around. Finally in desperation, he double parked on the street next to where the Subaru was and ran across the separating green lawn, dodging the sparsely-spaced shade trees. However, when he arrived, he found himself looking at an empty parking space. The Subaru was gone.

Frantically, he looked back and forth, searching up and down the street for any sign of the distinctive, green-and-gray car. There was none.

Frustration hung in his throat like an aching lump. He had missed his chance, maybe his only chance, to get the full license number of the car and clear himself. His fists clenched at his sides. An uncharacteristic impulse engulfed him. Suddenly he wanted just to pound something, anything. His right fist rose in readiness as his eyes alighted on the innocent trunk of a nearby tree. Then he thought about what he was doing.

He was letting the anger control him. This was unlike the person he knew himself to be. Inhaling deeply he opened his hand instead and circled the unoffending shade tree with his fingers. He leaned his head against the white bark and closed his eyes, determined not to let this latest setback defeat him.

Simon knew the continuing frustrations were taking their toll, but he mustn't lose his mental control. Without reason there was no hope. And he badly needed whatever hope he could muster. Gradually, his equilibrium returned. He leaned away from the tree and was just starting to turn back toward the street where the Toyota was double-parked when he felt the heavy hand alight on his shoulder. Instantly, his relaxed guard came to full attention as he swung around ready for a fight.

MERRY PACED IMPATIENTLY around the floor of Florida House, waiting for Simon to return and feeling the minutes drag by. She started to think of all the reasons why she should have insisted on staying and checking out the Subaru with him. She could have acted as lookout. She had a sharp nail file in her shoulder bag that could have been used to scrap away the mud from the obliterated license plate number.

Her head shook in renewed recognition of something she had experienced many times before. Only after an event did she think of all the clever things she could have said and done during it. Why was it that hindsight was always such a damn sight better?

She was so far sunk into self-recrimination that when the doorbell sounded, she jumped in surprise. She ran to the door in expectation that it would be Simon, only to stop on the threshold as other possibilities presented themselves. As the doorbell sounded again, she moved over to the balcony window and looked down at the street. Sitting right out front, baking under the afternoon sun was the ugly pea-green Toyota. Its presence caused her to rush back to the front door and swing it wide.

"Simon! Thank goodness it's you. I was so worried! What happened? Are you all right?"

Simon stepped through the door, quickly closing it behind him and smiling at the concern in Merry's words.

"I'm fine. I'm sorry I've been so long, but I ran into an unexpected delay."

Merry noticed the perspiration seeping through his light blue cotton shirt. "Come on into the kitchen while I fix us something cool to drink and tell me about it."

Simon nodded and followed her. While she poured the soda into two glasses, he told her about going back to the Smithsonian, having difficulty finding a parking space and how he ended up missing the Subaru.

"I shouldn't have let you take me home first," Merry said as she handed him his glass. "I should have insisted you pull over right then and take the opportunity that presented itself. If you've been looking for a parking space all this time, it's no wonder you couldn't get to the Subaru before it left."

Simon shrugged, a rueful smile on his face. "Actually, I wasn't looking for a parking space the whole time. Part of it I was trying to talk a traffic cop out of giving me a ticket for double parking."

Merry blinked in surprise. "You got a parking ticket?"

Simon nodded. "I'm lucky he didn't decide to take me in for threatening a police officer. I came real close to taking a swing at him when he approached me from behind and just laid a hand on my shoulder. I didn't know what to expect. He followed me from a side street where he had watched me illegally park. I think he was going to give me a piece of his mind along with the ticket."

Merry couldn't help but smile at the image Simon's words conveyed. She felt a whole lot better since knowing he was okay.

"You were able to explain your way out of it?" Merry asked.

Simon smiled and Merry could tell his good humor was back. "Except for the parking ticket. Still, I think I was lucky, considering the unexpected scare. And speaking of unexpected, I've been meaning to ask, how did you end up here in Florida House? I thought you were from Washington State?"

"I'm rooming with my friend Karen. She's a law clerk for one of the Supreme Court justices. She lives here temporarily. Her dad is dead, but when he was alive, Florida was his home and he was active in state government."

"How did your friend get permission to live here? I thought these state houses were only for visiting state-government personnel with business in D.C.?"

"Well, like I said, Karen's dad was an active, influential man in his state. So when Karen had troubles at home a month ago and needed to move out, a close friend in state government pulled some strings to let her stay here. Again, it's only temporary."

A sudden noise of a door closing from somewhere close by brought Simon instantly to his feet. "Who's that?" he asked.

Merry hurried to reassure him. "It's okay," she said. "It's just a prosecuting attorney from Florida. He's also here to argue a case before the Supreme Court. His involves police helicopter surveillance. His rooms are on the other side."

Simon relaxed back into his chair only to once again raise at the sudden ringing of the telephone. Merry was beginning to see how on edge he was, despite his assurances to the contrary. She reached to answer the phone.

"Merry, it's Laura. I've got that information you asked for last night. Do you have a pencil and paper? You might want to jot some of this stuff down."

"Good idea. Just a minute," Merry said as she searched for her shoulder bag. She spied it on the counter top and reached inside it to get a pencil and paper. Then she looked over at Simon and put her hand over the mouthpiece.

"Simon, this is the call I was expecting from my partner. Why don't you pick up the extension in the living room? She says she has the information about the dead man in the Smithsonian. I'll introduce you."

Simon nodded. "First name only and no profession," he said as he walked into the living room and reached for the extension. Merry nodded and put the phone back up to her ear. "I'm all set, Laura. I'm just waiting for a friend to pick up the extension."

"Is it Karen?" Laura asked.

"No. Just a minute and I'll introduce you."

She had no sooner finished her sentence when she heard the click of the extension phone. She made a cursory introduction and Laura and Simon exchanged polite hello's.

Merry cut back in. "And now that those formalities are done, what have you found out, Laura?"

"Well the man who was killed in the Smithsonian was an Ian Skabos, a European-born gem cutter. The police didn't find any identification on him but verified his prints with the FBI. He was carrying a hundred dollars and a hotel room key."

"You say Skabos was a gem cutter?" Merry said. "Like in diamonds?"

"Especially like in diamonds. He was a master at his art of duplicating the world's most beautiful gems. He would often discard a beautifully cut duplicate and start over again to create another because the first contained a single flaw. Many wealthy families were shocked to find him disreputable."

"Disreputable?" Merry said.

"Absolutely," Laura said. "He had been engaging in a second, secret business. It seems he was caught several years ago duplicating some expensive jewels here in the States, not exactly at the request of the owners."

"A confidence game?" Simon said.

"A switching game," Laura said. "He'd use photographs of famous jewels to duplicate them. Then his accomplice would worm his way into the good graces of the rich owners and switch their real jewels with Skabos's copies. The two thieves fenced the real jewels and the original owners often weren't the wiser."

"Except somebody must have wised up somewhere along the line," Merry said. "Otherwise how did Skabos get caught?"

"Actually, it was his younger accomplice who got caught," Laura said. "Right in the act, as they say. He was a well-dressed, attractive man whose modus operandi was to travel in the right circles to meet wealthy women. He would seek out and make love to the rich women who owned the gems, thereby gaining access to their bedrooms and their jewels. One night while he was making a switch of a fake for a real jewel, he turned around to see his latest conquest watching him with a loaded gun in her hand."

"And she turned him in?" Merry asked.

"Without a qualm, apparently. The FBI put a tap on his phone and discovered his connection with Skabos. When they picked Skabos up, he agreed to testify against his accomplice for a reduced sentence."

"His accomplice couldn't have been too pleased about that," Merry said.

"He wasn't. He vowed he'd get Skabos one day. That was thirteen years back. Skabos only served six months and then was released. He was caught less than a year later trying to fence some stolen gems and ended up going back to jail for more than eleven more years. He was only released from prison eight months ago."

"What happened to the accomplice?"

"Records show he was paroled after serving just under four years, his sentence shortened because of good behavior. He never reported to his parole officer, however. After he was released, he just disappeared."

"How can someone just disappear?" Merry asked.

"Well, he could have had help. There were whispers that both Skabos and his accomplice had dealt with organized crime connections when they were using fences for the larger gems.

If the accomplice was well connected that way, they may have slipped him into a new identity.''

"What was the accomplice's name?" Merry asked.

"John Kahr. *K—A—H—R*."

Merry made a note of it. "This is quite a bit of information, Laura. I'm surprised and most appreciative."

"Hold on, Merry. There's more. As a matter of fact, I'm only just now getting to the good part."

Merry was having difficulty holding on. "The good part? What do you mean?"

"Well, how Skabos died, of course! He was choked to death!"

"Yes, Laura. I know," Merry said, a little disappointed that the news wasn't new.

"You know someone shoved a whopping red diamond down his throat?" Laura asked.

Merry dropped her pen. She heard Simon's intake of breath. "What?"

"So you didn't know? Yes, the man was choked to death when someone shoved a replica of a famous red diamond down his throat. It was a very good copy of the Fire Diamond, just had a small flaw. Police had to find a gemologist to tell it wasn't real."

"A replica of the Fire Diamond?" Merry repeated, still trying to get the information to sink in.

"Yes, and I can tell you that really got the authorities' attention, wondering if Skabos wasn't up to his old tricks of substituting fakes for the real thing. Of course, somebody obviously got to him before a way to switch the Fire Diamond was devised. He was found in front of the jewel, you know. Oh, yes, of course you'd know. How stupid of me. You found him."

"Yes. I found him," Merry said, methodically repeating what she had heard while her brain pursued meaning behind it all.

"How's it going with the police?" Laura asked.

Merry readjusted her mind's focus. "Nothing new. But I think it might be time to tell you everything that's been happening."

Merry went on to explain about the two men who tried to grab her in the Smithsonian the morning before and who also tried again last night. "Each time if it weren't for Simon, they would have succeeded," Merry said.

The agitation in Laura's voice was barely contained. "For God's sake, Merry, why didn't you tell me you were in that kind of danger? You don't just need a lawyer. You need a body-guard!"

"Yes, I suppose you're right," Merry said. "Any ideas about how I might go about employing one?"

"What about your friend Karen?" Laura asked. "Her family has a home there. Perhaps they've had occasion to employ a few security personnel?"

"Of course! Mr. T.! From his description, he'd be perfect!"

"Mr. T?" Laura said.

"I'll explain later. Thanks, Laura. I'll call you tomorrow and let you know how things go in Court."

By the time Merry had hung up the phone, Simon was walking back into the kitchen. "It amazes me how your partner was able to find out so much so quickly," he said.

Merry smiled, feeling pleased she had been able to contribute to their collective bank of knowledge. "Laura has political friends with clout. What do you make of all that stuff about Skabos and his partner?"

Simon pulled out a chair for Merry and himself and they both sat down at the kitchen table. "Well for starters, I think it strengthens our thought about the Fire Diamond being the connecting link between our two mysteries. The fact that Skabos was a gem cutter and was killed with a replica of the Fire Diamond gives him a close tie to the jewel."

"But not to the deadly flu since he was choked to death."

Simon shrugged. "Yes, but we don't know if he was already dying of that flu. When you first described your experiences of yesterday morning to me, you said Skabos was beet-red in the face. That could have been from a high fever."

Merry wasn't convinced. "Wouldn't the medical examiner have discovered the flu when the autopsy was performed?"

Simon shook his head. "No. All a medical examiner is really interested in or has time for is establishing the cause of death. Once that's been determined, he goes on to his next case. Further effort spent in additional analysis is a luxury he can't afford.''

"I see. But Skabos was killed with a replica of the Fire Diamond, not the real jewel. Can you be sure he came into contact with the people who handled the genuine stone?''

"No, but I hope to meet with the curator of the gemstones at the Smithsonian tomorrow and maybe get some answers to that question.''

Merry drank the last of her soda and got up from the table to pace about the kitchen in thought. She moved with a smooth, effortless grace. Simon watched her absentmindedly reach up to reposition a recalcitrant blond curl that was dangling onto her cheek. The light from the window caught the fine sunny strands of similarly-colored hair on her raised arm, making her skin glisten.

He was thinking that he could feel content just watching her when he suddenly realized she was speaking and he had missed her first few words.

"What did you say?''

Merry stopped her pacing and paused to look at him, quizzically. "I was just going over that theory you proposed in my hotel room last night.''

Simon nodded. "Right. Go ahead.''

Merry resumed her pacing. "Well, you said it was possible that these two men were expecting to get something from Skabos and it was that something they were still looking for when they tore apart my furnishings. Does Skabos's murder change any of your thoughts?''

Simon shook his head. "Not really, except that your abductors' behavior points to them being the most likely suspects in Skabos's murder. A replica of the Fire Diamond suggests that the real jewel was their target. Whatever scheme they cooked up with Skabos must have gone wrong.''

"A falling out among thieves?'' Merry asked.

Simon nodded. "It fits. They must have had an argument and killed the gem cutter.''

Merry shook her head. "Don't thieves have their falling out after the theft when they argue over splitting up the spoils?''

Simon shrugged. "Maybe Skabos decided not to go along. Or maybe he refused to go along without a bigger cut.''

"But, still, wouldn't it have been more reasonable for the other two to agree to Skabos's demands and then murder him after the theft was accomplished?" Merry asked.

Simon smiled. "Spoken just like a logical lawyer. We can't be certain those two are as logical, however."

"Okay. Let me try to think this through," Merry said. "Let's say that these two men arrange for Skabos to make a duplicate of the Fire Diamond, thinking that they might be able to switch such a duplicate with the real diamond. So Skabos makes the duplicate and meets them to get his payoff. But something goes wrong."

"Yes," Simon said. "Your partner mentioned that the stone Skabos was choked with had a flaw. Perhaps these men noticed the flaw after giving Skabos his payment and tried to get their money back. A fight ensued and one of the men shoved the fake diamond down Skabos's throat."

Merry shook her head. "Except at that point the scenario falls apart. If the two men killed Skabos, why didn't they just grab the money back and run? Why did they stick around and try to grab me?"

"Perhaps someone interrupted or distracted them, giving Skabos time to get away. How long would you say he stood next to you before you turned to look at him?"

"I'm not sure. Half a minute to a minute I'd guess. He was just a shadow in my peripheral vision while I studied the Fire Diamond. When I finally turned to look at him, it was too late."

"Did you see anyone else? Or hear any movement behind you?" Simon asked.

Merry shook her head. "I was looking at the red diamond."

"I imagine Skabos saw you and tried to reach you before he choked to death," Simon said.

Merry shook her head dejectedly. "Fat lot of help I was."

Simon stood up. He put a hand over her arm in a comforting way and opened his mouth to respond when he was interrupted by the doorbell. He frowned at Merry. "Are you expecting anyone?"

Merry shook her head and walked over to the kitchen window, seeing a familiar maroon Ford. "Oh, damn, it's Sergeant Calder."

Simon looked around uneasily as though trying to find a means of escape. "Do you have to answer the door?"

Merry once again pushed aside her uneasiness at Simon's reluctance to meet with the police. She looked quickly around.

"You can step out onto the balcony. I'll close the glass door and draw the drapes behind you so he won't be able to see you."

Simon nodded and complied. Once he was out on the narrow balcony, she reclosed the glass door and drew the drapes. Then she took a deep breath and went to answer the door. Sergeant Calder stepped inside immediately, not waiting for an invitation.

His voice was smoothly sarcastic. "That was a fast one you and your friend Richfield pulled on me last night, Ms. Anders."

Merry closed the door then turned away from Calder's probing look, leading the way into the living room. She gestured to the couch and sat across it in a chair.

"You want to explain that very odd statement, Sergeant?"

Calder descended into the couch with a studied ease, careful not to sit on the back of his perfectly pressed suit jacket.

"I don't have to explain the fact that Ms. Richfield threatened senatorial intervention in my investigation last night if I did not let you go. What I couldn't check out until you gave me her name this morning, however, is that such senatorial intervention would be miraculous since her father, the former Senator Richfield, is not only no longer a senator but is also dead."

Merry really hated watching the smug smile on Calder's face. She was determined to wipe it off.

"Your statement is incorrect in several respects, Sergeant. First, Ms. Richfield threatened nothing. Second, she mentioned no names when she referred to appealing to a senator to ensure you remain within the bounds of the law. If you've checked on her family this morning, then you also know their wealth, power and influence still reach to many in Washington, despite her father's death."

The smile didn't get entirely wiped from his face, but at least it faded somewhat. His tone also showed signs of strain. "No one will interfere in my investigation. No one."

Merry shrugged, not wanting to provoke a fight. "As long as you conduct your investigation within the bounds of your authority, I don't foresee the necessity arising for intervention. Now, why are you here?"

Calder eyed her for a moment. "Last night you said nothing about what type of vehicle this mysterious stranger of yours was driving when he took you on this mad ride through the city streets. I need that information to complete my report."

Calder's question irritated Merry. Once again he was concentrating on Simon instead of the two men who pursued her. She shook her head in disapproval.

"I don't understand you, Sergeant. This stranger saves my life from two thugs who have physically accosted me and then shot at me, and instead of following leads to pursue them, you're constantly quizzing me about him. How can the type of car he drove possibly matter?"

Calder's tone began to sound labored, although his expression still seemed mild. "It matters. Now stop evading the question. What make and year was the car?"

Merry recognized a new 928 Porsche when she saw one, but she knew of no reason to admit that to Calder. The closer he got to identifying the car, the closer he could come to identifying Simon. She put on the most innocent expression she could muster.

"I don't know much about cars."

Calder's tone turned impatient. "If you don't know much about cars, then how could you tell you were being followed by a dark blue Cadillac?"

Merry knew she couldn't be caught by such an obvious trick. She leaned back in her chair. "The stranger told me, of course."

She could see Sergeant Calder was not pleased. Every tightened muscle around his mouth and eyes said so. "You must have at least seen the color," he said.

Merry put her arms over her head in a leisurely stretch. "Well, you know how tricky it is to distinguish color at night. Dark green, dark blue, even dark gray all look the same."

She could see her answers were beginning to upset Calder. He leaned forward toward her. His voice was harsher, more demanding. "Have you seen him again?"

Calder's question was unexpected. She tried to keep her tone steady as her fingers gripped the soft fabric of her chair. "Seen who?"

A muscle began twitching near Calder's mouth. His eyes squinted, leaving distinct lines on either side of them and making the sergeant look several years older. He was obviously not pleased. "If you don't stop playing these games, you're going to find yourself down at the station answering a set of very serious charges. Do you understand me?"

Merry's thoughts churned as she groped for a satisfactory answer to Calder's question. A sudden noise outside the kitchen balcony made any response unnecessary, however. Calder's head jerked in the direction of the kitchen as he jumped to his feet. "What's that?" he asked.

Merry tried to keep her voice and mannerisms calm, knowing the noise came from the balcony Simon was hiding on. "How should I know?" she said.

Calder marched purposely toward the kitchen, Merry following closely behind. He stopped at the kitchen table and picked up the second glass of soda that still sat there. Then he looked over at Merry and smiled a crooked little knowing smile. So fast Merry couldn't even follow the movement, he pulled a snub-nosed .38 revolver out of his shoulder holster and was pointing it at the draped balcony.

Her heart pounded against her chest as she moved quickly to Calder's side. She couldn't control the horror in her voice. "What do you think you're going to do with that gun?"

Calder ignored her. She watched him as he stalked the window that led out onto the balcony, circling his left hand around the dangling cord to the heavy drapes. With one rough pull, he snapped the drapes wide, exposing whoever hid there to his waiting gun.

## Chapter Nine

The surprised, tawny eyes of the gigantic ginger cat glowed at Calder and Merry as it sat on the wrought-iron railing, rudely awakened from its sun bath by the sudden pull of the drapes. Then as though becoming aware of the unnatural tension in the air, it meowed its indignation loudly and flashed them its fluffy tail as it headed down an impossibly narrow drainpipe.

Merry looked around Sergeant Calder in relieved disbelief to find Simon gone and with him the pea-green Toyota that had been parked on the street. As her knees started liquifying in reaction, she clutched the edge of the nearby kitchen table and sank down into a chair. Calder was still staring out the glass balcony door, swearing an ugly oath beneath his breath and reluctantly shoving his gun back into his shoulder holster.

By the time he turned toward her, Merry had regained her momentarily lost composure and was able to look him straight in the eye. "Well, if you're finished scaring neighborhood cats, Sergeant, I suggest you leave."

He was visibly upset, his normal calm stripped away by his disappointment at not finding her mysterious stranger. He leaned white knuckles on the kitchen table as he bent over it toward her. "Where is he?"

Merry opened her eyes as big and innocent as she could get them. "Where's who?"

Calder's voice was openly angry as he grabbed the second glass off the kitchen table and shook it at her, spraying the half inch of soda it still contained into an airborne arc around them. "Don't make me repeat myself. I want to see this figment of your imagination and I want to see him now. Where are you hiding him?''

Calder's demanding tone was making Merry angry. She rose to her now steady feet so she wouldn't be forced to strain her neck looking up at the man. Her tone was tinged with contempt. ''Don't be silly, Sergeant. If he's a figment of my imagination, how can you possibly see him?''

Calder stood before her caught in a white anger. Merry could almost see the color recede from his face from the tight constriction of his blood vessels.

She began then to suspect that if the police sergeant really had sufficient evidence to take her in, he would have already done so. The angry man she had just seen drawing his gun was not one who would hesitate to use any ammunition he possessed. Suddenly she felt very strongly that his earlier words and cocky manner must have been a bluff. And if it was a bluff, then it was about time she called it.

She assumed a condescending air. ''I'm expecting a lot of company and I no longer have time to waste chatting with you. I'll show you to the door.''

Merry didn't wait for Calder's reaction to her words. She turned and walked purposefully toward the front door, opening it and holding it expectantly. He remained standing in the kitchen for a moment more and then reluctantly started toward the open doorway. Before he passed through, however, he had one last parting shot.

His voice was calm again, but Merry could almost taste the audible arsenic with which it was laced. ''Before this is over, Ms. Anders, you will tell me the truth. Because if you don't, one way or another, I'll get you. That's a promise.''

Merry immediately shut the door, feeling the threat in his words reaching out like cold fingers along her spine. She leaned against the closed door.

*Terrorize*. That was the word. What right did Calder have to terrorize her? Policemen weren't supposed to act that way. They were supposed to serve and protect, not threaten. Why was Sergeant Calder doing this to her?

The answer was simple. He was trying to coerce her into giving him the information he wanted. Her sense of fair play reminded her that Calder was the law and that she was withholding evidence. Still, his way of trying to extract it was very wrong. He wouldn't be any closer to the killer or killers of Ian Skabos if she told him about Simon. Even with the truth about her abductors, the sergeant had not provided her with protection.

A sudden thought occurred to her. Calder hadn't even asked her to come down to the station to look at mug shots to try to pick out the men. He should have, shouldn't he? Wasn't that what they always asked witnesses to do on television crime programs? It made sense that her abductors might have served time, too, if they were mixed up with Skabos.

There was only one conclusion. Calder wasn't much of a policeman as Karen had said from the first when she pointed out that he had failed to test the skin beneath Merry's fingernails to use for future identification of the men.

Such police incompetence assuaged the remaining shreds of Merry's conscience. Her open nature abhorred the keeping of secrets, but in this case, it seemed the best decision. Besides, she had put her trust in Simon and she could not withdraw it now.

She plopped heavily onto the living room couch, questions racing through her mind. How had he gotten off the balcony? Where had he gone? Was he all right?

She had lied to Sergeant Calder about expecting a lot of company. She had done it purposely to leave the way clear for Simon to return. But he didn't.

It wasn't until three very long hours later that she received word of any type. It arrived at her door in the hands of a delivery man, a single envelope with her name written in bold script on the front. She signed for it, closed the door and then proceeded to tear it open excitedly. She found a ticket for a Shakespearean performance at the Folger Theatre with a short note clipped to its back.

Hope to see you tonight.

                                                    Simon

"MERRY, DON'T BE A FOOL! You can't go out tonight after everything that's happened these last two days," Karen said.

Merry, Karen and Joseph Freedman were having an early dinner together again, this time in the formal dining room at Florida House. Merry's intent to attend a Shakespearean play at the Folger Theatre was meeting with stiff opposition.

"But I'll have a bodyguard," Merry said.

"I don't care if Mr. T., I mean Charles, has agreed to accompany you. It's still a dangerous proposition going to this play. Tell her, Mr. Freedman. Talk her out of this insanity," Karen said.

At Karen's direct prodding against the outing, Joseph Freedman very carefully put down his fork and adjusted the glasses farther back on his perfectly straight nose. He obviously considered it his duty to comply.

"Ms. Richfield is quite right. You're taking an unnecessary chance. These men who have followed you seem most determined. Why give them another opportunity in which to accost you?"

Merry shook her head. "Don't let Karen involve you in this, Mr. Freedman. I already feel I've burdened you unnecessarily with my affairs stemming from that scuffle at the museum Saturday morning. On reflection I realize I should have kept the entire business to myself. It is a personal matter, after all."

Freedman stared at Merry with a guarded intensity. "Ms. Anders, I hope you understand that my regard for you extends far beyond our professional association. I consider your personal safety of utmost importance. Please do not take unnecessary chances."

Merry was surprised and a little touched at Freedman's words. Despite their formality, they seemed to hold signs of friendly concern. She gave him a small smile as she offered her rebuttal.

"Those men have no way of knowing where I'm planning to go, Mr. Freedman. Besides, the theater's right down the street, I'm meeting this friend, Simon, I've told you about inside, and Mr. T. will be with me. I'll be well guarded."

Charles was pacing around the living room at that very moment, studiously examining every figurine and painting. He had refused to join them for dinner, insisting he had already eaten a cow. Merry didn't doubt it for a minute after getting a look at the massive frame bulging out of his king-size suit when he delivered her belongings that afternoon.

"Look, Merry, I have to work tonight or I'd stay home with you and keep you company myself," Karen said, obviously not giving up on talking Merry out of her evening's plans. "Perhaps Mr. Freedman can work himself free and take my place?"

Karen looked at Joseph Freedman hopefully, but the man's face began to quickly redden behind his thin glasses.

"I'm very sorry, Ms. Richfield, Ms. Anders. I must catch a plane this evening. Something unexpected has come up. I have a very important conference in . . . in my New York office tomorrow."

He picked up his fork and studied his plate as though he was expecting to find a bug any moment in the remaining food.

Merry couldn't help but sound shocked. "You won't be in Court tomorrow when the case is heard?"

Joseph Freedman kept his eyes focused on his plate. "I'm afraid not, Ms. Anders. I hope it won't be awkward for you. I know this is a disappointment. Please accept my apologies. The situation is . . . unavoidable."

"Of course, Mr. Freedman. I understand," Merry said, somewhat subdued and not really understanding at all.

"Forget about tomorrow. I'm still concentrating on tonight," Karen said, turning the focus of attention away from the sudden strangeness in Joseph Freedman's behavior. "Why can't you and this Simon fellow and Mr. T. just stay here and watch television?"

Merry's glance turned away from the averted head of Joseph Freedman to the determined eyes of her friend.

"I already checked the *TV Guide*. According to it, the most interesting thing scheduled tonight is a 'To Be Announced' slot coming on at 11:30 on Channel 7," she said.

Karen laughed. "The programming can't be that bad?"

Merry shrugged. "Okay, I'm exaggerating a bit. But I've been looking forward to attending a play at the Folger Theatre ever since I knew I was coming to the capital. Being invited by this, uh, friend makes it perfect. I know I'm feeling a little sorry for myself, but I've had to give up on a lot of sight-seeing because of this craziness. I don't want this opportunity to pass by, too."

Karen sighed. "How are you going to get Charles in if the performance is already sold out?"

"Well, it doesn't really matter. Your Mr. T. isn't exactly a Shakespeare fan. We've agreed he'll park the car right out in front and spend the time listening to a scheduled ballgame on the radio. Much more to his liking, I'm sure. Remember, Simon is meeting me inside."

Karen seemed to be weakening. "Merry, are you sure this is what you want?"

"I'm sure. *Much Ado About Nothing* is the play, and I confess it's one of my favorites because it has a lot of comedic elements and a happy ending. Frankly, I could use them both about now."

"Well, I guess as long as Mr. T. is there..."

MERRY LOOKED UP at the graceful Georgian-marble building that housed the Folger Shakespeare Theatre and its adjoining library, feeling suitably impressed and understanding why the structure was listed on the National Register of Historic Places in Washington, D.C.

But she found herself really delighted to find the theater inside a cozy affair, probably accommodating no more than two hundred and seventy-five maximum, with the dark-stained wood seats spread before the small stage like reverent church pews. Its tiered balconies on either side looked up to a canopied ceiling, reminiscent of the atmosphere of an Elizabethan inn yard.

She felt herself step back nearly four centuries as she settled herself into her rustic balcony seat, worn comfortable by frequent use, despite its lack of modern-day cushioning.

She had come a few minutes early hoping to talk with Simon, but so far he was nowhere to be seen. She felt hopeful he wouldn't be too long. But as the play was about to start, he still hadn't shown. The murmur of a packed house died an instant death at the drawing of the heavy curtain.

Part one ended on a happy, upbeat note. The audience, now standing up for a short intermission, was full of smiling faces. As Merry got up to stretch, her aching muscles reminded her of her recent escapades. Then she got a much stronger reminder with the recognition of a familiar voice near her ear.

"Sorry I'm late," Simon said. "Had trouble finding a place to park."

Merry turned to find him beside her, the warm look in his eyes and the flash of his white teeth pumping her heartbeat into an eccentric beat.

"I'm glad to see you," she said. "I've been a bit worried."

"Me, too. How are you feeling? I've been concerned during these last few hours that you might have gotten ill and I wouldn't be around when I was needed. Still feeling strong, no fever?"

Merry nodded, a little disappointed his interest seemed so heavily professional. "What happened this morning? How did you get off the balcony?"

Simon shrugged. "I jumped off onto the raised patio area as soon as I realized Calder had come in to talk. It was only a five-foot drop. I didn't want to take any chances of his finding me with you. I drove off soon as I could get the keys in the ignition."

"Why didn't you come back after Calder left?"

"I parked around the corner and waited. He parked up the street from Florida House and watched its entrance for nearly two hours. I thought it might be a protective surveillance."

Merry shook her head. "That'll be the day."

Simon's voice sounded surprised. "Did he give you a bad time again?"

Before Merry could answer, the house lights dimmed, signaling the beginning of part two of the play.

Simon leaned over and whispered "later" into her ear, his warm breath and closeness threatening to melt the solid bones in her ankles. As they both gave up conversation temporarily and sat down, she redirected her outward attention to the play. But inwardly, Merry was finding that the simple pleasure of seeing him again made her ability to concentrate on other things more and more difficult.

When part two was over, he took her arm and led her to the lobby. "Well, what do you think of the performance so far?"

"If you're asking are the actors doing a good job, I've no idea. I'm afraid I'm very unsophisticated as a critic. All I can tell you is the story's fun, the portrayals seem light and unaffected and for those reasons, I'm enjoying it. I wish I could say the same about my conversations with Calder."

They walked slowly between the carved oak paneling of the Great Hall, which joined the theater entrance with the library entrance on the northwest side. There were only two other couples stopping at the exhibits of early Shakespearean art and artifacts and they were some distance away.

Simon was watching her face. "It didn't go well with Calder this afternoon?"

Merry shrugged. "My confrontations with the man seem to be getting worse. This time he insisted on knowing more about your car."

"My car? Why?"

Merry shook her head. "I don't know, Simon. At first I thought he didn't believe you existed. But this afternoon when he came by Florida House, he acted as though he did believe you were real and that you and I were part of some kind of murder conspiracy. What's wrong with the man, anyway?"

Simon detected the frustration in her voice and sought to lighten it. "'Stony adversary, inhuman wretch, uncapable of pity, void and empty from any dream of mercy,'" he quoted.

*"The Merchant of Venice!,"* Merry said. "And how apt a description of him. What a marvelous command you have of Shakespeare. However did you get it?"

Simon smiled, obviously pleased. "My parents were actors."

"Were?"

"Oh, they're still alive. Live in England now in a house previously owned by my grandparents. I only meant they're retired."

"Did they perform classic works?" Merry asked.

Simon nodded. "Instead of nursery rhymes, they practiced their Shakespearean lines on me. I've forgotten a lot of it, of course. But some of the descriptions were so vivid, they've stuck somewhere in the dark recesses of my mind, jump into my conversation before I realize it. What about you?"

"Oh, my mother's an English professor with a lifelong love of Shakespeare. She wanted both my brother and me to be conversant, so we often exchanged lines around the dinner table. We couldn't cheat. The lines had to be germane to the conversation and spoken accurately. Whoever slipped in the most lines got a dollar with dessert.''

"And your brother never won," Simon said.

"Wrong. He won nearly every time," Merry said. "And he's two years younger."

"What? No competitive spirit? From what I know of you, I would have thought otherwise," he said.

Merry smiled at the warm look that accompanied his words. "Well, I soon found I liked to turn the words around or mix them up with others to come out with new meanings and nuances. Misquotes, intentional or not, were against the rules, of course. But I thought it was a more fun game than the straight quote."

"More creative, certainly," Simon said.

Merry shrugged, although she was pleased he had interpreted her actions that way. "But definitely less profitable. Jack, my brother, saved up enough from his winnings for a down payment on a car when he was in high school."

"And he's a financial wizard today?"

Merry laughed. "Not hardly. He went on to become a college instructor in English literature and, heaven knows, they barely get a living wage."

"And big sister went into law. Why?"

"Oh, its order, its logic. If there was one thing studying Shakespeare at my mother's insistence taught me, it was that life could be full of unhappy endings when its players based their parts on raw emotions."

"So no raw emotions and unhappy endings for you. Just the pursuit of order, logic and...?" Simon's voice was deep, inquiring, interested.

Was he really interested in her, or was she just fantasizing?

"So you do want to keep a secret or two?" he said, bringing her out of her reverie. It seemed she didn't have to speak her mind. He was beginning to read it.

"I was just wondering why you asked?" she said.

"Because I wanted to know, of course. What else has been in your life besides order and logic?"

She thought about the things that gave her pleasure and knew she would like to share them with him. "I've spent a lot of time with a collection of progressive-jazz records, a small, second-hand sailboat named *Sea Star* and a fat goldfish I call Gus."

"And you're content with those?" he asked.

"No, not really," Merry said. "I'd like to be special to someone and have someone be special to me. I've always thought of a home and family as important. Still, circumstances haven't quite worked out that way."

"Hmm, I understand how work can intervene. I've always been too busy traveling around the country answering epidemic-aid requests, indulging that spirit-of-adventure need by looking for interesting puzzles, I suppose. What's your excuse?"

Merry could have used work as her excuse, but she knew it wouldn't be accurate. She decided the plain truth was going to have to suffice. "I've found it hard to fall in love."

"Why's that?" Simon asked.

The question was quite personal, but Merry found she didn't mind answering it. "The men I've dated don't seem to have the forthrightness and honesty I find I require. Someone who hides who they are is not the kind of person I want to spend my life with, and if that's all that's out there, then I'd rather be alone. Do you know what I'm talking about?"

His look was warm and thoughtful. "Yes, an open and honest relationship. We both know you're not one for hiding things."

"And you, Simon? Do you feel that way, too?" she asked.

Simon looked away suddenly, as though he had allowed himself to go too far. "I've gotten us off the subject of these two apes after you and we need to return to it. Do you feel safe at Florida House?"

Merry nodded, disappointed at his abrupt change of subject.

"Then the safest thing for you to do is to be ready and packed so you can get on a plane right after court tomorrow."

Merry felt surprise at his words. "I don't understand. I thought we were going to work together to get to the bottom of Skabos's death and the deadly flu. You said you had to observe me carefully to see if I developed Carmichael's fever."

He wasn't looking at her; he was staring straight ahead as they began to walk back toward the theater side of the Great

Hall. The other couples had now left. The play had probably started again, but neither of them was hurrying to get back.

He stopped and turned to face her, his outstretched hands lightly touching her arms. "Merry, I must continue to look for the secret behind Carmichael's flu because there is no one else who'll do it. But you don't have to find out who killed Ian Skabos. Let the police take care of it. Get out of harm's way. Those men aren't going to give up trying to find you."

Merry's voice was full of faith. "You've managed to protect me from them quite well up to now."

The feel of her warmth beneath his fingers, the nearness of her soft body, the trusting look deep within her eyes made him suddenly unable to remember all the reasons why she should be leaving. He found himself leaning down to her upturned face, wondering what her parting lips would taste like.

"Excuse me, folks. Thought you'd want to know. The play has begun again."

Simon straightened up quickly to face the young usher.

"Thank you," he said, wondering if he should shake the young man's hand or punch him in the mouth. Perhaps in time he might realize the handshake was the more appropriate since for him to become more involved with Merry was a definite mistake. But at the moment . . .

He offered his arm and Merry curled her own inside. He savored the feel of her by his side as they walked slowly back through the foyer toward the heavy wooden theater doors.

They stopped inside the darkened theater, quickly closing the door behind them so as not to distract the spectators from the players on the stage. Merry stood still with Simon at her side as she allowed her eyes to adjust to the lowered light.

When finally she knew she saw well enough to move through the crowded theater to her seat, she started forward only to stop instantly as Simon whispered in her ear. The tone in his voice sent a cold chill up her spine.

"Don't move. Very slowly now look to your right."

Merry obeyed and jumped uncontrollably at what she saw, thankful for Simon's steadying hands that quickly encircled her arms. Her abductors were standing no more than eight feet in front of her, scanning the audience carefully in the subdued light. Fortunately, their backs were to the door where she and

Simon had just entered. But any second now they might turn around and . . .

Before the thought could even register in her mind, she felt Simon's hands urging her backward, out the quickly opening door. They emerged back into the foyer and headed as of one mind toward the stairs, out of the theater.

"Do you think they saw us?" Merry said as they scurried down the entrance steps to the street.

"I don't think so, but when they don't find us inside . . ."

"I get the picture. My bodyguard's out here, though. We'll have reinforcements."

"Your bodyguard?" Simon said, obviously surprised.

Merry didn't waste her breath in answering. But when she ran confidently toward the curb to summon Mr. T., she was surprised and deflated to find both her bodyguard and the car gone.

"I don't understand it. Where did he go?"

Simon took hold of her arm. "I don't think we've got time to wait around to find out. Quick, come on!"

Merry followed Simon into the bushes around the corner. They made the hiding place without a second to spare, because just as they melted into their green camouflage, out rushed their pursuers from the Folger Theatre entrance. They paused at the bottom of the steps.

Merry and Simon stayed perfectly still, barely daring to breathe, as their pursuers carefully looked around, obviously trying to catch sight of them.

After a very long minute, the men mumbled between themselves and then took off down the street, fortunately in the opposite direction from where Merry and Simon hid.

As soon as they left, Merry asked the question that plagued her the most. "How could they possibly know I was here?"

He gave his answer with his exhaling breath. "Good question. Come on. My car's a few blocks away."

"We can walk to Florida House from here," Merry said.

"No. That's the direction those two apes went. Let's give them a wide berth. The car's safer at the moment. We'll take it and drive around a bit to give those two a chance to get lost."

They covered the distance to the car cautiously, looking down every alley and around every dark corner suspiciously. When they reached the car, Merry was surprised to find it was the Porsche.

"It's fixed? Already?"

Simon smiled as he opened the passenger's side for her.

"What, disappointed? Don't tell me you were getting attached to that pea-green Toyota? I had no idea. Perhaps they'd take the Porsche in trade for it?"

Merry shook her head. "Your sense of humor boarders on the bizarre. Maybe that's what makes you fun to be around."

Simon chuckled as he walked around the car to the driver's side and got in. He started the car and drove off slowly. When next he spoke, his voice sounded more serious. "Who was the bodyguard?"

Merry shrugged. "Remember when Laura and I talked about one earlier today and I spoke of Mr. T.?"

"Oh, yes, I do remember. I meant to ask you about him then but the information we had learned about Skabos totally drove the thought from my mind. Is he related to your friend, Karen?"

"Not related. He's employed by Karen's family as a sort of chauffeur and security man all in one. Been with them a lot of years. His real name is Charles but everyone calls him Mr. T. because of his physical appearance. I can't understand what happened to him tonight. He was supposed to be waiting for me right outside the theater."

Simon shrugged. "Well there's not a whole lot we can do about him now. I think our wisest move will be to get you back to the safety of Florida House. We'll just take a few more turns here and there and try to find a parking space near by."

They approached the street cautiously as Simon spoke again. "I haven't seen either of your two playmates about. I think you'll be able to enter safely."

They parked about a half block away. Merry could see lights were on in the apartment, but she wasn't sure if they were just left on or if Karen had come home.

Simon put a restraining hand on Merry's arm before getting out of the car. "We'll approach the front in much the same way as we did going into the hotel. You walk ahead and I'll stay behind to see you make it safely. In case there's trouble, have your keys out and ready. Don't wait for me. Run up the stairs, get inside and lock yourself in. Understand?''

She looked over at his face in the darkened interior of the car unable to see his expression, although she could imagine what it was like from the strained urgency in his voice. Directions to leave him on the street being attacked while she ran away were the last thing she wanted to hear. "But, Simon, what if—"

His hand gripped her arm more tightly. "No 'what if's,' Merry. You run up those stairs and you lock yourself inside the apartment. Got it?''

She inhaled deeply and nodded as she dug for her keys in her shoulder bag. He let go of her arm and got out of the car. She didn't wait for him to open her side, but slipped out and closed the door quietly behind her.

He nodded for her to go ahead and she walked slowly, looking around with each step. The street was packed with parked cars, any of which might hide within their darkened interiors someone waiting to pounce on her when she passed. Her shoulder blades pulled together as the nerves in her back tightened.

She looked nervously at the large bushes hugging the sides of the houses, imagining figures lurking behind them. The sound of her leather heels slapping against the pavement amplified in her own ears until they sounded like a loud, persistent clapping. Perspiration coated the keys in her hand.

But finally it was over and she was stepping in front of the brightly lit shamrock-green awning to Florida House. Just when she thought she was safe, she looked up to suddenly see a body hurling down the stairs straight at her. Her heart rocketed into her throat as she instinctively jumped back, out of the way.

Her movement halted the man who had been hurrying down the stairs in her direction and he quickly shortened his strides to stop in front of her. Her sudden fear turned into puzzlement as she recognized Sergeant Calder.

"What are you doing here?" she said, both dumbfounded and dismayed at having to see the man again.

His face was in shadow as he looked down at her. "I'm here because your neighbor called us concerning a break-in. It seems your apartment has been burglarized, as well."

Merry detected the surprised tone of the sergeant's voice, but at the moment she was more interested in getting to the facts of what had happened.

"The apartment burglarized?"

Calder nodded. "Your neighbor returned to his apartment this evening to find it ransacked. He was on the phone calling us when he saw two men leaving your apartment through the front door. They were gone when we got here."

Merry exhaled in some relief. "So, finally, someone else has seen and described the men who have been following me!"

Sergeant Calder shrugged. "Maybe. Your neighbor didn't get that good a look. We have a lot of burglaries in this city. The perpetrators could have been some of our regulars."

His continuing disbelief was becoming a real irritation to Merry. She really wished someone else had answered the call. And then she wondered why he had.

"Why are you here, Sergeant? I thought your department was homicide. Why should you concern yourself with a burglary?"

Although she still couldn't see his face, Merry could certainly hear the lick of impatience in his voice. "I concern myself with whatever I choose, Ms. Anders. And for your information, all subsequent events to a homicide case are under the homicide department's jurisdiction, despite whatever other department might normally handle them."

Merry still had questions. "All right. But how did you even know about the burglary?"

Calder exhaled, a sudden contempt lacing his response to her continuing questions. "Not that I have to explain myself to you, but I routed the case jacket to the desk sergeant in burglary. Standard procedure. He knew of the break-in at the hotel and your new address at Florida House. When we got the call about a break-in here, it was natural for him to call me. I am the lead detective on the case, after all."

Merry had to admit it sounded routine from what little she knew about police procedure. But it also sounded as though her movements were being watched quite carefully by the Metropolitan Police Department. If they were that interested in her, why couldn't they have spared an officer to give her some protection? The thought irritated her once more.

She turned, looking for Simon, but already knowing he would be gone. She tried to swallow her disappointment as she scanned down the street. She couldn't be sure because of the darkness of the night, but an empty space seemed to have appeared halfway down the block where the Porsche had been.

"Looking for someone?" Calder asked.

Merry ignored the man's question. "If you'll step out of my way, I'd like to go up to my apartment," she said.

Calder moved aside but began to follow Merry as she ascended the stairs. She turned toward him. "Where do you think you're going?"

"What's wrong, Ms. Anders? Have you all of a sudden decided you don't need police protection?"

His words surprised her so much she wasn't sure how to respond. Could the doubting Sergeant Calder finally have begun to believe her?

# Chapter Ten

It was like the destruction of her hotel room. Only this time, it was even worse because the victims were pieces of beautiful antique furniture, priceless in their workmanship and historical significance.

The wreckers had been thorough. She found each room of Florida House a shambles. Even in the kitchen, everything in the refrigerator had been opened and thrown on the floor. Merry walked carefully through the pots and pans dumped on the lovely tile to read a torn note from Karen still hanging limply on the door.

Merry,

If you beat me home, there's cold chicken in the frig. If not, you won't be reading this note and I'll have already eaten the leftovers!

I hope you enjoyed the play. *Much Ado About Nothing* isn't exactly a title that grabs, but I know the light touch is what you were in the mood for.

See you elevenish,
Karen

P.S. Save me a leg.

Merry jumped at a sudden noise and looked around to see Sergeant Calder, only then remembering his presence. He was leaning against the kitchen wall, his eyes traveling over the broken dishes and scattered food.

"The mobile crime lab folks have already been here. I'll need you to give me a list of anything that's missing."

"When did the break-in occur?" she asked.

"An hour and a half, maybe two hours ago."

Merry checked her watch. That would have been right after she left and right after Karen had written the note. Her roommate had placed it on the refrigerator, but had Karen actually left before the break-in? Did the two men find her at home? An awful churning grabbed at Merry's insides. Her eyes darted to the two numbers Karen had recorded for her next to the kitchen telephone. She grabbed the slip of paper and raced into her bedroom for some privacy from the policeman.

There was no answer to the Supreme Court's library phone. The unlisted number for Justice Stone's chambers rang six times. With each unanswered ring, Merry's nerves stretched anxiously. Finally, Karen's distracted voice said hello.

"Karen, thank God you're there!"

"Merry? Is that you?" Karen asked.

"Yes, yes, it's me. Karen, listen. The apartment has been broken into. It's a shambles. The police are here. Don't come home. It isn't safe. Go to your family's place in Georgetown tonight. You understand what I'm saying?"

"Yes, Merry. Of course. Are you and Charles all right?"

"I'm fine. But I don't know where Charles is, Karen. When I came out of the play, neither he nor the car was there. I have no idea where he went."

"That's . . . strange. There must be some explanation. What are you going to do now?"

"I'm going to gather up my papers and get out of here. Now that they've found me, Florida House is no longer safe."

"Come stay with me in Georgetown. My stepmother won't mind. She'll probably be even happier to see you than me."

"No, Karen. I've already complicated your life enough by taking your hospitality last time. This break-in was because of my presence."

"But, Merry, where will you go?"

Where, indeed? Merry thought. But she had to show a solid front for her friend.

"Oh, I have police protection now. I'll be safe in their custody," she said, not believing it for a moment.

"You'll give me your new address tomorrow?" Karen said.

"Of course. See you in court."

Merry hung up wishing she hadn't had to cut off what might be her one avenue of safety. But she wouldn't put Karen in jeopardy again by becoming a roommate. She started suddenly as she heard someone clearing his throat behind her. She jerked around to see Sergeant Calder standing in the doorway.

"I hadn't actually offered the protection bit yet, but you're right, I was getting to it," he said.

"Don't tell me you're actually starting to believe that those two men have been trying to abduct me?" Merry asked.

"I admit it's a possibility," Calder said as he advanced leisurely into the bedroom. As always, not a hair on his dark head was out of place, not an early whisker showed on his clean-shaven face. And the familiar cologne scent preceded him into the room. His voice was almost unconcerned, certainly not contrite. "You may have been telling the truth about those two men."

"So why have you assumed I wasn't?" Merry asked.

"Well, you've got to admit all this business about a mysterious stranger was pretty farfetched."

Merry inhaled deeply. "For the last time, Sergeant Calder, the man is real."

"So, okay. I'm willing to adjust my opinion. Produce him and I'll find you a safe hotel room for tonight."

The detective righted an overturned antique chair in her bedroom and sat down on it, looking more like an owner than a visitor to the premises. Merry shook her head in wonder as to how anyone could stay so neat and pompous all the time.

"Well, Ms. Anders? You want to tell me who he is?"

Merry exhaled heavily. "He's an innocent bystander in this, Sergeant, just like me. My coming forward and telling you what I know hasn't seemed to help my position any. Every time I turn around, I find those men pursuing me. They followed me to the Folger Theatre tonight. For the second time in two days, they've torn up the place I'm living in. You tell me what you're going to do about them first, and then maybe we'll discuss my mysterious stranger."

Calder's outward calm disintegrated at her words. He stood, his hands opening and closing at his sides, his voice only partly controlled. "Since when do you think you can dictate terms to me?"

Merry rose, looking eye-to-eye with the irritated man. Amazingly, she felt very calm and controlled. "I'm not dictating anything. I'm stating the facts. I'm a victim of several crimes under your jurisdiction involving physical and emotional injury and property damage and all you've presented me with is distrust and disbelief. If you want my cooperation, you'd better start showing me some of yours."

His eyes burned into hers in a fierce stare. "You want cooperation? I'll show you cooperation. I'm going to cooperate in every way I can to fry you and this stranger of yours. You don't really think I believe your story, do you? I know who killed Skabos. I know everything."

Merry marveled at the handsome face next to her, truly curious how far the ugly portrait in his attic had progressed. She could taste the hot anger warming the enamel of her teeth. "You're not welcome here. Leave."

Calder smiled, his anger seeming to dissipate as suddenly as hers surfaced. His tone became sugary sweet. "I take it you're refusing my protective custody?"

"I'd be better off with my pursuers if you're the metro police's idea of protective custody."

Her choice of words seemed to annoy him. "For your information, the metro police are the train guards. I'm a Detective Sergeant at the metro*politan* police."

"You could have fooled me, Calder. As far as I'm concerned, any one of those *trains* has more brains and compassion than you!"

Calder turned for the door, looking almost amused by her last angry retort, pausing briefly to lean against the frame to release his parting shot. "If you change your address, you'd better give the office a call and leave a number. You're still my number-one suspect in a murder investigation. Don't make it difficult for me to find you."

Everything in Calder's tone told Merry he was happy she had refused his bogus offer of protection. If he were to find her in the morgue the next day, she was sure the sight would disturb him less than a stain on his trousers.

"Get out," Merry said, no longer able to stand his offensive attitude.

As soon as he left, Merry grabbed a partially intact suitcase and began throwing her strewn clothing and papers into it. Getting the wrinkles out of her abused blouses and suit took secondary billing to the venting of her feelings.

Gradually, as her anger subsided, other thoughts intervened. She gathered the rest of her things more neatly into the suitcase and closed the top. Next, she reached for the telephone and dialed a number in Bainbridge Island, Washington. She barely gave her law partner a chance to say hello.

"Laura, I'm sorry to be calling you again after hours, but I've reconsidered your suggestion of engaging a criminal lawyer to represent me in this little matter of a murder. Do you suppose you could get me a couple of names?"

Laura's response seemed delayed by surprise. "Well, yes, of course. But what's changed your mind? Is everything all right?"

Merry sank onto the bed next to the phone. "Nothing's all right, Laura. The police think I conspired with Simon to kill Skabos. Those two men who have been after me seem to find me wherever I go, and on top of it all, I probably have caught a weird flu that's going to turn me beet red before I die."

Laura's voice sounded incredulous. "For God's sake, whatever are you talking about?"

Merry sighed as she leaned against the back of the bed, trying to let out her frustration and feeling of helplessness. She knew she had no right to be dumping everything on her partner this way. She tried to regain her sense of balance.

"Ignore me, Laura. I'm just babbling. No doubt partly due to the jitters about appearing tomorrow in court. Forget everything I just said except the part about the names of a couple of good criminal lawyers. The sooner I get those the better. Just to be on the safe side you understand."

Laura's voice took on a more natural tone. "Of course, I understand. I can have them for you by tomorrow morning. What time do you expect to return to Karen's place after court?"

Merry knew she had no intention of staying in Florida House tonight, much less returning to it tomorrow morning. But she didn't want to alarm Laura any more than she already had. "Uh, I'm not sure. Why don't I call you? That way you won't have to keep calling here trying to catch me."

"Sounds good, Merry. I trust your friend, Simon, is still around?"

Merry tried to answer Laura's question without lying. "We saw part of a play together tonight."

Laura's voice grew warmer. "Ah, do I detect a little romance in the air?"

Merry was trying to think how to answer Laura's question. Her intentions had definitely turned romantic, but had Simon's? His questions had gotten more personal. And there was that moment in the theater during intermission when he had held her shoulders so gently and leaned toward her almost as though he might—

"Merry, are you still there?" Laura asked.

"Yes, sorry. My mind wandered."

"Where? Are your worries so bothersome you can't take out a moment for a little frivolous conversation?"

"No, no. Of course not, Laura. What were you saying about Simon?"

"Well, from everything you've told me, I can't help wondering about him. His exploits against those two men who have chased you seem most courageous. Is he pursuing you?"

Pursuing me? Merry thought. How could he want to with two would-be abductors on her heels and a deadly flu probably coursing through her blood?

"'Who chooseth me must give and hazard all he hath,'" Merry quoted aloud.

"What was that?" Laura asked.

Merry sighed. "Nothing much. Just the words of a Shakespearean lawyer by the name of Portia. Seemed to fit, somehow."

Laura's voice sounded concerned. "You're beginning to worry me, Merry. You sound positively strange."

"Probably because I feel positively strange, Laura. But don't worry, it'll pass. Right now I'd better be going so I can be sure I get to bed early enough for a sufficient night's rest."

"Yes, get some sleep," Laura said. "You want to be fresh in the morning."

Merry said goodbye and hung up, feeling a little better for having talked with her partner. But as she finished packing, unwelcome thoughts of her current plight resurfaced. She was alone and in danger, and the only person to whom she felt she could turn to for protection was gone.

Once again he had vanished with the arrival of the police. After her last conversation with Calder, she was beginning to think she should vanish, too, at the sight of them. They were never there when she needed help. Only Simon was. Except tonight he had told her she should go back to Washington. Had that been his way of saying goodbye? She felt abandoned, and yet knew she had no right to feel such loss. Simon didn't owe her anything. She owed him.

She fought the sadness that threatened to drag her down. All she could do now was call a taxi and find another hotel. She reached for the phone, only to stop and whirl around at the sudden noise coming from the doorway, her heart in her throat.

"You sure this isn't the way you keep house?" a familiar voice asked.

Merry's startled look graduated into a relieved smile as she recognized Simon leaning against the doorjamb. A heavy, sad weight suddenly lifted from her spirit as she rushed over to him, happily giving him a hug.

His arms gave her a light hug in return before he gently extricated her limbs from around him.

"I'll say this for you. You certainly give a wonderful welcome, but I'm afraid it's come at a time when I can't enjoy it fully. We've got to get out of here."

Merry wouldn't have dreamed of arguing. She picked up her slashed suitcase, her shoulder bag and followed him out the door. They didn't even stop to turn off the lights in the apartment. But when Merry began down the stairs, she noticed the light there had apparently burned out. They made their descent in darkness.

Simon's voice was a whisper. "I'm parked on the next block," he said. "Your sergeant hung around a couple of minutes making calls on his car phone before he drove away, otherwise I would have been up sooner. For a while there I thought he intended on staying around long enough to tail you. Since he didn't, perhaps you're no longer a suspect."

Merry didn't feel like correcting his assumption since it would have necessitated a long explanation.

"Is your roommate okay?" he asked.

"Yes. She wasn't home when the break-in occurred. Our neighbor, the prosecuting attorney from Florida, called the police and got a look at the two men when they came out of the apartment. They'll be back, won't they?" Merry asked, keeping close beside him.

"Right about now," her companion said as he gently urged her behind yet another bush.

Merry was thinking that if she survived this trip to the nation's capital and anyone ever asked her what sights she saw, she'd at least be able to describe the bushes quite well.

She could feel her companion's breath on her neck, warm and comforting, as they both peered into the darkness beyond the streetlight. Always when he was by her side, the danger seemed less frightening. She was beginning to think that in all the world, he was the one person she trusted totally with her life.

Internal musings were immediately eclipsed by external reality. Merry's heart began to race as she caught sight of two figures stealthily moving toward Florida House from across the street. They had already searched the apartment. They had to be coming back for her. Suddenly she realized the darkened stairs had not been the result of a burned-out bulb. Simon must have removed or broken the bulb to give them cover for their escape.

She was glad for his foresight and experienced a renewed admiration for such resourcefulness.

She stood perfectly still, holding her breath as the men paused at the bottom of the stairs, watching, listening. She couldn't make out their faces clearly, but their physical outlines were familiar enough. A small shiver passed through her as the muted gleam from a streetlight flashed off the knife clutched in the shorter man's hand. Then they walked stealthily up the stairs toward the entry.

At the same moment she heard the door to Florida House being forced open, Merry felt Simon's hand on her arm, taking the suitcase from her hand, urging her to follow him. They moved quietly out of their hiding place behind the bush and ran the length of the block, trying to make as little noise as possible and only pausing when they reached the corner. Before he led Merry to his car, Simon peered back down the street.

"They haven't come out yet. Probably searching every closet for you. No doubt they'll be surprised to find you gone. Come on. We don't have a moment to lose."

They ran the next block full out, much less concerned with making noise than putting as much distance between themselves and the two men they expected would follow.

They were in the car and pulling away from the curb when Merry turned to look behind them. The blond man had just come around the corner at a run.

"He's back there!" she said.

"Yes, I see him," Simon said. "They must have split up trying to determine which direction you had taken. But that one may not be able to see the car too well. Even if he thinks it's us, we'll be long gone before he can join his partner and get back to their car for a pursuit. And just to make sure . . ."

The Porsche made a sudden leap, like some wildcat, and tore away, leaving a trail of burned rubber on the pavement and several of Merry's vital organs flattened against the back of the bucket seat. But it mattered little to her now. All that was really important was that they were safe and they were together. She kept that thought for another minute before others began to invade her mind.

"Where are we going?" she asked.

Simon shifted down into second to make a tight turn. "I suppose I can't talk you into the airport?"

"No. I have people depending on me. I must be in court in the morning."

"Your high ideals won't mean a thing if you're dead," he said.

Merry turned at his words. "So should I flee back to Washington State and leave my client with no representation before the Supreme Court? Is that what you'd do?"

Simon looked at Merry. "At least you'd be alive."

"But the question is, could I live with myself? Could you, if you made such a decision? Of course not. Your integrity would have you facing whatever problem that came your way in an honest, straightforward manner. You would never shirk a duty.''

A very serious note injected into Simon's voice. ''How could you know what I'd do?''

''By your actions, of course! Look how you've made your superiors angry because you refuse to give up on tracking Carmichael's flu. You put yourself on the line for others. You've certainly faced danger each time you've stepped in to save me from those two monsters. It's easy to see the kind of man you are. A man to admire, to—''

Merry stopped herself, realizing she had begun to get carried away and regretting her indiscriminate tongue. Her feelings for Simon were growing and she just wasn't the type of person who could hide them for long. Did he know how much she cared already? She glanced over at him. Whatever she expected, it wasn't the deep frown that was reflected in his eyes.

''Don't ever be so sure you'll know what any man will do in a given situation. We don't know ourselves.''

The continued seriousness of his tone gave Merry pause. What was it that caused him to say such things? She tried to lighten the suddenly solemn mood. ''Shakespeare must have said something profound to cover this situation, but for the life of me I can't think of an appropriate passage.''

He exhaled heavily before he spoke. ''Perhaps that's because the better quote comes from the Bible. Something about men and their feet of clay.''

A sudden sad quality in his voice made her heart ache. She shook her head. This was not the time to feed her spirit a diet of gloom and doom. Such nourishment never produced a happy outlook. She tried to refocus her thoughts on some positive action.

''Do you know of a discreet hotel where I might get a room for the night, someplace that wouldn't be inclined to give out my name for a bribe?''

Simon was quiet for a minute, in careful thought. Then he nodded as though he had made a decision. When he spoke his voice had regained its lighter tone.

''Yes. A very discreet place in a nice neighborhood with select clientele and reasonable rates. You could get a taxi to the court tomorrow. And I'll even cook you breakfast before you go, if you'd like?" he asked.

His last comment was a giveaway. "Your place?" she asked.

He looked over at her. "A separate room. A safe bed. In all respects."

Merry couldn't hide her immediate pleasure at the idea.

"I do feel safe with you, safer than I've ever felt with anyone. But this is an invasion of your privacy. I certainly wouldn't want to have some stranger coming to stay with me on the spur of the moment. And what if these men find I'm there? What if they break into your place next?"

"They won't find you there," he said.

"Is it a hotel?"

"No, it's a town home in Georgetown. Belongs to my brother. He's out of town with his family so he's lent it to me. It's his way of supporting what I'm trying to do here, even though he thinks I'm a fool."

Merry heard the frustration in Simon's voice again. "Hasn't there been any family member, co-worker or friend who's believed in your pursuit of this deadly flu?"

Simon shook his head. "My brother is the closest family member I have and his attitude is best described as tolerant. I haven't wanted to upset my parents by telling them all the troubles my pursuit has caused, so I've purposely kept them in the dark. My boss has become outright hostile and threatened my job. And my friends have hoped I'd just keep them out of it."

Merry frowned. "I'm beginning to understand how hard it's been for you to keep following up on the meager leads hinting of this deadly flu. You must feel worn out."

Simon smiled over at her. "Thank you for that, Merry. Having you understand somehow reduces the frustration quotient to bearable. Would it bother you if I don't take you to court tomorrow?"

"Of course not. Is that why you mentioned the taxi?"

"Yes. The curator of the gem and mineral collection at the Smithsonian will be in first thing tomorrow. I wanted to catch him the moment he walks into his office. I've got to get the specifics on who came in contact with the people handling the

Fire Diamond. There could be some very sick individuals out there who need help.''

"Have you made an appointment?" Merry asked.

"No. I plan to barge in first thing, flash my CDC credentials and not give him time to even think about checking with Atlanta. If all goes well I could meet you at the court later?''

"All right. My case is the second on the calendar. It will begin at eleven.''

"If I get to the curator soon enough, I should be able to make it to court in time for your presentation.''

"I hope so. You know, if I'm staying in Georgetown tonight, I should call Karen and have her pick me up on her way into court tomorrow. She's staying in Georgetown tonight, too.''

They were turning into some narrower, residential streets, lined on each side by crowded buildings, several stories in height. Merry hadn't really been watching where they were heading, but she was pretty sure they were in Georgetown now.

"Tell me who knew about your going to the play tonight," Simon said, distracting her attention from the scenery.

Merry understood what Simon was getting at. "I don't think we'll need to go through a list of names. I'm pretty sure I've already figured out how those two men found me at the Folger Theatre.''

"You've done some detective work of your own?''

She shrugged. "Just some thinking. They must have read a note Karen left me on the refrigerator door mentioning the play. So when they didn't find me at Florida House, they headed for the theater.''

"That explains the theater, but it doesn't explain how they knew you were at Florida House," Simon said.

Merry nodded. "Nor does it explain how they found me at the hotel.''

Simon seemed to consider her words. "Finding you at the hotel might not have been too difficult since you were registered under your own name. But finding you at Florida House took concerted effort.''

He paused, giving Merry an opportunity to ask a question of her own.

"How did you find me at the hotel? I thought you told me I was successful in losing you with that trick of having the taxi stop at the other hotel?" she said.

"Yes, you did throw me off at first. But it wasn't hard to pick up your trail again. I knew the name of the cab company and where it had picked you up, so I just called the dispatcher to get the final destination."

Merry exhaled a frustrated breath. "Then those two men could have done the same?"

Simon nodded.

"So that explains how they might have found me at the hotel. The only place it doesn't cover is Florida House. Is it possible they tracked us from the Smithsonian Museum this morning?"

Simon shook his head. "I don't see how, but I suppose we have to consider it."

Merry went over the route they had taken in her mind, trying to remember if she had seen a blue Cadillac along the way, knowing the green-and-gray Subaru had been parked. Simon was right. It didn't seem possible that they had been followed. But if they weren't, how did the men find her at Florida House? She sighed.

"Tired?" Simon asked.

"A little," she said.

"Then you'll be happy to know we're here," he said as he pressed the garage-door opener and drove into the narrow, single-car garage. The door closed behind them and a light stayed on overhead. Merry wasn't sure she could get out on her side without hitting the door of the Porsche against the side of the concrete wall.

"Sorry," Simon said, recognizing the reason for her hesitancy. "I leave more room on this side out of habit. Normally, you see, I'm not carrying a passenger. Here, give me your hand. You can slip out this way."

Merry grasped his outstretched hand firmly as she maneuvered over the gearshift and out the driver's side. As she struggled under the steering wheel and across the second seat, he placed his other hand around her, trying to guide. She stood up, out of the car, to find she was almost folded in his arms only a step away from an embrace. She inhaled and then sighed at the wonderful, clean soap scent that seemed so much a part of him.

"There goes another sigh," he said. "You must be tired. Are you noticing any unusual weakness?"

The message in his words brought her possible infection forcibly to mind and whisked away her pleasurable feelings at his closeness. She stepped back, aware her face felt flush and her knees a little weak.

Oh, God, she thought in sudden awareness of her state. Are these the first signs of Carmichael's flu?

## Chapter Eleven

Simon leaned back and removed the cold, round knob of the stethoscope from Merry's chest and unplugged his ears. He smiled at her as she quickly rebuttoned the top of her blouse, feeling the blood rise up her neck despite the fact that throughout the very proper and virtually fully-clothed examination she had just received she kept reminding herself that Simon was a doctor.

"Your heart sounds strong. Your breathing is clear, your pulse regular, your blood pressure only slightly above normal. That small rise in your temperature could be due to many different things, even the anxiety you must be feeling because of your possible exposure."

Merry exhaled in some relief. "So I'm generating my own symptoms?"

Simon smiled. "Maybe. I think what we both could use right now is a brandy."

Merry watched Simon place the stethoscope in his bag and close it. He got off the powder-blue sectional they were sitting on in the living room of his brother's town home and walked over to a portable bar standing in the corner.

As soon as Merry had entered the house, she could see it was decorated by someone who could only be described as a "blue" person. Everything from the carpet to the wallpaper to the furniture was in varying shades of blue. And although Merry gravitated more toward warmer tones, she had to admit that the furnishings were expertly coordinated and very tastefully done.

She watched Simon as he poured brandy into two snifters on top of the ceramic bar, and she remembered the feel of his fingers as they gently probed the lymph glands in her neck. She probably shouldn't be at all surprised the thermometer said her temperature was elevated or the blood-pressure machine had inched above normal. She tried to put her mind on something else as Simon leaned over to hand her a brandy and she once again caught the clean, natural scent of him.

"Feeling okay?" he asked as he sat across from her.

Merry took a sip from her snifter, realizing Simon must be detecting her reaction to his nearness and that she had to make a more concerted effort to refocus her thoughts.

"I'm fine," she said. "This is good brandy, thank you. Have you had time to do any more thinking about what we learned from Laura this afternoon?"

Simon nodded. "I admit it's occupied most of my thoughts. Still, although we know a lot more than we did before Laura called, there's a lot I find confusing and incomplete. Has anything new occurred to you?"

"Not new exactly," Merry said. "But I've begun to have some doubts about our earlier assumptions."

"How's that?" Simon asked.

"Well, we know Skabos got out of prison about eight months ago. We know that he was found with a fake Fire Diamond stuck in his throat, probably a fake diamond he created when you consider his expertise and history. Would it be reasonable to assume he might have acquired my pursuers as new partners since getting out of prison?"

Simon nodded as he took a sip of his brandy. "I'd say it's probable. He'd need new partners. Still, it doesn't look like he chose his new associates too well, either."

Merry considered his words for a moment. "So we're saying Skabos teams up with those men to somehow heist the Fire Diamond. They get angry and the gem cutter ends up choked to death by a replica of the diamond."

Simon looked over at her. "You don't sound convinced."

Merry shook her head. "I suppose those men must have been the ones who killed Skabos, but something has been bothering me ever since we discussed that possibility this afternoon."

"Which is?" he asked.

"Why would they use a replica of the Fire Diamond as a murder weapon?"

"It was handy?" Simon suggested.

Merry shook her head. "We know they've got guns—knives, too. Why didn't they use them?"

Simon shrugged. "Gunfire could have been heard. A stabbed man might cry out from a knife wound. And we can't be sure they had either a gun or knife on them Saturday morning. Frankly, I think if they had had either, they would have tried to use one or both on me when I tried to pull them off you."

Merry nodded at the logic of his reasoning. "All right. Let's leave that point for a moment. Let's assume they killed Skabos. They've searched my room at the hotel and Karen's apartment looking for something. We've surmised it was either jewels or money."

Simon sipped some of his brandy. "Actually, since we now know Skabos's history, the logical conclusion is that they were looking for the money they advanced him to replicate the stone. They were angry he flawed the diamond and they wanted their money back."

Merry frowned. "But there were two of them, Simon. If their physical hold on Skabos was strong enough to shove a fake diamond down his throat, why wasn't it strong enough to just grab back the money they had paid the gem cutter?"

Simon shook his head. "I don't know. From the way you just described the probable scene, I admit I don't see why they couldn't have just taken the money. Are you going somewhere with this?"

Merry pursed her lips and nodded thoughtfully. "Yes, but bear with me a moment as I pursue something else that's been bothering me. Remember when Laura told us about Skabos she said the police found a hotel room key and approximately one hundred dollars in cash on him?"

Simon sat forward as the import of Merry's words sunk in. "That's right. If Skabos only had one hundred dollars on him, what happened to the payoff?"

Merry nodded. "Yes, that's been bothering me. If Skabos didn't have the money on him and neither did I, did it ever exist? Have we been assuming an exchange took place that never did?"

Simon put down his brandy glass. "If those men weren't after the money, why have they been tearing your places apart? What could they hope to find?"

Merry sat forward, a new gleam in her eye. "What is small and valuable and could be hidden in the shoulder pad of a suit?"

"You mean the replica of the Fire Diamond?" Simon asked.

Merry nodded. "Yes. What if they had come to meet Skabos in the gem room expecting to get the replica of the Fire Diamond? What if Skabos was killed before they got it?"

Simon shook his head. "Wait, that doesn't make sense. If they killed Skabos, they'd have to already know the replica was shoved down his throat. They wouldn't be tearing your stuff apart looking for it."

Merry nodded. "Except, what if they didn't kill Skabos?"

Simon picked up Merry's train of thought, his voice reflecting a new eagerness. "Yes, what if they didn't? They weren't immediately there when Skabos came to stand next to you. It wasn't until after he had collapsed on you that they appeared. Could it be someone else killed the gem cutter?"

Merry nodded. "It fits. If they weren't the ones to kill Skabos, they wouldn't have known the replica was used as the murder weapon. They may have wanted to retrieve it when they found Skabos dead so as to cover up the attempt to replicate and steal the Fire Diamond. Or they may have wanted it because they are still planning to go through with the theft."

Simon nodded eagerly. "Yes, that could explain it. Merry, I think you've hit on something. Only if they didn't kill Skabos, who do you suppose did?"

Merry sat back in the sofa, the brandy she had drunk suddenly filling her with a warm lassitude. "Beats me," she said.

Simon watched her yawn and got to his feet. "And speaking of beat, I think we both are. What do you say we head for bed. Your room will be the one on the left at the top of the stairs."

She followed him up the narrow staircase and into yet another blue room. It had a king-size bed and two dressers. He put her battered suitcase next to a nightstand and took some of his clothes out of the closet.

Merry shook her head as she began to understand what he was doing. "I can't take this room. It's obviously the one you've been using," she said.

Simon shrugged. "Not tonight. There's room in the closet and this top dresser drawer on the right is empty. The bathroom is out the door here, first room on the left. It's the only one, so knocking is probably a good idea. Is there anything you need?"

Merry immediately thought of her suit, the one she was going to have to wear the next day.

"Do you by any chance have an iron?"

He nodded and left. Merry had her suit and a blouse out and laying on the bed when he returned. He had brought an ironing board, as well, and set it up for her.

"What are you going to do about the missing shoulder pads?" he asked.

Merry eyed her suit critically. "Maybe if I stuffed and pinned some Kleenex inside the lining?"

"I've got an idea," he said and left again. He reappeared with a coat slung over his arm and pair of scissors in his hand.

"I never wear this coat anymore," he said as he snipped the restraining threads holding its shoulder pads in place. He then handed them to her. "Try these."

Merry fitted them loosely in place of the shredded pads and looked at them, trying to judge the effect.

"I better try the jacket on before I sew them in," she said.

He helped her on with her suit jacket and stood behind her as she studied the fit in the large dresser mirror.

"Well, what's the verdict?" she asked.

"Hmm. Yes, I think you'd make a good linebacker for the Green Bay Packers."

She grinned. "It's overpowering, isn't it? But I believe I'm almost tempted. Picture it. Here comes two big shoulder pads walking into the Supreme Court of the land with a tiny little head sticking above and two spindly legs beneath. What a comedy. Wouldn't you want to be there? Just to see the looks on their faces?"

He was watching the look on her face, the light dancing in her translucent-brown eyes. So open. So full of good humor.

He was thinking how lovely her smile was. How much he liked its feel.

He turned her around to face him and leaned down to gently brush her lips with his. The impulse had rushed him into one quick kiss before rational thought could intervene. But the moment he tasted her, he leaned down for more, folding her in his arms. For a second unconscious moment he luxuriated in the feel of her lips responding to the demand from his, of her soft body melting into his hard flesh. Then several sharp reminders bit savagely into his attention, causing him to wrench back in painful memory. His hands quickly moved her to arm's length.

"I'm sorry." His words sounded husky and choked as he forced them out from a tightened throat. "Good night." He released his hold on her arms, walked out of the room and closed the door behind him.

Merry stumbled over to the bed and sat down, feeling flushed and overly excited. Her body trembled all over, but this time she was sure it wasn't from any deadly flu. The diagnosis of her current fever was all too readily obvious. That had been some kiss. She had willingly, wholeheartedly flowed into his arms, urging him closer, savoring his taste, thrilling to his touch.

She inhaled deeply, still feeling the blood tingling through her body and feeling perplexed by his behavior. Where were the follow-up embraces, the words of affection and endearment that were the natural accompaniment to a man and woman sharing such a moment?

Was he worried about catching the deadly flu she might have? It was possible, but in her mind unlikely. He had been exposed before and hadn't contracted it. Somehow she just didn't believe the fear of further contagion had caused him to pull away from her willing arms. So what was the reason?

The nagging reminders of his numerous refusals to face the police surfaced suddenly in one large, festering boil of suspicion. She had refused to seriously listen to the doubts, but the time had come when Merry realized she had to face them. Simon Temple was hiding something, something that made him avoid the police, something that had sent him from her arms tonight.

Her mind reeled at the possibilities, afraid to seriously consider a particular scenario. He had saved her life. Whatever else he was involved in, whatever else he had done could not mitigate his efforts on her behalf. She must not presume to judge him. She did not have all the facts. He had treated her with care, trust and respect. Her sense of fair dealing dictated she show him nothing less in return.

Unfortunately, no amount of brave and logical self-talk could ease the sad little lump that had become lodged in her throat. His Bible quote about feet of clay kept whirling through her mind. He had been trying to tell her something. What could it have been?

She looked down to see she was sitting on her already-wrinkled blouse. She got up and took it over to the ironing board. Might as well busy herself with getting ready for tomorrow. She had a feeling she wasn't going to sleep much tonight.


"JOSEPH, DO YOU THINK it was wise coming here tonight?" Laura asked.

The president of Freedman Diamonds shrugged his bare shoulders against the rumpled sheets and repositioned his glasses back across his nose. Then he reached over to pull the woman with the tousled chestnut hair closer to his side.

"We've waited long enough. The time has come to act."

Laura sighed as she snuggled up against Joseph Freedman. "Won't Merry become suspicious?"

"I told her I was going to my New York office. She won't get wise until it's all over."

Laura licked dry lips. "She's been my good friend these past years. I'm beginning to feel guilty."

The tall, attractive man leaned over to gently kiss his bed companion on the tip of her nose.

"Remember what I told you before, Laura. There are endings to everything. Some things you must put behind you now."

Laura watched Joseph's hand coming to rest on the top of hers. She raised worried eyes to his.

"We're doing the right thing, aren't we?" she asked.

Joseph Freedman nodded. "The only possible thing," he said.

"And Merry?" she asked.

Joseph Freedman shrugged. "We have to go ahead with our plans. She's bound to find out why you sent her to the capital alone. It's not something we can keep from her much longer. Too much has happened."

"Then, tomorrow?" Laura asked.

"Yes, after tomorrow it will be all over," Freedman said.

"WELL, TODAY'S THE DAY, Karen. Thanks for picking me up," Merry said as she got into her friend's car Monday morning in preparation for their drive to the Supreme Court.

Karen smiled good-naturedly. "It has its price, you know. What happened last night? Why did you leave the theater early?"

Merry told Karen a slightly edited version of the events of the previous evening.

"But how did they find you and what were they looking for?" Karen said.

"I've asked myself the same questions, Karen. I don't know. It's got to have something to do with what I told you about the dead man, Skabos."

Karen shook her head. "Well at least the police have come to their senses and are finally giving you protection. Is that one of their safe houses that I picked you up at?"

Merry shifted uneasily in her seat as she remembered once again awakening that morning to find Simon already gone, a cryptic note left on the kitchen table explaining he was getting an early start. She had found it at seven and knew the real reason he had left early was because he had wanted to avoid seeing her. The realization had hurt.

"Merry, did you hear what I said?" Karen asked.

Merry shook her head. "You asked a question?"

"Yes. I asked if that was a police safe house I picked you up at."

"No. That's where my friend Simon is staying."

Karen looked over at her passenger in disbelief. "What? I thought you told me the police were giving you protection?"

"I didn't want you to worry, Karen. Sergeant Calder hasn't changed in either his demeanor or manners. I wouldn't have felt safe with any arrangements he may have been willing to make.

He still doesn't believe there are two men after me. All he wants to hear about is Simon because I won't tell him his name. At least Simon has been there when I've needed help.''

Karen shook her head. ''Merry, I'm not sure I like this. Simon's unwillingness to go to the police has me very uneasy. You should have stayed at our place in Georgetown last night. We're close to you, family, really. You seem to be putting a lot of confidence in this man.''

''What's wrong with that?'' Merry asked.

Karen shrugged. ''It doesn't feel right. You've just met him, after all, and you've been taking everything he says on faith. Doesn't it bother you that he won't face the authorities? And why is it that the CDC isn't backing him in this quest for a supposedly deadly disease? Is this man hiding something?''

Karen's words fell into the gaping hole of doubt in Merry's belief system, bringing a frown to Merry's normally open countenance. She tried to hold on to an even tone. ''He has some personal concerns he's trying to work out. It's been very frustrating for him not being able to properly track and identify this deadly flu.''

Karen studied her friend's frowning face. ''Ever since those men broke into Florida House last night, I've been having some second thoughts about Simon. He knew where you were staying, Merry. Can you be sure he isn't in cahoots with those two men in some way, trying to confuse you into trusting him? Can you be sure he truly is the hero you keep painting him to be?''

Merry knew her inner belief came through in her voice. ''I may not be sure of everything, but I'm sure he's a hero.''

''And the reason for this certainty?'' Karen asked.

'' 'I have no other, but a woman's reason; I think him so because I think him so,' '' Merry quoted.

Karen shook her head. ''No, Merry. I'll accept no quotes from Shakespeare this time. And you above all people shouldn't be falling back on that 'woman's feelings' argument. You're a lawyer, trained to deal in the logic of facts. You should be able to rise above that emotional nonsense.''

Merry shook her head. ''I can't totally rise above my emotions, Karen, even when they aren't supported by the facts. I'm human, and that means fallible. Still, in this case, I believe my emotions are backed by the logic of Simon's actions. He's saved me from those men several times over, when the police wouldn't even take the fact of those men seriously. Logically, how can I not trust him?"

Karen shook her head. "I don't know, Merry, but something doesn't seem right. Charles was beside himself last night when he returned at the end of the play to pick you up and couldn't find you. He had only left for a couple of minutes to get something to drink when you took off without him. And why? Because this Simon of yours said to."

"So that's where Mr. T. had gone," Merry said, ignoring the rest.

"Merry, are you listening to me? Anytime this Simon says to, you jump as though you're part of a kid's follow-the-leader game. Simon says jump into his car, Simon says leave the play, Simon says stay at his place. Do you understand me?"

"Karen, relax. He's on my side."

"You say he's on your side, but how can you be sure? Think about what Laura told you yesterday. This accomplice of Skabos's, this handsome man who charmed the ladies. Remember how this Simon appeared so suddenly at the Smithsonian Museum? Didn't it occur to you that this man you now call Simon and that man, John Kahr, could be one and the same?"

"No."

"No what? No, it didn't occur to you or no, they aren't the same?"

"No, it didn't occur to me, because no, they're not the same."

"What evidence makes it untrue?"

"I don't need evidence, Karen. I just know it," Merry said.

Karen shook her head sadly. "Well, all I can say is that Simon has a lot to answer for."

"What do you mean?" Merry said.

"I mean he's managed to turn one of the most logical minds I've ever met into mush in just two days," Karen said.

Merry laughed. "It has been just two days, hasn't it?"

"Oh, for heaven's sake, Merry, listen to yourself. Two days go by and all of a sudden it doesn't matter to you that a man is hiding something so important as to make him avoid the police."

Merry sighed, unhappiness creeping into her voice. "Oh, it matters. It matters very much. But I can't believe he's a criminal. The way he has risked his life for me has been courageous. The way he has treated me has been so gentle. He's a man who knows right from wrong."

"Are you sure?" Karen asked.

"I couldn't care this much for him if I wasn't."

"And how much is that?" Karen asked.

How much, indeed? Merry thought as they descended into the private garage beneath the Supreme Court building.

SIMON LOOKED AT HIS WATCH. It was already after 10:50. His attempt to bluff his way into the office of the curator of the Smithsonian's gem and mineral collection had failed miserably. The curator had had to fly out on urgent personal business and had not even come into the office that morning. For an hour and half Simon had waited for him only to finally learn he waited in vain. His frustration had mounted considerably.

Now he only had a few minutes to make it to the Supreme Court. He'd have to drive there directly if he hoped to keep his word and be on time for Merry's presentation. He gunned the Porsche and fought his way through the city's heavy traffic.

Five cups of black coffee already this morning and he still didn't feel revived. Maybe after he put Merry on a plane this afternoon, he could relax. The thought didn't furnish any additional energy. He would be happy to have her safely out of D.C., but he wouldn't be happy to see her go out of his life.

But it had to be. He kept reminding himself of that fact the night before as he lay sleepless, thinking about how her lips had tasted and how she had felt in his arms. And remembering that all the time she was in the next bedroom.

He glanced at his watch. Time was getting short. He took a chance and parked illegally, deciding a ticket was preferable to being late. But when he turned the corner to join the line waiting to get into the court, what he saw made him retreat. There on the steps of the Supreme Court building were the two men.

They were poised on either side of the main steps, positioned behind two large, seated marble figures. The female figure on the left, *Contemplation of Justice*, and the male figure on the right, the Guardian or *Authority of Law*, seemed incongruous symbols for two such thugs to hide behind.

They weren't looking down the stairs in his direction. They were looking up toward the entry where Merry would emerge after her case was over. He had just one chance of warning her. He'd have to join the waiting crowd without being seen by the two men and get into the building in time to stop her walking into their hands. He took a deep breath and started forward.

MERRY SAT WITH THE OTHER lawyers in the Supreme Court of the United States waiting for her case to come up and her chance to speak. She was shaking like a leaf.

It had always been this way, even back in grade school. No matter how prepared she was for what she was about to say, there was something about getting up in front of people that always made the moments before almost unbearable. And yet, amazingly, as soon as she got up to speak, all the nervousness went away and then the problem became trying to be succinct.

But this morning at a few minutes before eleven, her nervousness was also generated by other concerns. Simon had still not shown up.

Periodically she looked back to study the faces of the observers, while the Florida prosecutor presented his case. She was getting more anxious by the minute and more impatient. She had to think of something else.

Merry's attention drifted to the classical Corinthian architecture of the room up to the suspended ceiling clock halfway between the four massive marble columns behind the nine justices. It was too old to be battery operated. So that meant the rod suspending it must have an electrical cable. But what happened if there was an electrical outage? Or, at the end of October when the country went off daylight saving time? Who was it that climbed what must be twenty-five feet up to reset the clock?

She smiled at the thought of some poor guy swinging off an extension ladder, trying to reach the clock. Maybe there was another way up? Thick velvet drapes lined the room like a warm coat. Perhaps it was the same somebody who cleaned those drapes?

Suddenly, their deep-red color brought to mind the Fire Diamond and her relaxing musings ceased. Everything about these strange events surrounding her over the last couple of days also seemed cloaked in the Fire Diamond's spectacular light. Skabos had died in front of it, with a replica of it shoved down his throat. In its wake followed a deadly flu. And it was in front of the fabulous jewel that Merry had been grabbed and thrown into this continuing danger that made no sense.

A short recess signaled the end of the oral arguments for the first case and brought Merry's mind back to the present. With only a minute or two before she was to go on, the nervousness of her momentary appearance clutched at her insides, erasing all thoughts from her head. Which was why she jumped uncontrollably when the hand was laid on her shoulder.

"I'm sorry, ma'am," the young courtroom guard said. "Didn't mean to startle you, but a gentleman gave me this note for you. Said it was most urgent."

Merry took the folded note and stared down at it for a moment in surprise. "What gentleman?" Merry asked, looking up, but the guard was already gone and she was being called to present her case. She rose on unsteady feet.

SIMON WATCHED MERRY GET UP a little hesitantly to approach the lecturn, his unread note still clasped in her right hand. Just before she addressed the assemblage, she slipped the note into the pocket of her suit jacket.

His stomach muscles tightened in alarm. If she didn't read it, she would walk out of the courtroom at the noon recess right into the hands of her abductors and there would be nothing he could do about it.

# *Chapter Twelve*

Simon's knowledge of courtroom procedures extended to the black-and-white reruns of *Perry Mason* he caught occasionally on a local TV channel. He didn't know what to expect of a presentation before the Supreme Court. As Merry began to speak, he immediately recognized her assured tone and marveled at her ability to project her voice so that each syllable was clear and distinct throughout the large courtroom.

"The State of Washington argues that the Freedman Diamond Company's personal delivery of a diamond to a customer involves the establishment of a company presence. And because of this interpretation of presence, my client's company is being told such transactions are subject to business, occupation and sales taxes levied by the State."

Simon listened to Merry explain the logic behind the need for a personal delivery of a custom-cut diamond by a gemologist. Since gemologists were the only professionals who could tell the difference in gem quality, such delivery assured both the safety and the authenticity of the stone. Items of such value could not be shipped by conventional means, so transportation provided by special messengers should not be construed as business presence.

Simon watched the eight men and one woman, noting the forward position of their obvious attention. Merry's legal argument seemed sound. But Simon could see it was really her presentation that was making the difference. She had a way of saying something, a quality in her voice that lent believability. It was as though she was able to wear her inner convictions for all to see and hear. He had admired that same openness in their personal dealings. It seemed equally as effective with the men and woman of the Supreme Court.

When Merry's thirty minutes were up, Simon listened to the state attorney present the case for the other side. His logic was also good, but he lacked that special quality of believability. Simon watched the justices' attention spans wander as the state's attorney droned on. How much of a difference would Merry's presentation make?

When it was all over and the justices had asked their questions of both sides, Simon decided that Merry's belief in her subject had carried the day. Of course, he knew he wasn't exactly objective in the matter.

He watched her gather up her papers in preparation to leave and willed her to remember the note he had sent her before beginning to speak. As though she had received his silent signal, she suddenly reached into her right pocket and pulled it out. As he watched her read it, he breathed a sigh of relief knowing she'd be safe. Now it was time for him to exit with the other gallery spectators and try not to be seen by the two watching and waiting men. That could prove very, very tricky.

A FROWN WAS FORMING on Merry's forehead as she headed directly for where Karen sat on the edge of the lawyers' area as soon as the noon recess was announced. When Karen held out her hand in congratulations, Merry took it and pulled her out of earshot of the other lawyers milling about in casual conversation. Karen's eyes reflected her startled expression.

"What's wrong, Merry?"

"I've got to get out of here. And I can't go out the front door. The men who have been after me are outside."

Karen's voice rose in a breathless disbelief. "I don't understand. How can you know that?"

"Simon sent me a note. He saw them there and he sent me a message through one of the courtroom guards. Karen, they're waiting for me. Is there a back way out of here?"

Karen thought for a moment and then nodded. "Yes. We can go down the elevator to the garage and drive out in my car. Do you want me to take you to the airport or the police?"

"Neither. I have an appointment at the Capitol," Merry said.

"The Capitol? An appointment? I don't understand. Who are you going to meet there?"

"Simon, I hope," Merry said.

Karen looked over at the worried look on her companion's face. "You hope? What's wrong?"

"I'm afraid he's in danger," Merry said.

WHEN KAREN LET HER OFF in front of the Capitol, Merry headed directly for the rotunda to join a tour group as Simon had instructed. His note told her he would meet with her somewhere along the way, if all went well. And if all didn't go well? Merry firmly pressed that thought down.

But as the tour progressed farther and farther through the beautiful marble hallways, Merry found herself totally inattentive to the guide as she became more and more concerned. Where was Simon?

Had her abductors spotted him outside the Supreme Court? Had they caught up with him? Merry tried to remind herself worrying wasn't going to get her anywhere. She tried to calm down as her tour group entered the Supreme Court Chamber, the room in the Capitol Building that had been the meeting place for the Supreme Court before its separate structure had been built.

Merry stopped in the outer room to read aloud a quotation from Thomas Jefferson. "For Heaven's sake discard the monstrous wig which makes the English Judges look like rats peeping through bunches of oakum."

Merry started at the sound of a small laugh just behind her. "I'm glad Thomas Jefferson was able to convince American jurisprudence to forget the wig."

"Simon!" Merry said as she turned at his voice. She was overwhelmingly relieved at his presence and the warm look in his eyes. After his abruptness of the night before and his early departure that morning, she had been thinking he might never look at her that way again. For once in her life she was content to not say a thing and just bask in his warm gaze.

He smiled as he reached out to smooth back a strand of her hair with his fingers. "Yes, I'd hate to think of a wig covering such nice hair. By the way, what's oakum?" he asked.

"A plant fiber, I think," Merry said as she reached out her hand to clasp his arm. Her heart was slushing sillily in her chest. She felt the tears come into her eyes. "I'm so glad to see you."

He stared down into her moist eyes a moment more, feeling the warmth of her hand, wondering how he could get this carried away by someone simply telling him she was glad to see him. If only things were different. If only he could change the past. But of course, he couldn't.

He cleared his throat, trying to control his tone. "You were great in court," he said. "I was most impressed."

The tour group had finished in the Supreme Court Chamber and was turning toward Merry and Simon, the sound of their feet audible on the creaking, clear plastic that lay over the thick red carpet, protecting it from wear.

Simon withdrew his hand from Merry and stepped back. "We'd best be on our way," he said.

They made their way through the lingering crowds and found the nearest exit. As they were walking to Simon's car, he reviewed their next steps. "I'll drive you back to Georgetown now and pick up your things. Then we'll drive to National Airport and you can get on that plane back to Washington. There's nothing to keep you here now. We can stay in touch by phone over the next few weeks just to make sure you don't develop any symptoms of Carmichael's flu."

Merry shook her head. "It's no use, Simon. I'm not going to be any safer in Washington than I am here. I knew that as soon as I got your note in court."

Simon was surprised at her words. "What do you mean?"

She sighed. "My pursuers know who I am and where I'm from. Don't you see? Since they knew I was going to be in the Supreme Court today, they must know the rest. If I fly back to Washington, what would prevent them from following?"

Simon listened to her words and found himself nodding. "Damn it, you're right. They must know. And they probably are tenacious enough to follow you wherever you go. I've been fooling myself thinking you would be safe if you could just leave D.C."

They reached his car and got in, both in thought. Simon was the first to speak. "Then we go on as we first agreed. We continue to work together until we find both the cause of the deadly flu and the mystery surrounding the murder of Ian Skabos.''

He turned to her then, his eyes full of strength and determination. ''Deal?''

Merry felt her pulse race as she took his outstretched hand and shook it firmly. His warmth flowed through her and she suddenly got the impression something strong and unbeatable had just been forged between them. It was a heady feeling.

''Do you know, at this moment I feel sorry for those men,'' she said.

He gave her one of his soaring smiles and suggested lunch. She agreed readily. He selected a Chinese restaurant a few blocks away and soon they were enjoying dim sum and hot tea.

Simon looked across the table at her thoughtfully. ''Do you still feel as you did last night that your pursuers might have been after the replica of the Fire Diamond?''

Merry nodded, her mouth full of noodles. Simon went on. ''Well, my attempt to see the curator of the gem and mineral collection this morning fizzled, but I've been thinking I might work his absence to my advantage,'' Simon said. ''Are you game to help me give it a try?''

Merry nodded enthusiastically.

''Okay, we'll tackle his assistant. Perhaps we can ask two kinds of questions. One kind can lead me to the people who have handled the stone and might therefore have contracted Carmichael's disease. The other kind can probe how a diamond like that might be duplicated.''

Merry swallowed to clear her mouth. ''Yes, of course. How did the replica get reproduced? One of the things I read in *Gemletter* about the Fire Diamond was that there were no pictures of it available. Wouldn't Skabos have had to handle the stone in order to make such a good reproduction of it?''

Simon nodded. ''Maybe the assistant curator can tell us how Skabos could have gotten access to it. If he came close enough to others who had it in their possession, he'll definitely be added to my list of those possibly afflicted with Carmichael's flu.''

''You have your credentials from the CDC. How will you explain me?'' Merry asked.

Simon smiled. "You're my invaluable assistant. Don't worry. If I do this right and put on a pompous, demanding air, no one's going to ask for your identification."

Merry felt assured by Simon's confident manner. They headed to the Smithsonian right after lunch, quickly learning that Margaret Whatley was the assistant curator for gems and minerals. Simon boldly marched into her office with Merry in his wake.

"Whatley?" he asked in a loud voice flashing his credentials, "I'm Dr. Temple, CDC. This is my assistant, Anders. We've got a very serious problem here. Your boss was supposed to meet with me about it, but his secretary advises me he's been called out of town on a personal emergency. I'm going to need your help."

Without waiting for an invitation, Simon plopped down in one of the chairs in front of Ms. Whatley's desk. Merry took another and watched the disordered look on the face of the neat-looking woman who had risen from behind the desk.

She was short, dark-haired, round, about fifty with a nervous habit of chewing her lower lip. She kept busy at the task as she eyed the two people who had just charged in on her.

"Did you say CDC?" she asked.

Simon leaned back in his chair as though he owned it. "Yes. Epidemic Intelligence Service Officer from the Centers for Disease Control. Naturally, I had to come in person because of the seriousness of the matter. But then I expect the curator no doubt apprised you of my impending arrival."

From the look on Ms. Whatley's face there was no doubt that Simon's statement was news to her. She remained standing behind her desk.

"I-I was not told of your visit, Dr. Temple. I'm sure the curator—"

Simon waved away whatever she was about to say. "Well, perhaps not. It did happen over the weekend and the curator knew of the need for secrecy in the matter. Still, I should think you could be trusted, as long as the curator is unavailable, that is. Sit down, Whatley. I'm prepared to fill you in."

Merry watched Ms. Whatley descend into her chair on command and gained a new respect for Simon's brash approach.

"The man who died in front of the Fire Diamond Saturday had symptoms of a contagious disease, as yet unidentified. I need to know everyone who that man had contact with at the Smithsonian."

Ms. Whatley munched feverishly on her abused bottom lip at Simon's words. "A contagious disease? But I thought the police said he had been murdered?"

Simon nodded. "He was. I said he showed symptoms of a contagious disease, not that he died of one. Now, Ms. Whatley, what was this man's business with the Smithsonian?"

Ms. Whatley looked very uncomfortable. "He had no business with us, none at all. The man was just a visitor, strolling through the museum as any other visitor might. His murder on the premises was a most unfortunate occurrence."

Merry watched Simon raise an eyebrow in obvious disbelief. "Really, Ms. Whatley? How odd then that this 'visitor' by the name of Skabos was choked to death by someone shoving an almost-flawless forgery of the Fire Diamond down his throat."

Merry could see that Ms. Whatley was surprised at their knowledge. Her voice sounded dismayed. "How did you find out who he was and how he was killed? The police haven't released that information."

Simon shrugged professionally. "We were called in when the medical examiner did his autopsy and found evidence of this contagious disease. Did you expect us not to know how the victim died?"

His comeback was so smooth and automatic that if Merry had not known better, she would have believed every word he said. It was discomforting for her to learn how smooth and polished a liar Simon was.

"Now what can you tell me about this disreputable gem cutter's attempt to steal the Fire Diamond?" he asked.

Ms. Whatley's expression became even more alarmed. Her bottom lip took some new stabbing by her front teeth. "They told you too much. No one was to know these things. I shouldn't be talking to you."

Simon leaned forward in his chair. "Are you telling me you're not going to cooperate with the Centers for Disease Control in trying to avoid a serious epidemic?"

Ms. Whatley looked trapped. Merry couldn't help but feel sorry for her. She decided to speak up and concentrated on keeping her voice even.

"Ms. Whatley, everything you tell us will be kept in the strictest of confidence. We have no wish to embarrass the Smithsonian. We only wish to save lives. We are relying on you not to mention the reason for our visit, too. News of our investigation might give rise to unnecessary panic. So you see, we trust your discretion. Won't you trust ours?"

Merry's words seemed to release the bars from Ms. Whatley's caged expression. Her muscles relaxed, sagging her round body into an unresisting lump in the oversized chair. Her new tone was subdued.

"Naturally, the police alerted us when they found out how this man died," she said. "We were astonished to find out who the man was. He had done some gem verification work for us many years ago. That was all before his being charged with that diamond-theft business he got involved in, you understand. Anyway, the medical examiner's office called for our assistance in determining if the stone was a real diamond. But as you say, it turned out to be a quite clever fake."

Simon allowed a long pause after the assistant curator had had her say before he asked his next question. "Well, Ms. Whatley?"

"Well, what?" she asked.

"Was an attempt made to steal the Fire Diamond?" Simon asked.

Ms. Whatley's tone was emphatic. "No, Dr. Temple. No such attempt was made. And if one ever was, it would fail. Our security is top-rate."

"And exactly what measures are you using to keep the Fire Diamond secure?" Simon asked.

Ms. Whatley's short, straight dark-hair shook vehemently at the sides of her round head. "That information is confidential, Dr. Temple. I don't care who you represent."

Merry could see that the question upset the assistant curator. She hurried to take over the questioning for a while to ease the tension that had surfaced.

"I understand the Fire Diamond is a fairly recent addition to the Smithsonian collection," Merry said.

As Ms. Whatley turned her attention to Merry, her face seemed more relaxed. "Yes. It was donated by a wealthy patron just about a month ago."

"Who was that?" Merry asked.

It was another question that seemed to upset Ms. Whatley. Her tone once again became challenging. "The gift of the diamond was intended to be made anonymously. I will not violate the benefactor's confidence."

"Of course not," Simon said. "If those were the conditions of the donation, naturally we wouldn't want you to."

Merry was a little surprised at Simon's capitulation on that point. She thought he should have pressed for the identity of the donor in order to track the deadly flu. But she didn't have much time to think about it because the conversation was moving on.

"How was the gem brought to the museum?" Simon asked.

Ms. Whatley glanced back at him. "By armed guard, directly from the home of the benefactor after it had been examined by two gemologists from the museum."

"They examined it at the donor's home?" Merry asked.

"Yes. They checked its weight and classification. It was placed in its protective glass case and has remained there ever since."

"You mean the gemologists brought it back with them right after the examination?" Merry asked.

"Not right after," Ms. Whatley said. "Proper transportation and arrival times had to all be worked out. The Fire Diamond remained safe under guard at the benefactor's home until suitable arrangements could be made."

"How long did those arrangements take?" Merry asked.

"I don't remember, exactly. Two or three days, maybe."

"I need the gemologists' names, Ms. Whatley. And the names of the guards who transported the diamond," Simon said.

Ms. Whatley nodded. "They should be in the file. I'll get them for you before you leave."

Simon nodded. "Have any Smithsonian employees associated with the diamond in any way come down with flulike symptoms since the diamond's arrival?"

Ms. Whatley shrugged. "I have no way of knowing that, Dr. Temple. I can consult the recent attendance records of those Smithsonian employees involved in the diamond's transfer and display. That will tell me if they have been absent because of illness. However, my suggestion would be that you take down all their names and telephone numbers so that you can check with them directly and be certain of the facts."

Simon nodded.

"You say the gemologists checked the diamond's classification?" Merry asked. "Did they come to any conclusion on a definite color category?"

Ms. Whatley looked suspiciously at Merry. "Why should that be of interest to you?"

Merry smiled. "Because I find diamonds fascinating, of course. Don't you?"

Ms. Whatley grunted noncommittedly. "A panel of experts will be meeting in a month's time to make such a determination."

"How do you think it will be classified?" Merry asked.

For once, Ms. Whatley seemed pleased with a question. It had to be because her opinion was being sought.

"It's an unusual stone, of course. But all this talk about a new color grade is ridiculous. Photoluminescence has been known for many years in other diamonds. Just look at the blue in the Hope Diamond. Besides, most luminescence is a non-factor in the color-grading scale. And whereas there is no doubt its red heart enhances the 'fire' of this diamond, that's hardly reason to change standards we've all fought a long time to establish."

"I understand your point of view," Merry said. "Do you happen to have a picture of the jewel?"

Ms. Whatley seemed almost mellow now. "Yes. I believe there are several in the file. Just a moment."

Ms. Whatley got up and moved over to a file cabinet in the back of her office. She looked through some folders for a few minutes before selecting one and extricating it from the file drawer. She brought the material back to her desk and sat down. When she opened the folder, the pictures were on top. She handed them to Merry as she consulted the attendance records of the Smithsonian employees who had anything to do with the Fire Diamond.

"No absences, Dr. Temple. Not since the diamond was transported to us. Here, you can use this pencil and paper to take down the names of those involved."

Simon took the offered supplies and quickly wrote down the names Ms. Whatley rattled off along with the employees' addresses and telephone numbers.

Merry shuffled through the pictures of the Fire Diamond, taking time to study them carefully. Photographing diamonds was always a difficult business because of their capacity to redirect light falling on their surface. But this artist had done a beautiful job, as flawless as the depicted gem.

Merry waited until Simon had written down the information he needed before asking the assistant curator her next question. "Were these taken by a Smithsonian photographer?"

Ms. Whatley looked at her. "No. Mr.... I mean the family that owned the Fire Diamond last arranged for these photos to be taken. The family donated them along with the diamond."

"Who's the photographer?" Simon asked as he shoved his recently taken notes into his shirt pocket.

"I have no idea. I told you the family donated the photos at the time the Fire Diamond came to us. The museum had nothing to do with their commission."

Merry turned the photographs over quickly, noting the name of the photographer stamped on the back before repositioning the pictures and handing them to Simon.

"When will the diamond be removed from its display case for its next examination?" Simon asked.

Ms. Whatley had begun to look suspicious. "Probably in a month when the panel of experts meets to officially decide on its classification. Dr. Temple, these seem like strange questions for the CDC—"

"A history of events surrounding contagion are important in gaining a perspective on the spread of any disease, Ms. Whatley," Simon interrupted. "By the way, how have you been feeling lately?"

It was an effective aggressive move. Ms. Whatley's suspicious look turned quickly into one of alarm. "Me? I feel all right. I never went anywhere near the dead man. I—"

Simon waved away the rest of her response as he got to his feet and started for the door. "We'll be in touch," he called over his shoulder.

Merry was scrambling to her feet to follow when Ms. Whatley quickly circled her desk and almost ran to the door to reach out to Simon for the photographs of the diamond he still held. Simon surrendered them, looking surprised that Ms. Whatley was making a fuss. The assistant curator clutched the photos to her bosom as though they were her endangered children.

"Just one last question, Ms. Whatley," Simon said as he stood inside the doorway. "Do you have any idea of how this man Skabos gained access to the Fire Diamond?"

Ms. Whatley stepped back as though Simon had slapped her. "What are you trying to imply? The man never got any closer than any other visitor to the Gem Room. What an absurd question!"

"Really, Ms. Whatley? Then how do you explain his ability to replicate the diamond so well that it took a gemologist to tell the difference between it and the real thing?"

They left Ms. Whatley nervously devouring her lower lip and frowning as she obviously contemplated Simon's last question. After they left the building, Simon paused and turned to Merry.

"So what do you think?" he asked.

Merry thought about his question as she looked up at the thick gray in the sky's gathering clouds. "You were right when you told Ms. Whatley that the dead gem cutter had to have come in contact with the Fire Diamond. Skabos could never have made such a replica without a detailed examination of the real jewel. But I don't see how he could have gotten his hands on it considering the fact that, according to Ms. Whatley, the Smithsonian knew who he was and his background."

"Maybe all he needed was some very good photographs of it," Simon said.

Merry's eyes gleamed at Simon's words. "Of course! That's why you were asking about the photographer!"

"Yes," Simon said. "If we could find the photographer, we might even be able to find out who had access to those excellent pictures. I'd be interested in how well the photographer has been feeling recently, too. However, running down that one particular photographer doesn't seem too feasible. If only our Ms. Whatley had been more informed on that subject."

Merry smiled over at her companion. "The photographer's name is Sara Jones. Her studio is located on K Street here in town."

Simon turned to her with a look of wonder. "How could you possibly know that?" he asked.

Merry smiled smugly. "Simple. When you asked about the photograph and I could tell you were interested in who it was, I thought of looking at the back of one of the prints. Most photographers stamp the name of their studio on the back of their work. Sara Jones was no exception. Shall we drive by or call?"

Simon looked torn. "Ms. Whatley gave me the names of six Smithsonian employees involved in the transfer or display of the Fire Diamond. I'd like to follow up on them first."

"But didn't she say that according to the attendance records none had been out ill?" Merry asked.

Simon shrugged. "I don't know how long it might take before symptoms appear. I at least need to make contact with them and let them know of their possible infection. Then I can follow up with each to see if the disease develops."

Merry nodded. "Right. How are you going to approach them?"

"Let's use one of the phone booths over there and see who we can reach. We can tell them they've been exposed to a new strain of flu and get their cooperation for tests if they begin to feel ill."

"Shall I take three names?" Merry asked.

Simon shook his head. "No, let me call and do the talking. If any of this gets back to the CDC, I don't want you implicated."

It was just as well Simon had insisted on talking to the employees himself. On the fourth call he found that a guard who had been positioned in the offices when the Fire Diamond had been brought in had reported out ill that morning with a high fever.

"What else have you noticed besides the fever, Mrs. Thomas?" Simon asked the man's wife, trying to keep the excitement out of his voice.

"He's been feeling weak, Dr. Temple. And his neck seems to be quite swollen. Is it the new strain of flu you just told me about?"

"It might be, Mrs. Thomas. Has he seen a doctor?"

"No. Our medical plan doesn't cover doctor visits. Cliff has been trying to tough it out, hoping it would go away."

"I'd like to examine your husband, Mrs. Thomas. May I come to your house? There would be no charge for the visit."

"You mean make a house call?" Mrs. Thomas's surprised voice asked. "Yes, of course you can see him. Come right away, doctor. I'll give you directions."

The Thomases lived in the city and Simon and Merry were at their house in just a few minutes. Merry could feel the excitement flowing through her companion, like something almost tangible. His posture was erect, his movements quick and sure. He asked her to wait in the car as he rushed into the sick man's house with medical bag in hand.

Merry settled back in the passenger's seat and waited expectantly. However, it was only a short time later when she saw Simon slowly reemerge from the Thomas home with a dejected look on his face. Merry could tell at once that his hopes had once again been dashed. He set his medical bag in the back seat and got into the Porsche next to her.

"Mumps," he said. "Poor guy looks like a chipmunk with enough nuts stored in his cheeks for two winters. Damn."

Merry searched for something to say. "We still have two more names to call."

Simon shook his head. "No. After I examined Mr. Thomas, Mrs. Thomas let me use the phone to call them. They're both feeling fine."

Merry shook her head. "I never thought I'd be sad to find out that someone wasn't sick. Where to now?"

Simon started the engine to the Porsche. "Let's drive over to see the photographer, Sara Jones. Didn't you say her studio was on K Street?"

"Yes, that's right. You know her address also tells us the donor of the Fire Diamond was someone from the Washington, D.C. area, otherwise a local photographer wouldn't have been used."

Simon didn't respond to Merry's last logical assumption, which disappointed her. She had felt somewhat proud of her deduction. When she looked over at his profile, she realized he looked a little sad and decided he probably still had his mind on his dashed hopes of locating the deadly flu.

"I'm sorry, Simon. I almost wish I'd get Carmichael's flu for you so you'd be able to locate the infectious agent and put an end to all this frustrating business."

He circled her arm with his warm hand. "Thank you, Merry. I think that's the nicest thing anyone has ever said to me. But I'd rather never find the answer than have you infected. That goes without saying, doesn't it?"

Merry's sigh turned into a smile. "Even if it does, I'm still glad you said it."

SARA JONES WAS A TALL, big-boned thirty-year-old with stringy red hair, large nose, ruddy complexion and crooked teeth. She had on one pink and one blue sock, yellow tennis shoes and a calf-length, pale-green dress of totally creased cotton. The gray cardigan sweater pulled over her slumping shoulders was missing a button.

Merry's first impression was that she was a bag lady who had wandered in off the street. But despite the obvious fact that Sara Jones took no interest at all in her own appearance, the photographs that lined her studio wall were elegant and exquisite, reflecting the beauty that dwelt in her mind.

"Can I help you?" she asked in a low and pleasant voice.

"Yes," Simon said. "My name is Whatley. I'm an assistant curator from the Museum of Natural History. You were commissioned to photograph the Fire Diamond several months ago by our benefactor of the jewel. I'm here to get some additional prints of your excellent photos."

Merry remained quiet at this outright fabrication, gulping down her unease, trying to remind herself that they intended no harm with their ever-increasing number of lies.

Sara Jones's forehead creased into two deep red lines. "I'm sorry, sir, but the negatives and prints of the Fire Diamond were stolen over three months ago in a burglary. I filed a report with the police, of course, and called the family to explain. They advised me they would arrange for me to see the diamond again if more pictures were needed."

Merry's brow puckered. "That's odd, Ms. Jones. None of the family mentioned your call to us. Would you check your records to see who you spoke to?"

Merry wondered if her ploy to discover the name of the donor would work. She watched Sara nod and bring out a cardboard box from underneath the counter. Merry could see it was filled with a collection of receipts. The photographer began to search through them.

"I hope you don't mind my saying so, Ms. Jones, but you look a little pale," Simon said. "Have you been feeling all right?"

Sara looked up from her search. "I'm never ill. I'm pale because I never get out in the sun."

Simon and Merry exchanged looks as Sara resumed her search. After a minute or two, the photographer seemed to have located the paper she was seeking.

"Yes. Here it is. I always attach any subsequent notes to my original receipt. It was on July 22 when I spoke with Mrs. Diane Richfield concerning the theft of the photographs."

Merry began to see white spots in front of her eyes as the shock of the photographer's words flashed in her brain.

"At her Georgetown home? 555-6767?" Merry asked.

Sara and Simon both looked at Merry, but it was Sara who spoke. "Yes. That's the number," the photographer said.

Simon and Merry thanked her and were back out in the street before Simon asked the inevitable question. "How did you do that, Merry? How did you come up with Georgetown and the right number?"

Merry's mind was still reeling from the shock of her discovery. She looked over at Simon, a little wide-eyed. "Mrs. Diane Richfield is Karen's stepmother."

Simon frowned. "You mean your friend? The law clerk for a Supreme Court justice? Are you telling me her last name is Richfield?"

"Yes. Her stepmother must have been the bereaved widow who donated the Fire Diamond to the Smithsonian. And Karen's father must have been the multimillionaire who died a month ago after he came into possession of the stone! My God, it all fits, yet I'm finding it so incredible!"

Simon was frowning. "So am I. She didn't tell you anything about her family's connection to the Fire Diamond?" he asked.

Merry shook her head. "Not a word. I know she was unusually quiet on the occasions I discussed the Fire Diamond, but until now I didn't realize why. Except that I'm still not sure why. Why didn't she tell me, Simon? What's going on?"

# Chapter Thirteen

Simon shook his head at Merry's questions. "I don't know."

Merry knew her voice was octaves too high, but she didn't seem able to bring it back to normal tonal range. "If it was Karen's family that possessed and donated the jewel, if it was her father who displayed those weak and shaky symptoms, then they all might . . ."

Simon rested a comforting arm around her shoulder. "Yes, I know, Merry. They might have all been infected."

Merry nodded. "We've got to find out, Simon. I've got to talk to Karen and discover why she hasn't told me about her connection with the Fire Diamond."

Simon shrugged. "Then it's back to the Supreme Court?"

Merry shook her head. "She'd be in the Justice's chambers by now. The only way I could get in is to contact her by telephone first and have her come to the entrance to direct the guard to let us through."

"Do you want to call her from here?" Simon asked.

Merry shook her head dejectedly. "I don't have the number. It's on a piece of paper back at Florida House."

Simon shrugged. "Then it's off to Florida House we go. Your chariot awaits, my lady," he said with a small bow toward the Porsche. As she got in, however, Simon noticed he had been unable to make her smile this time.

When they were in the vicinity of Florida House, Simon watched carefully for anyone lurking about. He saw no one.

"You've still got your key?" Simon asked.

Merry pulled it out of her purse. "Right here."

"Okay, let's go," Simon said. "You ahead, me behind, just like before."

Their approach to the apartment was uneventful. They found it in the same disarray in which Merry had left it the night before. She headed immediately for her bedroom where she remembered she had left the slip of paper with the telephone numbers on her nightstand. Simon followed her through, pausing to stop in the doorway to look at the mess of thrown knickknacks and bedding all over the carpet.

"Can I be of some help?" he asked.

Merry nodded. "You could retrieve my American Express card."

Simon leaned against the doorjamb smiling. "Don't tell me you left home without it?"

Merry paused in her search to smile at his comment. "Not home. The restaurant the other night. Karen picked it up for me and put it in one of her dresser drawers in her bedroom. I keep forgetting to get it back. Would you go to her bedroom, it's the next door on the right, and look for it while I try to find the piece of paper with her number on it?"

"I'm on my way," Simon said.

It took another moment or two for Merry to locate the elusive slip of paper, which had been hiding beneath the telephone. She went to join Simon. As soon as she entered Karen's room, she found him searching the last drawer of a bachelor chest. She could see he hadn't had any luck so far.

"Why don't you check that nightstand over there and I'll check this one?" Merry said as she moved toward the bed.

Simon nodded and began wading his way through ripped bedding and strewn clothes toward the nightstand closest to him. As Merry started for her nightstand, however, she inadvertently stepped on a picture frame, both feeling and hearing the crunch of glass beneath her shoe.

"Oh, damn," she said as she leaned down to pick up the ruined picture. A very thin Senator Daniel Richfield stared back at her through the cracked glass of the frame. She hardly recognized him from the robust man she remembered meeting at her brother's wedding years before. The last few years had certainly aged him quickly. She was just about to set the pic-

ture on the bed out of harm's way when she saw the faces behind the senator and gasped in shock.

"I've found your American Express card," Simon said as he
turned and held up the missing card in his hand, obviously not
having heard her exclamation over the sound of the closing
drawers. One look at Merry's face, however, and he dropped
his hand.

"Merry? What is it? What's wrong?" Simon said, hurrying
to her side.

Merry was having trouble getting the words out. "Look at
this picture. It's Karen's late father—and Mr. T."

"So?" Simon said as he looked over her shoulder.

"Well, don't you see? There, in the background. It's those
two men who have been following me! My God, Simon. Karen
knows my abductors!"

Simon took the picture from Merry's hands and studied the
images for several moments. "If Karen has had some role in
this business, it would explain how the two men were able to
find out where you were staying. She could have told them you
were at the hotel and then at Florida House. From her they
could have learned you would be at the Folger Theatre and the
Supreme Court the next day."

Merry dropped onto the nearby bed, aware Simon's words
made sense but not wanting to accept them. "No, Simon. Not
Karen."

Simon sat down beside her, his voice gentle but firm. "Karen
was the one who knew where you were on all of those occasions, Merry. It makes sense."

Merry shook her head. "No, it doesn't. If Karen was the one
who told them, why did those men search the other occupied
apartment here? She would have been specific about which
apartment to search."

Simon shrugged. "They might have misunderstood her. Or
they might have ransacked the other apartment in an effort to
throw the police off. Other explanations might fit. But I'm
finding it difficult to identify another explanation for those two
men being so well acquainted with Karen's father that they
posed in a picture with him, a picture Karen keeps on her
nightstand."

Merry sighed in defeat. "Yes, I can't help thinking the same thing. And Mr. T. was in that picture, too. Remember when we left the Folger Theatre and he had gone? Perhaps he had driven off on purpose. It might have been that he, too, is in league with my abductors."

Simon looked over at Merry when he recognized the defeat in her tone. Her expression was one of deep sadness. He hated to see her hurt and disillusioned about her friend. More than anything he wanted to gather her in his arms and offer her comfort and protection from the pain. But he knew he mustn't. He had to try to keep his voice even and unemotional.

"Can you think of any reason why Karen would be behind this attack on you?" Simon asked.

Merry shook her head. "It can't have anything to do with me, personally. It has to be because I just happened to be in the wrong place at the wrong time."

"In front of the Fire Diamond Saturday morning?" Simon said.

Merry nodded. "Karen did talk to me about her recent estrangement from her stepmother. She said something about her stepmother giving away her father's possessions right after his death. Karen was angry that her stepmother hadn't consulted her beforehand. Do you suppose Karen was referring to the Fire Diamond? Do you suppose she wanted the jewel?"

"Could be," Simon said. "Maybe her father had even promised it to her one day. Certainly as a member of the family, she would have known Sara Jones had been commissioned to photograph the diamond. Since your pursuers apparently had some connection with the family, she might have gone to them and elicited their aid in stealing the photographs and securing a diamond cutter to duplicate the original."

Merry sighed. "Oh, God. I guess it is possible."

Simon flicked his finger at the picture he still held. "These two men strike me as the type to take orders, not to originate them. I've been thinking another brain was at work here. And a Supreme Court law clerk certainly has enough smarts to be orchestrating a diamond theft."

"But how has Karen planned to do it?" Merry asked.

"I don't think we're going to know that until we have a chance to examine the security system in the Gem Room."

Merry got slowly to her feet. "Let's go."

Simon winced at the sadness in her voice. Without conscious thought he rose from the bed and put his arm about her shoulders, hugging her to him. She rested against him with a sigh and he found himself immediately fighting mounting desires to hold her closer and to kiss away her disappointment. He gently but quickly moved her to an arm's length leading the way from Florida House.

They drove directly to the streets surrounding the massive Smithsonian complex, finding a parking space just a couple of blocks away. They headed straight to the Museum of Natural History, making their way immediately upstairs and into the Gem Room. As they stood in front of the Fire Diamond, Merry once again felt its magic to mesmerize.

"It is certainly beautiful," Simon said from beside her. "The cut diamond is so much more spectacular than the original rough stone Carmichael showed me. But we'd best get to the reason why we've come here, checking out the security system. There are instruments that could cut through this thick glass in a matter of seconds. However, I can't imagine there isn't an alarm system that would alert the guard if the glass was compromised."

Merry nodded. "Yes, there must be one. Besides, I think it would be a bit obvious walking in here with such a glass cutter under your arm don't you?"

Simon nodded.

Merry was looking up. "What about that ceiling-mounted camera?"

Simon followed her pointing finger. "Yes. Another precaution. Well, the area looks well protected to me. I think it would be very difficult for someone to seriously contemplate stealing the Fire Diamond from here and getting away with it."

Merry nodded. "We should have guessed as much. After all, the Hope Diamond is right over there and has been for years. It would be pretty silly for the Smithsonian to have put it on display all this time without adequate security precautions."

As Merry looked over at the Hope Diamond display, however, her attention was diverted by the two men who were conversing beside it. She felt the shock of recognition like a douse of ice water down her back.

"Simon!" she said, as she grabbed his arm. One of her abductors, the dark-haired man, was standing no more than fifteen feet away talking with James Tritten, the security guard.

Simon raised his hand to cover hers.

"It's all right. I see him. Let's step in back of this couple over here. We'll be less conspicuous."

Merry nodded and exhaled the breath she had sucked in so quickly. Much to her relief, the man seemed too intent in his conversation with James Tritten to notice anyone else in the room.

"Simon, that's the security guard who came on the scene Saturday after you saved me from those two men. He's also the one who later told me about the millionaire's wife donating the diamond because she thought it killed her husband."

"He is? Then what is he doing talking with that thug?" Simon said.

"I was just asking myself that same question," Merry said.

Simon looked around at the gathering visitors. "This place is beginning to fill with people. I think we've accomplished everything we can. There's a way out through the fine-china section over there. Let's try to exit unobtrusively that way."

Merry nodded, following Simon's lead. But in order to leave the Gem Room, they had to walk very close to the man and James Tritten. Merry felt the nervous perspiration collecting on her skin as she approached within just a few feet of her attacker. She caught just a snatch of conversation, but it was enough to tighten her stomach muscles into a sickening knot.

"She came back the next day," James Tritten was saying. "I might be encouraged to tell you about it."

Merry watched her abductor slip James Tritten some money. "How's that for encouragement?" he said.

Merry and Simon moved past, through the China Room, down the stairs, across the Rotunda and out the door. As they descended the steps to the Mall, Merry spoke for the first time, noticing her voice was somewhat breathless.

"They were talking about me," she said.

Simon nodded. "I heard. But was it as accomplices or was your pursuer just trying to get more information about your whereabouts?"

Merry shook her head in discouragement. "How will we know? I used to think law could be frustrating. But this investigative business we're in seems so imprecise, so unending in its possibilities." She looked over at Simon. "I guess I'm beginning to realize I'm ill equipped for it. I can't even tell who's friend or foe."

Simon's tone was steady. "Still, no matter how ill-equipped we might be, the only other option is to give up, and when you think about that one, you'll find it's really no option at all."

Merry looked at his face, seeing for the first time the tiny lines of pain about his mouth.

"Simon, it's at times like this, when I remember all the frustrations you have had to endure over the last two years, that I can't help but admire your spirit and tenacity. What's kept you going?" she asked as they headed for the car.

"Hope, Merry. The simple hope of eventual success. Even the saving of one life would make it all worthwhile."

His words reached past her discouragement. She knew then that even when all else was gone, as long as hope remained, there was still a chance. She turned toward him, a new energy in her voice.

"You've helped me to think clearly again. I'm going to call Karen so we can go see her. I'm going to tell her everything I've found out and ask her what it means."

"You think it wise to show your hand?" Simon asked.

"Why not? What have I got to lose? If Karen really is in on this thing, her knowing I know can't put me in any more danger than I'm already in. Besides, it might shake her up and push her into making a mistake. Isn't that what the detectives do on TV?"

Simon smiled. "Yes, but they know what the script calls for next. Still, you're right in that I can't see we lose anything by it. There's a telephone booth over there."

Merry's telephone conversation with Karen was cryptic. Karen agreed to let her in to the justice's chambers for the talk she insisted they had to have, but she balked at Simon coming along. Merry finally agreed she would come by herself.

"I don't like it," Simon said as he drove her to the front of the Supreme Court. "You'll be alone with her. What if—"

"I'll be okay," Merry said, hoping she was correct. She was feeling more and more unhappy about her loss of faith in her friend. By the time Simon had dropped her off and Karen had led her back to the justice's chambers, Merry had taken several deep breaths to gain strength to say the words she must.

"Karen, I know your father owned the Fire Diamond and your stepmother donated it. Please tell me what's going on."

Merry watched Karen's face fall as she heard her long sigh. The thin woman sank into a thickly padded chair. "Damn, I'm sorry, Merry. I guess I should have told you the first time you brought it up, but I just couldn't. I kept hoping you wouldn't find out and the whole thing would just pass away and be forgotten."

Merry couldn't believe her ears. "Pass away? Be forgotten? For God's sake, Karen, those two thugs of yours have tried to kill me!"

Karen's eyes grew into two large dark holes as she leaned forward in her chair. Her voice was a hoarse croak. "*My* thugs? What are you saying? I know nothing about those men after you!"

"Then why did you have a picture of them on your nightstand?" Merry asked.

"On my nightstand? Are you crazy? I never had a picture of any thugs. What's going on?"

"Karen, I went back to Florida House today to get my American Express card from your dresser and I saw a framed picture of your father, Mr. T. and two men. Those two men are the same ones who tried to grab me in the Smithsonian and who have been stalking me since. Now, who are they?"

"Oh, my God! You can't be serious?" Karen asked.

"Deadly serious. I wasn't seeing things. I repeat, the two men who have been following me and the men in your father's picture are the same. Please, Karen. Please be honest."

Karen shot to her feet, her voice splintering under the ax of Merry's accusation. "I have been honest! That picture was the only possession other than my clothes that I took from our Georgetown home. When my father was gone, I wanted to have it as a remembrance. Don't you remember how he hated candid shots, succumbing only to posed pictures in front of a camera? I couldn't stand those stilted, unnatural photographs. I snapped that picture the day before his death. I liked it because it caught that elusive smile of his I loved so much.''

Karen sounded sad and sincere. Merry didn't think she was that good of an actress to be faking her emotions. She began to start hoping there was an explanation. ''Who were the two men in the picture?'' she asked.

''The men with Mr. T. were private security personnel who had been hired a few months before to guard the Fire Diamond. I didn't even know them! I still don't!''

''They were hired to guard the Fire Diamond? Who hired them?'' Merry asked.

Karen waved her hands helplessly. ''I'm not sure. I assume my father.''

''Did Mr. T. know them? Recommend them maybe?'' Merry asked.

''No, I don't think so. He treated them as strangers. They were just two hired men. Merry, you've got to believe me!''

Merry exhaled her distrust, finding she was very glad to release it. ''I do believe you, Karen. But why didn't you tell me about the Fire Diamond if there was nothing to hide?''

Karen's sparkling animation in her own defense suddenly fizzled. She sank back into her chair.

''Karen? Did you hear me?'' Merry asked.

''Yes, Merry. I heard you. I did have something to hide.''

Merry shook her head. ''But I don't understand. If you knew nothing about those men, what could you have possibly wanted to hide?''

Karen sighed heavily. ''Just about a week before my father acquired the Fire Diamond, I overheard him in the library talking with Joseph Freedman.''

''Joseph Freedman of Freedman's Diamonds? The man whose firm I represented in the case before the Supreme Court?''

''Yes, Merry. I know I gave the impression I never met him before he came to Washington to deliver your briefs on the case. And in truth, we really had never met until you both came to D.C. for the court case. But the first time I saw Joseph Freedman was in my father's study when they discussed the transfer of the Fire Diamond several months ago.''

"Karen, am I understanding this right? Was it Joseph Freedman who sold the Fire Diamond to your father?" Merry asked.

"Yes."

Merry shook her head in disbelief. "But he never said a word! Every time I brought up the jewel, he never once let on that he had had it in his possession once, much less that he had been instrumental in selling it. Why not?"

Karen's dark head nodded. "Yes, Merry, I know, but I wasn't surprised. You see the transaction transferring the Fire Diamond to my father was an illegal one. Joseph Freedman sold something he didn't legally own. Ever since I overheard my father and Joseph Freedman's conversation in the library that afternoon, I've been afraid of exposure."

"What exactly was it you overheard?" Merry asked.

"Well, I was just passing by, you understand. I never went into the room where they were discussing their business, so I only caught bits and pieces of the conversation. But one thing I heard clearly. Joseph Freedman told Father that he must never tell anyone who he bought the diamond from. He kept repeating the same warning. 'The bill of sale will have a fictitious name on it. If I'm ever asked, I'll deny having sold it to you.' Those were Freedman's exact words."

"And you thought that was because Freedman was not the legal owner and therefore had no right to sell the Fire Diamond?" Merry asked.

Karen lifted her thin shoulders. "What else would have caused Freedman to extract that promise from father and to deny his part in the transaction? And since father obviously obtained the diamond by giving such a promise, he knowingly became the receiver of stolen property. Considering the value of that property, had he lived and the particulars of the transaction become known, he could have been prosecuted as a felon and given a prison term."

Merry now understood the pain in Karen's voice and the reason for her previous reluctance to disclose what she knew about the Fire Diamond. Merry suddenly felt ashamed for her suspicions of her friend. She moved over to Karen's chair and leaned down to put her arms around the distraught woman.

"Karen, I'm so sorry. I've suspected you of some pretty rotten things and all you were attempting to do was protect your father. Can you forgive me?" Merry asked.

Karen's voice was sad and heavy. "If you suspected me, it was my own fault for not telling you the truth from the start. I wanted to explain about Freedman, too, so you would know the kind of man you were representing. But I knew if I told you about him, I would have had to tell you about my father. I've been dreading people finding out what he did. He was such an honest man up to then. I'm so ashamed for him."

Merry felt her friend's pain and immediately resolved to extinguish it.

"Karen, you're too hard on both yourself and your father. You've been living with so much agony over your suspicions that you've blinded yourself to the real evidence. All you know of your father's possible duplicity in the receipt of stolen goods is fragments of an overheard conversation."

"What do you mean?" Karen asked.

"Well, think about it. How can you be sure of your facts or the conclusions you drew from them? Did Joseph Freedman say at any time that he was not the lawful owner of the Fire Diamond?"

"Well, no but—"

"Did your father at any time say he was purchasing stolen property?"

"Not exactly."

"Think it through. What you overheard was the seller of the Fire Diamond asking the buyer not to disclose the fact of their agreement. Admittedly, the fictitious name of the bill of sale and the secrecy of the negotiation are irregular, but Freedman may have insisted on those things for perfectly legitimate reasons. Nothing was specifically said about the Fire Diamond's transaction being illegal."

Her friend's expression was still doubtful. "Merry, I know what you're saying sounds right, but . . ."

Merry gave Karen's shoulder a little shake. "I know, Karen. You've been dwelling on one explanation so long it seems to be the only possible one. But it isn't. It may not even be the most likely."

Karen obviously wasn't convinced, but her voice was lighter. "I really hope you're right. I'd like to think my father wouldn't be part of something illegal."

Merry smiled at her. "Remember, we're all innocent until proven guilty beyond a reasonable doubt. He deserves that reasonable doubt, doesn't he?"

For the first time in their conversation, Karen hugged Merry back. "Thank you, Merry, for calling me friend and for being one to me. You'll never know how much this means."

Merry gave her friend one last hug before she straightened up again.

Karen was smiling. "I feel so much better and yet, I still can't help wondering. How can we find out what was going on between my father and Joseph Freedman?"

"By asking Joseph Freedman, of course," Merry said. "Could he have arranged for those two security guards at the time of the sale of the Fire Diamond?"

"Well, yes," Karen said, "I suppose so. But it seems more logical that my father would just have called our regular security company and asked for some guards for the diamond."

"Your regular security company?" Merry asked.

"Yes, the one that supplies a twenty-four-hour guard at the entry to the grounds surrounding our house in Georgetown. We've been using the same firm for years, although at the moment I can't remember their name. Other than the gate guard, we have some wired alarms around the doors and windows for protection, but special guards would have been arranged for separately."

"So you think your father would have gone through them?"

"Yes. Most likely. Unless Joseph Freedman had suggested some men he knew. Such a suggestion would have carried a lot of weight with father."

"And if Joseph Freedman suggested the two who have been following me as security guards for the Fire Diamond, then he might be spearheading their attempts to grab me. It could also explain how those men have found me so easily. Freedman knew I was at that hotel, Florida House, the Folger Theatre and the court this morning."

"But why would Joseph Freedman do that? What could he possibly want from you?" Karen asked.

Merry sighed deeply. "I don't know. But I've got to find out if he's behind this madness."

"But how?" Karen asked.

"Can you check with your stepmother and find the payment receipts for the security guards' salaries? If the checks were made out to your regular security company, we'll know your father selected the men," Merry said.

"And if they were made out to someone else, then maybe Freedman set this whole thing up with my father. Maybe he never meant for my father to keep the Fire Diamond. Maybe he meant to steal it back through those two men. Do you really think that's possible, Merry?"

"Yes, it's possible. I'm going to call Freedman now at his New York office and pose some probing questions to him. I'll put the call on my credit card. Can I use your telephone?"

Karen nodded as Merry picked up the instrument. "When do you think you'll know about the receipts for the guards?" she asked as she dialed Freedman's New York number.

"I'm not sure," Karen said. "I've got to stay here at court at least a couple of more hours. Diane is out shopping, so calling and asking her to look would be of no use. Can you call me tonight? Say after six?"

Merry nodded as she heard Joseph Freedman's secretary crisply answer the phone.

"This is Meredith Anders. I need to speak with Mr. Freedman. It's urgent."

"I'm sorry, Ms. Anders," his secretary said. "Mr. Freedman is in Washington on business."

"No, he's not," Merry said. "He left Washington last night for business in New York. Would you please check to see if he left a number where I might reach him?"

"I have checked, Ms. Anders. As a matter of fact, I spoke with Mr. Freedman long-distance this morning. He advised me he was still in Washington and wouldn't be returning until late in the week. You must have misunderstood his intent. Would you care to leave a message?"

Merry tried to absorb the news. "No," she said to the secretary as she hung up, more confused than ever.

"Merry, is everything okay?" Karen asked.

Merry looked over at her. "No. I'm beginning to really wonder about Joseph Freedman. His secretary just told me he's not in New York. According to her, he's still in Washington."

"So he lied to you about going to New York," Karen said. "Could it be he wanted an excuse to be gone when those two men came after you at the Folger Theatre and the Supreme Court? Was he establishing an alibi for the time in which you were to be attacked?"

An uncomfortable line etched itself between Merry's eyebrows. "He did seem uneasy about something when he told us last night that he had pressing business that would keep him away from court this morning, didn't he?" she asked.

Karen nodded. "Yes, I think so. Merry, if he's behind all this, whatever are you going to do?"

## Chapter Fourteen

Simon rubbed the back of his neck thoughtfully when Merry had finished relating her conversations with Karen and Joseph Freedman's secretary. He leaned against the side of the Porsche where it was parked across from the Supreme Court.

"You've told me that Freedman Diamonds is a New York-based company," he said. "But you've never mentioned how Joseph Freedman picked your particular legal firm to represent him on this case?"

Merry shrugged. "Well, it was a case that had to be argued in the Washington State courts, so it was natural for Freedman to engage a local law firm in the state. I'm not sure why he selected us since I wasn't in on the initial interview. Laura gave me the case after her first couple of meetings with Freedman."

"So he approached your law partner first? Did he know her before?" Simon asked.

Merry rubbed her forehead, almost as though she was trying to rub away the frown that had appeared there. "No, not personally I don't think. But now that you ask that question, I do seem to remember Laura saying something about Freedman having known her late husband. It's not a clear memory, so I could be wrong. Do you think it important?"

Simon shrugged his broad shoulders. "I don't know. I'm just trying to get a grip on this thing. Perhaps it would be a good idea to call your partner and ask her about Freedman. You can explain your concerns regarding his connection with the Fire Diamond. There's a public telephone booth right over there."

Merry nodded her agreement, walked over to the phone booth and placed a credit-card call to her law partner. Laura answered her personal line on the third ring.

"I'm glad you called, Merry. I've got the names of those two lawyers I promised you. Got a pen ready?"

Merry had forgotten about the lawyers. Since being in Simon's company, she felt amazingly safe and secure. But she didn't want to let Laura know getting a lawyer didn't seem nearly as important anymore, particularly after all the effort she realized her partner had probably made to secure the names for her. So instead she reached into her shoulder bag for a pen and something to write on.

"All set," she said.

She wrote down the names on the back of an envelope as Laura dictated them to her and then put the envelope back in her shoulder bag.

"Have things gotten any better since we talked last night?" Laura asked.

Merry remained purposely vague. "Somewhat. Laura, what do you know about Joseph Freedman?"

There was an uneasy pause on the other end of the line before Laura answered. When she finally did reply, Merry could hear a new, almost unsteady tone in her partner's voice.

"That's a strange question for you to be asking. I'm not sure what you mean by it?"

Merry tried to keep her voice even. She didn't want to unduly upset her partner and friend. "Well, for starters, why did Freedman pick our firm to represent him?" Merry asked.

"For heaven's sake, Merry, Freedman came to us over two years ago and you're just asking that question now?"

Merry got the sudden, uneasy feeling that Laura was avoiding answering her question.

"I know the question sounds strange and is definitely overdue, but I'm asking it. Why did Freedman pick us? Did he know your late husband, Ed?"

Laura's voice was tight. "Yes, Merry. Joseph, ah, Freedman and Ed were business acquaintances."

"Business?"

"Ed purchased a diamond broach for me from Freedman Diamonds for our tenth anniversary, the year before he died.

When Washington State began to unfairly tax Joseph Freedman's business ventures within the state, it was only natural for him to seek out our firm for representation.''

"I see," Merry said, hearing not just the words but the uneasy and almost defensive tremor in her partner's voice. Laura was hiding something from her, she was sure. Merry tried to keep her voice calm.

"Had you ever met Freedman before he contacted you about this legal business?" Merry asked.

A small hesitation. "Yes. He was at a party in D.C. when Ed introduced us and told me Joseph had designed the anniversary broach," Laura said. "We talked part of that evening about his business."

"Did he ever mention the Fire Diamond?" Merry asked.

"The Fire Diamond? Of course not. The first time I heard about that gem was when you called me and told me a man had fallen on you in front of it. Now, Merry, I've been patient. I've answered your questions. Now you answer mine. What is this all about?"

Laura's voice had gone from defensive to something that sounded like fear. Merry was getting more alarmed by the moment as she tried to keep her voice calm.

"Just one more question, Laura. Where is Joseph Freedman?"

The other end of the line had gone deadly quiet.

"Laura?"

Laura's voice came back upset. "How should I know? Merry, what is this all about? Why are you questioning me this way?"

Merry swallowed uncomfortably at the sad, accusing tone in her partner's voice. She couldn't hide her thoughts and intent from her friend another second. She sighed.

"Laura, I'm sorry. But things here have been getting stranger and stranger. I found out Joseph Freedman was involved in the sale of the Fire Diamond and I—"

"Merry, I'm sorry, but I've been keeping a client waiting for lunch," Laura cut in. "I hope this can wait because I really must go. Good luck with those lawyers. I'll talk with you later."

And with that she hung up, leaving Merry with a loud, very disturbing dial tone in her ear.

Merry knew something was wrong with her law partner. Very wrong. Did she really have a luncheon appointment, or was she really just putting Merry off?

Merry immediately dialed the law firm's number. Disguising her voice, Merry asked for Laura Osbourne, identifying herself as Mr. Freedman's secretary.

"She and Mr. Freedman have just left for a late lunch," the secretary said. "May I take a message?"

Merry fumbled to replace the receiver without responding to the secretary's question. She felt the blood draining from her face.

Simon was leaning against the telephone booth watching her expression. "Merry, what is it? What's wrong? You look like you've just lost your best friend?"

Merry turned her white face slowly toward her companion. "I think I just have," she said.

They walked around the block as Merry told Simon about her call to Laura, and they discussed again what Karen had told them about the two men and Joseph Freedman.

Simon was shaking his head. "You've heard all these conflicting stories. What do you believe?"

"I just don't know what to believe anymore," Merry said. "First, Karen seemed to be lying to me and it looked as though she was in back of all this madness. And then Freedman lied to me and he became the most likely suspect. Now Laura has lied to me and I think it might be both Laura and Freedman working together. I don't know who to trust, who to believe anymore."

Hurt by her pain, Simon reached out his hand to touch her, and then remembering all he was up against, drew it back. He tried to use his voice to reach her and soothe away her hurt. "At least you know Karen is still your friend. And we should be considering her welfare. Since it was her father who last possessed the Fire Diamond, she may have been exposed to Carmichael's flu. Did you find out how she's feeling?"

Merry raised contrite eyes to Simon's face. "No. I was so caught up in finding out about how she knew those men that I'm afraid I completely forgot about the flu. Some friend I am."

"Come on, Merry. Don't beat yourself. You have had a few other things to be concerned about. Why don't you give her a call now and relieve your mind?"

Merry nodded and headed back to the telephone booth. A moment later she was talking again with Karen. She didn't mince words as to why she had called.

"Since your father actually owned the Fire Diamond, you know you may have been exposed to the deadly flu I told you Simon is tracking. How are you feeling?"

Karen's tone was easy. "It's okay, Merry. I'm fine. Frankly, I wasn't even around the house much those last few months. Justice Stone kept me pretty busy."

"How about your stepmother?" Merry asked.

"Diane is feeling okay. She wasn't around my father much, either, during that last month. She was out of the house most of the time doing charity work. She used to complain that ever since my father had gotten his new toy, all he ever did was take it out of its black metal box and play with it, anyway. I know she didn't regret sending them both to the Smithsonian."

"Your father played with the Fire Diamond?" Merry asked.

"All the time. He was quite proud to possess it. Told me he liked touching the stone. Said it felt warm and alive."

"How was he feeling, Karen?"

"Fine. Oh, I think he had a little indigestion, but nothing serious. Only reason I even remember that was because Dr. Lewis's office called to confirm an appointment he had made. I asked him then what it was about and he explained that it was only a little indigestion. His very words."

Merry's interest was instantly peeked. "Your father went to see a doctor?"

"Just for the indigestion, Merry. It was nothing."

"Karen, think about it. Why would your father make an appointment with a doctor just for a little indigestion?"

The quiet on the other end of the line indicated Karen was thinking. Her next words underlined the new conclusion she had drawn.

"Merry, you may be right. Normally Father had to be dragged to a doctor. He wouldn't go willingly for just an upset stomach. What's wrong with me? Why didn't I see it?"

"We all want to take the assurances our loved ones give us," Merry said. "The last thing in the world we want to believe is that they're sick. And I think it's the last thing in the world your father would have wanted you to worry about."

"Oh, God, something was really wrong with him, wasn't it? He had caught that flu, hadn't he, Merry?"

Merry was licking dry lips. "Let's not jump to conclusions, Karen. Let's take it a step at a time. Can you get this Dr. Lewis to see me and Simon? This afternoon?"

"Give me a minute. I'll put you on hold while I try to contact him on another line."

Several minutes passed before Karen came back on the line. She sounded out of breath, as though she had just run a red-tape marathon. "His full name is Dr. Paul Lewis of Bethesda Naval Hospital. He'll see you briefly only if you can get right over there."

Merry barely took time to thank Karen before hanging up and hurrying out the telephone booth to tell Simon of her conversation. Within just a couple of minutes they were on their way to meet with the doctor.

Merry looked over at Simon, feeling his renewed excitement at the expectation of once again getting a lead to Carmichael's flu. "It's nice to have your smile back," she said.

"When I'm with you, it's never far away," he replied.


DR. LEWIS WAS good to his word and kept Simon and Merry waiting less than a minute before having his receptionist call them into his office. About forty-five, Dr. Lewis was a slender, balding man of medium height and had sharp, fine features. He fingered an empty pipe in well-shaped hands as he looked at Simon's credentials from the CDC with a puzzled frown.

"Now you're the last people I expected to see on this case," he said as he motioned them to take seats.

"Why do you say that?" Simon asked.

"Because there didn't appear to be anything here for you, of course. You have come to discuss the late Daniel Richfield, haven't you? I did understand his daughter correctly?"

"Yes," Simon said. "But, I don't understand your surprise. It's very possible that Richfield came in contact with a deadly flu I've been tracking, Dr. Lewis. Since he came to see you just prior to his death, I thought you might have run some tests that would be helpful in determining if he had been so infected."

Dr. Lewis had listened to Simon's explanation with his elbows on his desk and his chin resting on his steepled fingers. He now removed their support and watched Simon's face with curious eyes.

"You know he died as the result of injuries received in a hit-and-run?"

Simon nodded. "Yes. But I also know he was ill prior to his death. I know he came to you to have that illness treated. Can you tell us what you found?"

Dr. Lewis scratched the back of his head with his empty pipe. He seemed disappointed, as though he had expected Simon to tell him something for which he eagerly awaited. He leaned back in his chair.

"Well one thing is for certain, Dr. Temple," he said. "I did not find Daniel Richfield suffering from or infected with a deadly flu. However, you might be interested in what I did find. Here's the result of my tests."

And with that, Dr. Lewis opened a file he had on his desk and handed Simon a computer printout. Simon sat quietly and read it for a few minutes before raising startled eyes to the watching Dr. Lewis.

"Nausea, vomiting, diarrhea, fever, low white-blood-cell count. They are the same symptoms I've been tracking, but these cell ionization results are new. Are you sure of your findings and subsequent diagnosis?"

Dr. Lewis nodded as he reached over to retrieve the printout. "I did extensive tissue sampling just as soon as I began to suspect. You see, I've treated this type of sickness before in my career with the navy. Nothing I can talk about specifically, you understand. But when I saw Richfield, noticed the clumps of his hair falling out, well I suspected right away. The tissue samples I later sent to the lab confirmed my suspicions. I was going to tell him the next day."

"Going to tell him?" Simon repeated.

Dr. Lewis nodded as he sucked on his empty pipe. "He was dead by then, you see. The hit-and-run. Not that it made much difference. The exposure had resulted in a lethal dose. It was just a matter of time before he died of radiation sickness."

"I'VE BEEN BLIND, MERRY," Simon said. "It was right before my eyes these last two years and I hadn't seen it."

They were walking back to where the Porsche was parked in front of the hospital. Merry's mind felt as clouded as the increasingly overcast sky. She didn't feel she had followed what had gone on at all.

"I don't understand what Dr. Lewis meant by radiation sickness? Or why he had someone from the Nuclear Regulatory Commission quietly run a check on Daniel Richfield's whereabouts during the last few months? Was he saying Karen's father had been a victim of fallout from some nuclear testing?"

Simon shook his head as they made their way through the crowds of people milling about. "No. I realize that's what most of us associate radiation sickness with, but a human being can also be made ill by coming into contact with a radioactive substance. That's why Dr. Lewis said the NRC had done a sweep of Richfield's home and car."

"But I'm sure Karen didn't know or she would have told me," Merry said.

"They did it quietly because they didn't want to cause panic. They were satisfied he hadn't picked it up from something at home so they didn't think it important to tell Karen or her stepmother. They couldn't have guessed. You see, the symptoms of radiation sickness are quite general, reflecting our bodies' tissue sensitivity to exposure. The gross symptoms of nausea, vomiting, diarrhea all represent damage to the gastrointestinal tract, a vulnerable site."

"And a lower white-cell count?" Merry asked.

Simon nodded. "Yes. Radiation damages the blood-forming organs, too. White blood cells are the body's defense against infection. When their replication is impaired through radiation overdose, an individual may succumb to any minor infection."

"So all this time you've been chasing a new flu virus, it hasn't been a virus at all?"

Simon nodded. "Exactly. It's been radiation sickness. And that answers so many questions as to why people coming into contact with other people who had the symptoms didn't contract the illness. Radiation sickness isn't something that's transferred from one human being to another. It's transmitted by a radioactive substance of some kind."

"Substance?" Merry said.

"Metal more than likely."

Simon's words rolled around in Merry's head. "Since this radiation sickness has followed the Fire Diamond, could it be the black metal box that housed the stone?"

Simon sounded excited as he halted and grabbed hold of Merry's arm. "The black metal box? It's still around?"

Merry nodded. "I can't be sure it's the black box you told me Carmichael had, but Karen said her father took the Fire Diamond out of its shiny metal box all the time. If it's the same one—"

"Yes, Merry, that could be it! I remember the metal was shiny. I thought it looked unusual. Perhaps that's the substance of transmission. Perhaps the black box is made of a radioactive material. Does the Richfield family still have it?"

"No. Karen mentioned that her stepmother had donated it to the Smithsonian along with the Fire Diamond."

Simon nodded. "That would explain why the NRC found nothing when they did a sweep of the Richfield home." He quickly checked his watch. "Hmm. Too late to go back to see our Ms. Whatley today, but first thing tomorrow we shall definitely charge her office once again. God, I hope this is it. I hope this is one search that is coming to an end."

Merry looked up at the spark in his eyes and slipped her hand into his. "Me, too," she said.

Simon squeezed her hand for a moment before releasing it. "Let's put the radiation business on the back burner. We still have your pursuit by those two men to consider. Why don't we take a drive and try to sort out what we can?"

Merry nodded as they approached his car. They got in and drove away. Merry didn't take note of the direction. Other thoughts were controlling her.

"Well, if what we think is true and those men were after the replica of the Fire Diamond, then they must hope to steal the original. However, we've looked at the Gem Room and I can't help but think that stealing the Fire Diamond from the Smithsonian would be pretty difficult. Maybe the only way it would be possible is if they had an inside man."

Simon nodded. "You saw that guard, Tritten, talking with one of those thugs. From your conversations with him, can you judge the sort of person he is? Would you say he's the type to play a part in a diamond robbery?"

Merry shook her head. "I can't judge the character of a person from a brief acquaintance. It doesn't look as though I've done too well even with people I've known for years."

Simon looked over at the frown on her face and the unhappy curve to her lips, and heard her small sigh.

"You don't deserve the self-reproach. You've done very well considering all you've been through."

"Thanks, Simon. You always know the right thing to say. Perhaps if we could review what's happened, starting with when Skabos fell on me in front of the Fire Diamond, I could see some logic in my involvement in this mess."

Simon pursed his lips in consideration. "But in light of current information, maybe Skabos falling on you in the Gem Room wasn't the beginning. Maybe the beginning was when your partner, Laura, gave you the Freedman Diamonds case?"

Merry frowned. "But how can the case have anything to do with the Fire Diamond murder? It was only by chance that I was in the museum that morning. How could Laura or anyone else have known I would be in that specific place at that specific time? And Skabos certainly didn't select me specifically to fall dead on."

Simon looked at her in mocked critique, reaching out a hand to gently squeeze her arm. "Hmm, I don't know. You look and feel nice and soft. If I was going to fall on someone, I think I might select you."

Merry chuckled, happy for Simon's renewed spirits and willing to indulge them. "Just the same, it was very impolite of him not to ask first. But seriously, the point I was trying to make is that I don't see that a plan to steal the Fire Diamond has anything to do with my presence in D.C."

"Well, maybe it doesn't tie in, but why did your partner give you the case? She admitted to knowing Joseph Freedman and she was the one who had done the initial interviews," Simon said.

Merry shook her head. "I can't explain it other than the Freedman Diamonds case was considered a major one and I have been handling the major cases for the firm since Laura's husband died in an accident. She's had a hard time adjusting."

"You're certain her husband died accidentally? No hint of foul play?" Simon asked.

Merry turned to Simon, a new dismay dressing her face. "Oh, please, don't get me doubting that or I'll be left with no illusions whatsoever. Besides, the plane crash was well investigated. Ed Osbourne was a U.S. congressman, and the Federal Aviation Administration takes a particularly thorough interest in crashes involving political figures," Merry said.

"And the cause of that crash?" Simon asked.

"Very clear-cut. Pilot error."

"Okay, so your partner's husband died in an accident. But why have both Joseph Freedman and your partner told you lies concerning Freedman's whereabouts, and why has Laura kept what appears to be a closer relationship with Freedman secret? Considering Freedman's earlier clandestine involvement with the stone, couldn't they be in on a conspiracy to steal the Fire Diamond?"

Merry shook her head. "I guess they could be, but it doesn't seem reasonable and it's not something I really want to consider. Laura took me into her firm right out of law school. She's been more than a mentor. She's like the older sister I never had. And Joseph Freedman has always seemed like such a courteous man. Why would either of them do such a thing?"

"Money," Simon said.

"But they both have comfortable incomes. Why would they risk it?" Merry asked.

"Comfortable is a relative term," Simon said. "No matter how much money some people have, they never feel 'comfortable.'"

Merry sighed. "I suppose you're right. Neither of them has struck me as being that way, though. And we don't know if Skabos had any dealings with Freedman."

"No, but it wouldn't be a difficult meeting to arrange for someone in Joseph Freedman's position, would it?" Simon said. "He's a diamond merchant. He probably would have known of the dead gem cutter's talents. If he wanted the Fire Diamond copied, Skabos would be just the unscrupulous person to hire."

"So he hires Skabos to copy the gem, but he doesn't like the one produced and he kills him?" Merry asked.

Simon shrugged. "The gem cutter may have gone to the Smithsonian Museum for payoff and instead of money, Skabos got the flawed copy shoved down his throat to keep him eternally quiet about the arrangement."

Merry was shaking her head. "I don't know, Simon. I'm trying to picture the quiet, almost shy Joseph Freedman shoving a fake diamond down Skabos's throat. It's an image that just won't take shape in my mind."

"I know it's hard to imagine most people we know becoming violent," Simon said. "But if Freedman had hired the two men to take care of Skabos, he wouldn't have had to do the actual killing himself."

"But why kill Skabos that way?" she asked. "If Freedman had hired those two men to eliminate the gem cutter, surely they could have found a less dangerous way? Besides, I thought we had already decided that since they were still looking for the replica of the Fire Diamond, they couldn't have been the ones to have killed Skabos."

Simon rubbed his forehead vigorously, almost as though it was a bottle from which he expected a genie to emerge. "Yes, and no matter who killed the man, that would seem to be a foolish method to use. Why would Skabos have been killed that way? Perhaps if we could determine the answer to that question, this whole business would seem clearer."

Merry watched as Simon pulled the Porsche off the George Washington Memorial Parkway into a recreational parking lot in front of the C & O Canal and National Historic Park. He found an empty space and turned off the engine.

"I'm tired of driving. Would you like to sit in the car or walk?" Simon asked.

"Let's stretch our legs a bit. Exercise always seems to improve my thought process. Just give me a moment to slip on some walking shoes I always carry in my briefcase," Merry said.

Her feet in comfortable shoes, Merry joined Simon in walking on the grass adjacent to the thickly vegetated bank of the canal.

She crinkled her nose. "What's that smell?"

"It's the canal," Simon said. "Not exactly pleasant, is it? If I had remembered that you had been blessed with such a good sense of smell, I wouldn't have come this way."

"At the moment considering the odor, I think *cursed* would be a more appropriate adjective than *blessed*. What's in the canal to make it smell so?" Merry said.

He chuckled. "Better not to know, I think. I was only here once before and the same distinctive, ah, fragrance filled the air then, too."

"You're not from D.C. are you?" Merry asked.

"No. My family's originally from New Jersey. As I mentioned before, my parents are in England now, my brother settled here and I'm currently living in Georgia."

"You say that as though you haven't put down roots."

"They're not deep enough that I couldn't be transplanted," he said with a smile. Merry was just beginning to read a personal message in his words when his smile faded and his voice resumed a more formal tone.

"We'd better get back to the discussion of this Fire Diamond business. I think we left off with the question of why Skabos was killed with a replica of the stone."

Merry was once again disappointed that Simon kept an emotional distance between them, but found the idea of discussing it with him awkward. How did you ask someone why he doesn't want to get closer to you? She sighed and refocused her attention on Skabos and the Fire Diamond.

"Well, either someone planned his murder or it occurred on the spur of the moment," she said. "Since he was killed the way he was, I guess we have to assume it occurred without premeditation. So someone met Skabos in the Gem Room for some unknown reason, fought with him and ended up killing him."

"I wonder why they picked the Gem Room as the place to meet?" Simon asked.

"Yes, good question. If the individuals were partners in crime, one would think they would go someplace less public to conduct their business. It's almost as though Skabos and whoever killed him were looking for neutral ground," Merry said.

"Just what I was thinking," Simon said.

"Could that mean their partnership was a tenuous one, with mistrust on both sides," Merry said. "Perhaps this person who met Skabos was his old partner, John Kahr? A meeting between those two would certainly be calculated with caution."

Simon nodded. "Yes, that's possible. Certainly neither of your pursuers fit the physical description. This John Kahr was a smooth character from what your partner, Laura, said. But that does raise a question in my mind. Would you consider Joseph Freedman good-looking? The type of man women would go for?"

"I suppose he's attractive," Merry said, at first not connecting his question. When she did, it obviously caught her by surprise. "You mean Joseph Freedman could be John Kahr?"

Simon nodded. "I think it's possible. How long has he been president of Freedman Diamonds?"

"I'm not sure," Merry said. "Let me think. The company incorporated about eight years ago. And it was just about nine years or so ago when this man Kahr was released from prison and disappeared. If he did have organized crime connections, those connections might have helped to establish his phony identity and given him the money to start his company."

Simon nodded. "And a diamond company would have been sort of a natural, wouldn't it?"

Merry nodded reluctantly. "But if Freedman and Kahr are the same man, where does my partner come into the picture? How could she possibly be in league with such a criminal?"

"I don't know, Merry. But she's obviously lied to you about Freedman. You know her better than I. What do you think?" Simon asked.

Merry shook her head. "I don't know what to think. Nothing is making sense. Everybody seems so full of secrets. No one seems to be the genuine article anymore."

"The genuine article," Simon repeated.

Merry looked up at Simon's words, noticing the sudden glassy imprint in his eyes, as though thought had turned him completely inside.

"Simon, what is it?"

Simon's eyes refocused on her face. "Do you remember what your partner said over the telephone about Skabos? How he was such a perfectionist that he would discard a copy containing even a single microscopic flaw?"

"Yes, of course," she said. "Go on."

"Well, what if Skabos made two copies of the Fire Diamond, one with a flaw and one with no flaws? What if both copies were given to the person who commissioned them?"

Simon's words were confusing Merry. "You mean the person who asked for the copies wanted a flawed copy?"

"No, but what if the deal meant Skabos had to turn over all replicas, flawed or not?" he said.

"So what you're suggesting is that Skabos may have made a flawed copy on the first try. Okay, I agree from what we know, Skabos would have worked until he had a flawless copy. But even if he did and the second unflawed one exists, what does having more than one copy of the Fire Diamond mean?"

"Where is the other copy?" Simon asked.

Merry shrugged, as though she had been hoping for more than this mundane question. "Why, it's probably being held pending the expected switch with the real stone, of course."

"Unless the person who killed Skabos took the flawless copy and is hiding it from those two men?" Simon said.

Merry was still confused by Simon's line of questioning. "But why? Why would someone in league with these two men double-cross them before the diamond was stolen? Wouldn't this person need their help in the actual theft?"

"Maybe not. If it was their inside man at the Smithsonian who killed Skabos and stole the second copy, perhaps he doesn't need their help anymore and decided to cut them out of the deal. That inside man would be happy that you were implicated in the murder and theft. He might have even helped implicate you."

"You're talking about the security guard, aren't you?" Merry asked.

"Well, we know he's had contact with one of them."

"Yes," Merry said, "and he would probably know about the plans for the diamond to be removed from its protective case and examined in a month. Perhaps he's waiting to make the switch?"

"Perhaps," Simon said. He seemed to be in deep thought.

"You know, Simon, a switch makes more sense to me than an assault on the diamond display case. Remember, Skabos and John Kahr were switch experts, not the break-in types of burglars. I think Skabos might have been waiting until just the right time to replace the original with the fake."

"Unless the switch has already been made," Simon said.

Merry stopped in her tracks and she reached out to grab Simon's arm at her sudden realization of what he was getting at.

"But of course! Why didn't I think about that before! Ms. Whatley said that the diamond was verified at the home of Karen's father and not transported to the Smithsonian until a day or two later. There would have been plenty of time for a switch!"

Simon nodded. "And the Fire Diamond was left in the hands of the armed guards who had already been hired by Karen's father before his death—the two thugs after you."

Merry took his statement to its obvious conclusion. "They could have easily taken the original diamond and substituted the fake. And if so, there's a fake on display in the Smithsonian and the Fire Diamond has already been stolen!"

"Yes. The more I think about it, the more likely it seems. An earlier theft of the Fire Diamond would explain why the murderer wasn't concerned that the second fake was found as the murder weapon. While the authorities beefed up security for a possible theft, he was already in possession of the real jewel and leisurely making arrangements for its disposition."

Merry frowned. "No, Simon. Something's wrong. If my pursuers stole the original and the flawless fake is on display and the flawed fake was used to silence Skabos, why are they after me? Why the relentless pursuit and the trashing of my rooms? What is it they think I have?"

Simon scratched his right ear thoughtfully. "You're right. What are they missing?"

Merry shook her head. "Maybe the right question is what are we missing?"

A raspy voice suddenly shot into the air between them, causing Merry to whip around to face its owner, instant fear gripping her insides. "No, the right question is, where is it?" the dark-haired man said.

# Chapter Fifteen

"How did you find us?" Merry heard herself say to the two men who stood so confidently behind the strength of their guns.

The dark-haired one snickered. "Picked you up in front of the Supreme Court. That Porsche with a Georgia license plate stands out like a sore thumb. Thought we'd follow you to a less-conspicuous spot. Here will do just fine for what we've got to settle. Now, where's the Fire Diamond?"

Merry had never known such fear or confusion as she did at that moment looking into the cold, stony eyes of the men before her. She heard Simon's voice from beside her as though he were at the far end of some deep tunnel.

"The woman gave it to me. It's me you want. Let her go."

Merry watched the meaning of his words cause a momentary flicker of divided attention on the faces of the two men before her as their bodies physically reoriented toward Simon. The barrels of their guns had also perceptively turned in his direction.

"Get out of here, Merry!" Simon said.

Merry stepped sideways two paces, obedient to Simon's command but feeling dreadfully stiff and confused. The two men with the guns seemed unsure for a moment as to whether they should try to detain her.

"Grab her!" the shorter one said finally. "No one's leaving here until we find out what we need."

The blond one seized Merry's arm in a viselike grip, dragging her to his side. She went like a little rag doll, hardly aware now of the pain shooting up her arm. Her senses seemed to be shutting off one by one, as though the valve on each was being steadily turned to zero. Even if she had wanted to run away, she didn't think she could have gotten her anesthetized body to cooperate. Was this nature's way of lessening the final pain of death for the helpless prey?

Both men turned back to face Simon as soon as Merry was in tow. She looked at him, too. He had tried to save her and now he stood there alone, unarmed, facing two drawn guns, with no room to maneuver. He couldn't give them what they wanted. He was going to die.

A lick of strong protest shot into her numbed mind, serving to clear it. He must not die! That sudden resolve pushed aside the fear that had initially immobilized her spirit. She felt a surge of strength from a healthy dose of fresh adrenaline.

"Where is it? You've got three seconds," the man guarding Simon said as he moved in closer to his cornered prey.

Both of Merry's enemies had their backs to her now. She was an insignificant fly that could be swatted anytime. Their attention was fully on the man before them. If she was going to do anything to stop them, it had to be now. She was ready, her body shaking with its pent-up need for action.

With all her new-found might, she lunged sharply into the taller one. Her move caught him entirely off guard as he lost his balance and plunged sideways, knocking the other man to the ground.

The blond man released Merry's arm as he grabbed for the ground to break his fall, but he kicked out a leg, knocking her off her feet. The next thing she knew she was sliding down the steep bank and landing with an unceremonious plop in the murky water. She went under.

Merry felt herself being pulled down, as though something was reaching from deep in the murky waters to drag her to its dark bottom domain. Frantically, she kicked, her arms flailing the thick water, pushing hard toward the surface. She broke through, relief pouring over her as she opened her eyes and gasped for breath. But her relief was short lived as ahead of her on the shore she saw that the blond man had recovered and was aiming his gun at Simon. She screamed in horror at the same moment Simon kicked the firing gun out of his attacker's hands and made a lunge down the bank in front of her.

"Dive! Swim!" Simon yelled to her as he dove directly over her head into the water.

"You shot me! You fool, you shot *me*!" the dark-haired man screamed at his partner as Merry slipped beneath the water and quickly pushed away from shore.

She kept underwater, swimming as strongly and swiftly as the remaining adrenaline allowed her, until a lack of breath let her continue no longer. She fought her way to the surface for air in rising panic.

Breaking the water, she gasped for breath. Then she started as she felt something grab her arm. She had no breath to scream, but she turned, ready to fight. Fortunately she found it unnecessary as Simon's wet face emerged beside her.

"Merry, you must swim. Quick! Follow me!"

She nodded and moved in the direction of his quickly retreating body. He had a powerful crawl, but somehow she managed to keep up, more out of desperation than out of real expertise as a swimmer.

She didn't waste her energy on trying to watch where they were heading. She left that part up to Simon. Nor did she waste time looking behind them. Knowing her pursuers were out of sight or right on their heels ready to shoot at them was almost of no importance since she couldn't do anything about it. All she could control was her flight through the dirty, stinking water.

And it was more than enough. After only a few minutes she felt very tired. Her clothing was dragging her down with water-saturated weight. Her arms and legs were leaden bars she kept trying to lift. Her shoulders ached violently with the effort. But she went on. As long as Simon swam by her side, she told herself she could do it. And somehow she did.

Even so, it seemed an eternity. When they finally crawled up a bank downstream, Merry collapsed against the scratchy weeds, her raspy, painful breathing loud in her ears. She closed her eyes, as though keeping them open another moment was just too much effort. She lay there feeling as much dead as alive. But as the moments passed, her strength gradually returned. She opened her eyes to look at Simon.

He was lying on his side, his head propped up on a hand, little rivers of water flowing through his dark hair, a small smile on his face as he looked at her with his very blue eyes.

It was a warm, gentle, loving look. It made her forget her recent fright, her desperate swim to safety, the awful putrid smell that still lingered on her sopping wet clothes.

Then the look and the moment were gone and he was on his feet, reaching down a hand to help her up.

"If you're all right, we'd best be leaving."

"Have we lost them?" she asked as she gladly took his hand, warm and strong and feeling so right in hers.

"Only for the moment. We have to keep moving," he said.

She raised herself to her feet, but as soon as she stood, an awareness of what she must look like in dripping hair and clothes flashed into her mind. She released his hand as the thought of what he was seeing distressed her. He quickly read her changing expression.

"What's wrong?" he asked. "You're not hurt?"

Merry shook her head as she surveyed her clothing. "Only my pride. I must look awful."

She immediately felt his warm hand clasp her shoulder. "You look brave and courageous to me. I've never seen two more attractive features. You were great back there. When you knocked those men down, you saved our lives. No amount of canal water can ever dampen that kind of beauty."

She looked up into his eyes, finding all the necessary warmth to renew her spirits. Her thoughts were jumbled, but before she had a chance to clearly focus on any, she was distracted as he urged her up the bank.

"Where are we going?" she asked.

"My brother's house in Georgetown is all that comes to mind. By foot, too. We're quite a distance downstream from the car and on the opposite side of the canal. Besides, even if we could reach the Porsche, I don't think it would be a wise destination."

"They'll probably stake out the car, won't they?" she asked, as they began to make their way to a nearby jogging path.

"Afraid so. I hate to let it just sit there for a while, but I guess we have no choice. I'm really fond of that baby."

"Really? I never would have guessed," she said, smiling, and enjoying his returning sheepish grin.

But he was frowning by the time he asked his next question. "It's getting chilly under this overcast. I'm sorry I'm not wearing some clothing I can offer you."

"What about finding a phone booth and calling a taxi?"

Simon shook his head. "We'll be walking through a residential area. There aren't any phone booths. I'm afraid we'll have to walk the few miles."

"Are we talking just a few or quite a few?" Merry asked.

He looked at her sideways and smiled. "Always the precise lawyer, I see. About four miles in all. We have to keep out of sight so we'd best avoid any major thoroughfares. You can bet our pursuers will be on the lookout."

"But the shorter one was shot," Merry said. "I heard him yelling. Won't they concentrate on taking him to a doctor?"

"Maybe. But then at least one of them will be back in this area looking for us. You can count on it. We've got to put as much distance as possible between ourselves and the canal while we try not to catch pneumonia at the same time."

Merry felt the brisk breeze whipping more strongly through her damp clothes, chilling her wet skin.

"At least it isn't raining," she said.

Simon looked up at the darkening sky. "I hope you didn't tempt fate by declaring that so boldly."

"Nonsense. Believing in fate is illogical," Merry said.

"Ah, 'There are more things in heaven and earth, Horatio, than are dreamt of in your philosophy,'" Simon quoted.

She laughed at his newest quote from *Hamlet*, but the thick, fat raindrops began to pelt them less than a minute later.

The light rain quickly thickened and Simon wrapped his right arm around her and drew her to his side, indulging himself in the immediate warmth and pleasure of the closeness of her body.

"I hope you don't mind, but I was cold," he said, smiling down into her pale, wet face.

Merry didn't say anything but snuggled against him and sighed. It left his heart aching for all the things he knew they could not share. He matched his steps to her shorter ones, and soon they were walking in unison against the driving rain. He allowed himself to luxuriate in her feel for several moments more before attempting to speak.

"'Your silence most offends me, and to be merry best becomes you; for, out of question, you were born in a merry hour.'"

"That's what the Prince says to the talkative Beatrice in *Much Ado About Nothing*, isn't it?" Merry asked.

"Yes. And it's what I'm saying to the talkative Meredith Anders on the streets of Washington, D.C., on this wet and rainy Monday night. Talk to me, Merry. It will help to mitigate the 'slings and arrows' of our latest 'outrageous fortune.'"

Merry's wet face smiled up at him. "From Hamlet's famous soliloquy. Do you know how many clichés Shakespeare originated? They could probably fill a book."

Simon reached out and gently smoothed the soaked strands of stray hair out of her eyes. "Why don't you tell me about them?"

It was all the coaxing Merry needed. Soon she was launched into one of her favorite subjects, the Shakespearean origin of many phrases and expressions so common in everyday conversation. When she had run out of those that came immediately to mind, Simon supplied a few more.

They were both so caught up in the exercise that the miles passed unnoticed. Suddenly, she looked up to see they were walking up the steps of his brother's Georgetown home.

"We're here?" she asked as he withdrew his arm from around her to reach into his pocket to retrieve his keys. She was amazed to find a hint of disappointment in her voice.

"Didn't realize you liked to walk in the rain so much," he said with a smile as he unlocked the door. "We don't have to go in and dry off, you know. We can circle the block a few more times, or even walk back to the canal and jump in for an evening swim, if you'd prefer?"

Merry moved past him into the house, shaking her head. "You're an unbalanced, totally insane man and I should feel sorry for you. But despite your obvious diminished capacity, no motions for special favors will be entertained. I get dibs on a hot shower first."

To punctuate her statement, she ran up the stairs and headed for the bathroom. Simon watched her, smiling, still feeling the warmth of her body where it had curved into his.

"THAT HOT TOMATO SOUP and crackers tasted wonderful. I didn't realize I was so hungry," Merry said as she stretched out on the carpet in front of the living room fireplace, wrapping her robe around her cotton pajamas.

Simon still wore a towel around his neck, a remnant from his recent shower. He used it to rub his hair a few more times, trying to get the excess moisture out.

"I'm not much of a cook, but I've learned how to open a can. And a bottle. How about some brandy to ward off the onset of the pneumonia we've both been tempting?"

"Yes, please," Merry said as she leaned her head against the front of the couch. "Oh, this feels so good. I never realized how much I appreciate being clean and dry and comfortable before."

Simon poured their brandy into small snifters and came to sit next to her on the carpet, the towel now discarded. She looked over at the teasing gleam in his eye.

"Ah, I'll never understand women," he said. "Give them exciting gun fights, smelly canal soaks and rainy walks, and all they want is safety, a bath and dry clothes." Simon looked at the ceiling, his hands raised in mocked prayer. "Oh, God, why didn't you make woman first, before you had learned to be so sensible?"

She laughed at his teasing use of her earlier mock prayer and then noticed the time on the wall clock above the fireplace's mantelpiece. "Oh, I almost forgot. I've got to call Karen to find out how those two men got into her father's employ. Mind if I use the phone?" she asked as she reached for the instrument sitting on the coffee table.

Simon nodded as he picked up their dishes and headed for the kitchen. Merry dialed Karen's number in Georgetown. After verifying who was calling, a servant brought Karen immediately to the line. Her friend's voice sounded relieved.

"Merry, I'm glad you called. What did Dr. Lewis say?"

Merry explained about the diagnosis of radiation sickness. She went on to explain about their suspicions that it could be from the black metal box that housed the Fire Diamond.

"It's so hard to believe," Karen said.

"Well, we'll know more when we can get the box tested tomorrow," Merry said. "I'll keep you informed. Did you find out about how those men became employed to guard the Fire Diamond?"

"I checked the records and found out that they were secured from the same company that supplies our regular gate guard, Night-Light Security. Apparently, my father arranged for them himself, so at least that let's Joseph Freedman off the hook."

"Do you have the number of this company?"

"You won't need it," Karen said. "I already called them, I was so upset. I told the manager the men he sent us were hoodlums. He acted shocked, tried to excuse his company's involvement by insisting the two men were new to their firm but had come highly recommended from a New York security company."

"Did he check out their references?" Merry asked.

"Yes, by phone. Or so he says. Supposedly, the other firm gave them high praise. But he thought it strange that after the men had finished with their job of guarding the Fire Diamond, they quit."

"Strange, indeed. What names were they working under?" Merry asked.

"They called themselves Smith and Wesson," Karen said.

Merry shook her head. "Smith and Wesson? Like in the gun manufacturer? And Night-Light Security didn't find that strange? Yes, I'm a bit upset at them, too. Oh, well, thanks, Karen. I'll call you tomorrow and let you know if anything's new."

As Merry hung up, Simon returned to the room after doing their few dishes. Merry immediately filled him in on Karen's information.

Simon frowned as he sipped his brandy. "So, Karen's father arranged for the security men himself. Still, anyone who knew he was purchasing the diamond could have planted the men at the regular security company he used and paid off somebody at the New York company to recommend them."

Merry nodded. "I don't suppose there's any way for us to find out how many people knew. Since the Fire Diamond transaction was so clandestine, I can only guess that underworld types were the most likely to receive news of its movement and subsequent ownership."

"Probably," he said. "Still, after what those men said to us this evening about our having the diamond, I think we're going to have to reconsider our previous suppositions."

"Yes," Merry said, taking a sip of her brandy. "If they think I have the diamond, it has to be because at least your earlier assumption was correct. The thieves have already switched the real diamond with a fake."

Merry looked over at Simon. "What went wrong, do you suppose?"

Simon shrugged. "I would venture to guess that our two persistent chums have been double-crossed."

"By whom?" Merry asked.

"Whoever is in back of this business. The person who met Skabos in the Gem Room Saturday morning and killed him just before you got there," Simon said.

Merry nodded. "Someone meets Skabos. Steals the real Fire Diamond. Shoves a fake down his throat. Then takes off before those men arrive. Which is why they decided I had to be Skabos's accomplice, since I was the only other person he appeared to have contact with at the Smithsonian that morning."

"Who was on hand to do all that?" Simon's rhetorical question **was** asked aloud.

"James Tritten, the security guard," Merry said.

Simon looked at her. "You say his name very doubtfully. I would have thought he was the most likely suspect."

Merry shook her head. "He's a security guard. What does he know about diamonds?"

"What does he have to know to steal one?" Simon asked.

Merry twisted a recently-shampooed curl around her index finger, studying it as though it was an important piece of evidence. "Still, I've been thinking. My whole court case today rested on the fact that only an expert is qualified to tell a real jewel from a good fake. Skabos could have, of course. But I doubt either of those men have such expertise.''

''So?'' Simon asked.

''So I think the fourth person involved in the Fire Diamond theft is someone who can tell a real jewel from a fake. Otherwise how could any of them have trusted what Skabos was doing? He could have slipped them a fake.''

Simon shrugged. ''Maybe he tried to. Maybe that's why the fourth person killed him.''

Merry nodded. ''The killer must have left almost at the same moment I entered the Gem Room and started to look at the Fire Diamond. Only an instant before, he would have shoved the replica down Skabos's throat. I can't remember seeing anyone, but I was so intent on getting to the diamond, I could have brushed right past the man and never known it.''

Simon took a sip of his drink. ''I wonder if that's really the way it happened?''

''Well despite how it happened, I think maybe we shouldn't wait until tomorrow to contact the Smithsonian,'' Merry said. ''Maybe we should try to reach someone tonight.''

Simon's face looked puzzled. ''Why tonight?''

''To see if they are really displaying only a replica of the Fire Diamond. If the real Fire Diamond has been taken, they'll have to contact the police right away. And if they've got a radioactive black metal box lying about, I suppose there's some agency of the government that needs to be notified. What do you think?''

Simon looked away for several moments as he considered her words and sipped his brandy. ''I think you'll have to contact the Smithsonian without me,'' he said finally.

She swallowed an uncomfortable lump that had begun to congeal in her throat. She could feel the emotional wall being erected between them again. ''It's the police, isn't it, Simon? You can't face them. You're in trouble?''

He got up and moved over to the fireplace, leaning against the mantle, his face averted from hers. ''Yes.''

Merry heard a volumefull of unhappiness in his one word. It crept inside her and seemed to constrict the blood vessels flowing to her heart, making it pump painfully in her chest. She got up and went to stand next to him by the fireplace.

"Please tell me, Simon. I've . . . got to know."

He turned to study her worried face for a moment and then exhaled heavily and nodded as though he had made a decision. She followed his pointing hand and sat down on the blue sectional again, tucking her feet beneath her. For several minutes she watched him stare into space as he appeared to be getting his thoughts together.

"When I first told you about my efforts to discover the reason for Carmichael's disease, I omitted something. It was something . . . important."

Simon paused and Merry could hear the labored beating of her heart as it tried to overcome the heavy dread coursing through her arteries.

After what seemed an eternity, Simon went on. "About a month ago I was at the Centers for Disease Control in Atlanta when I heard a rumor about the Fire Diamond having been bought by a wealthy American. I was excited. The last lead I had was in Europe almost eight months before. I had begun to despair until this word came. I left Atlanta, following the rumor to the Georgetown home of former Senator Daniel Richfield."

"Richfield?" Merry repeated, leaning forward in her surprise and sudden hurt. "You knew Karen's father was the millionaire involved with the Fire Diamond and you never told me?"

Simon shook his head. "No, Merry. I knew it was Richfield, all right, but I didn't know he was Karen's father. You never told me Karen's last name. The first time I realized she was Richfield's daughter was when you mentioned it outside the photographer's studio. It was only then I knew of the connection. It came as big a surprise to me as it did to you."

Merry nodded, relieved Simon had not kept the information from her purposely. She leaned back against the couch again as he went on.

"Anyway, I drove up to the Georgetown residence to meet with Daniel Richfield. Only, when I got to the security gate, I saw a man sprawled out on the sidewalk in front of it and a car crossing into my lane, heading directly for me."

Merry's surprise laced her tone. "You saw the accident?"

"Not exactly. I must have gotten there just after it. My attention was mostly focused on the green-and-gray Subaru swerving into my lane and heading for me. He couldn't have seen me because he had us on a collision course. I twisted the wheel of the Porsche as hard as I could to get out of the way and he ended up smashing into the Porsche's front fender before he gunned the Subaru and drove away."

Merry nodded her head in understanding. "So that's why you said the green-and-gray Subaru was connected to the Fire Diamond. It was the car that killed Karen's father!"

Simon nodded.

"What did you do?" Merry asked.

Simon exhaled. "My first thought was to get to the injured man. I grabbed my bag and ran to him, but after a moment or two of working on him, I could see it was no use. He was dead."

"The impact with the car killed him?" Merry asked.

Simon shrugged. "Yes. He had a deep gash in his chest. But he also had a very pronounced redness to his skin, like he had been suffering from a fever prior to the accident."

"You thought he might have Carmichael's flu?"

"Yes, as soon as I recognized him. You see at first I had no thought that the man was Richfield. But after I started working on him, well, I had seen pictures of Senator Richfield, and although this man seemed thinner, I knew he was the Senator Richfield I had come to talk to, the man who had purchased the Fire Diamond."

"What did you do then?"

"Once I realized he was dead, I knew I couldn't do anything for him. I was just getting back to my feet when the security guard at the gate came out. He took one look at me, my dented car, the fallen man and he began yelling that I had hit and killed his employer."

"You told him about the other driver, of course?" Merry said.

Simon shook his head. "No. All I could think about or do was look at my front fender. It was dented and splattered with blood, you see. When the other car hit mine, the impact had transferred the blood to my fender. Suddenly, I knew how things would look. I was the only one who had seen the green-

and-gray Subaru and all the evidence remaining at the scene looked very much as though it was my car that had hit Richfield. And the man's death was clearly not an accident.''

"You mean the driver of the Subaru—" Merry began.

"Richfield was standing on the sidewalk, Merry. The driver of that Subaru deliberately jumped the curb to hit him."

Merry was beginning to understand what happened next. "You left the scene of the hit-and-run?"

Simon exhaled a heavy breath. "I knew I had to find that Subaru and fast. I jumped into the Porsche and headed in the direction the other car had gone."

Merry gulped, the import of Simon's story making her very uneasy.

Simon nodded at the expression on her face. "I know I was wrong, but my car was not the one that hit Richfield. Technically, I had not even seen the accident. I knew that unless I could prove the Subaru existed, the police would think . . ."

Simon's voice trailed off but the implication that they would think him guilty echoed about the room as if he had said the words.

"Merry, I wanted time to find the green-and-gray Subaru so I'd have something concrete to give to the police. But I lost it. Then I thought that since my brother owned a body-repair shop, I could use his contacts to locate the car when it was brought in for repairs. Only my brother's search through the records and with his contacts for the next couple of weeks yielded nothing. The green-and-gray Subaru was never brought in for repairs."

"But it didn't have a dented fender when we saw it," Merry said.

Simon shrugged. "The owner must have taken it out of state or paid someone to fix it without any paperwork."

Merry was shaking her head. "Simon, if all the police have is the security guard's statement, they'll never know about the other car and driver. They'll go on thinking it was you who struck Daniel Richfield. They might be looking for you. You must tell them the truth."

Simon exhaled. "I did, anonymously. I wrote a letter the day after Richfield's death, explaining the circumstances but not giving my name, of course. I described the vehicle that hit

Richfield to the best of my recollection. I even gave them a partial license-plate identification, a Maryland plate, the first two letters of which were *SC*. I didn't see the driver, but I gave them all the other details.''

''And you left it at that?''

Simon shrugged. ''I thought it was just a matter of time before I located the Subaru and got a complete license number. With that the police could have identified the owner of the car. Unfortunately, the thugs managed to get the car fixed without a regular repair shop making out records. After two weeks of no luck, I realized it had become too late to come forward.''

''Too late?'' Merry repeated, the unbidden image of clay feet coming to mind.

''It is unless I can produce some evidence to clear myself. When I told you about pursuing Carmichael's flu before, I didn't tell you the suspicion I was faced with by the police in Europe. When I showed up after Mabunda was mugged and killed, I was detained for two days in a European jail for suspicion in his death. His theft of my passport and my claiming his theft of Carmichael's diamond cast enough doubt in the mind of the authorities to jail me first and ask questions later. And although they finally had to release me, they made it very clear they still thought me guilty.''

''But this is America, Simon. Due process is—''

''Fallible,'' Simon said. ''I wasn't just a passing motorist on the day I witnessed Richfield's hit-and-run. I was coming to see him for the express purpose of tracking down the owner of the Fire Diamond. In the police's mind, they would know I knew of him, had an interest in him. That alone would have made my story suspect. Without a trace of the Subarau, well . . .''

''But you could have told them about Carmichael's flu, how you were tracking it,'' Merry said. ''As a matter of fact, with that knowledge they would have had to accept your story.''

Simon shook his head. ''Would they? I doubt it. Not even my boss at the CDC believes it.''

''But the missing Fire Diamond. If the one on display in the Smithsonian has really been switched . . .''

''Then I don't want to be around when they find out,'' Simon said. ''I'm the one who's wanted for questioning in the death of its last owner and possessor. Don't you see, Merry? If they find out the diamond has been stolen, who do you think they'll suspect? I've been the one on its trail for two years. I'm the one they can place at the scene of its last owner's murder."

"But you're innocent," Merry said.

Simon shook his head wearily. "The police are just human beings, Merry. They go with whatever information and suspect they've got. In this case, I'd be their first and last stop."

Merry considered Simon's story, beginning to understand the kind of trap he was in. The evidence did point to him. If she didn't know him as she did, would she be so willing to believe in his innocence?

She shook her head in confusion. She had always thought going to the police was the only thing an innocent person should do. After the last couple of days dealing with Sergeant Calder, however, she had begun to see the police weren't always that reliable. It was an extremely disquieting lesson to learn.

"Are you sure the Metropolitan Police are looking for you?" she asked.

"They're looking for me, all right. They had a description of me and the Porsche sent out over the police bands the day of the hit-and-run. I know because I was listening."

Merry shook her head in dismay. "Oh, Simon."

Simon shrugged as though he was balancing a heavy weight on his shoulders. "I was lucky the security guard didn't get my license number. But I decided I couldn't rely on any more luck. I put the Porsche in my brother's shop and had him order a replacement fender. I kept the damaged fender sealed in a plastic bag to maintain the evidence. Then I went back to Atlanta, waiting for the new fender to come in and for word on the movement of the Fire Diamond. Last week I heard it had been donated to the Smithsonian. That's why I came back."

"And immediately got embroiled in a mysterious death and the abduction of a woman by two men in front of the Fire Diamond. No wonder you didn't stay around to talk with the police," Merry said as she shook her head sadly. "I'm surprised you stepped in at all to help me, considering the chance you were taking."

Simon studied Merry's frowning face as he leaned back on the sectional. "Are you really surprised?" he asked, standing above her.

She heard the sad, inquiring tone in his voice and saw the serious look on his face. Shaking her head, she smiled up into the clear blue of his eyes.

"No, Simon. I'm not really surprised you helped me. You're a courageous man and a chivalrous one, too. Your nature wouldn't have let you do anything else."

He leaned down to her smiling face, cupping it with his hands, kissing it tenderly, feeling her arms circling around his back, urging him closer. It was an urging he could no longer fight against. She had just accepted the worst about him and had understood all his actions. It was too powerful a combination. All his tenuously controlled passions rose in one swelling mass, engulfing him in his need of her. As he drew her to him, those passions swept away all thought save that which told him of her uncensored response.

Merry's senses reeled at Simon's touch and feel. She had wanted this man and now he was a part of her, as necessary as her breath, pulsing inside her like the steady beat of her blood, joined to her in a physical fulfillment like none she had known before. She was swept away in its power, consumed in its joy and oblivious to all else around her. All her feelings coalesced in that moment of their joining into one coherent thought: At long last she had found love.

SIMON AWOKE TO FIND MERRY cradled in his arms, in front of the living room's fireplace. He looked down at her sleeping face and felt his heart swell.

He was just about to lean down to kiss her awake when all the pleasure of his recent joining with her was wiped out with the sudden memory of the blade on the bottom of the pendulum still swinging over his head. How could he say to her all the things that filled his heart knowing that at anytime his identity could be discovered by the police?

He had been selfish embroiling her in his troubles. By doing so, he might have even made her an accessory. The very thought turned his stomach. When they came to arrest him, they could arrest her. How could he subject her to such disgrace?

There was only one thing he could do. He had to go to the police and face the consequences of his earlier actions. Unless he could free himself of this blot on his character, he could never hope to be a part of her life. And if he couldn't free himself? He had no choice. There was no other way to protect Merry, and that must be the sole guide to his actions. Now.

Carefully, he rose from beside her. Gently he wrapped his robe around her. She stirred for a moment in some dream far away and he held his breath. If she were to awake now, he didn't know if he had the words to make her understand what he must do. He thankfully exhaled his held breath as she cuddled up to his robe, still a captive of dreams.

He dressed quickly and found himself stealing one last glimpse of her sleeping form and hoping he would be there to greet her when she woke in the morning, but fearing otherwise. Sadly, he silently stole out of the house.

MERRY WAS FLOATING on some lovely blue lake, the warm sun brushing the waters with its radiating heat, when all of a sudden a huge shadow covered the sun and the waters began to swirl black and murky, pulling on her arms. A dreadful fear gripped at her heart as a terrible sense of foreboding invaded her subconscious. She woke from the nightmare, feeling her heart pound and a cold sweat pop out on her skin, only to find that it hadn't been a nightmare at all.

Her startled eyes blinked up into the ugly face of her dark-haired pursuer, who was pulling on her arm and dragging her to her feet as he pointed the barrel of his gun at her heart.

# Chapter Sixteen

Shaking, still not quite aware of where she was or what was going on, Merry pulled Simon's robe about her as the hard fingers of her abductor bruised the flesh on her arm and his raspy voice grated in her ears.

"Here she is!" he yelled. "I found our little sleeping beauty in front of the fireplace."

Merry didn't have to wonder for long who he was calling out to. At that moment the other man came stomping down the stairs from the story above. He had obviously been checking the bedrooms. Somehow her abductors had found her here. But where was Simon? She knew of only one way to summon him and it fit in well with her current terror. She screamed.

"Damn banshee! Shut up or I'll give you something to scream about," the shorter one said as he stuck his gun in his pocket and savagely cupped her mouth with his now-free hand. The blond man was quickly at her side, pinning her arms behind her back to free his partner's other hand.

"She's got to tell us where it is," he said to his companion.

Merry tried to think through the terror pounding at her heart. Surely Simon heard her scream. Surely he should be calling the police even now. Perhaps if she could stall these men for a while, she could give Simon time to come to her rescue.

The dark-haired man's hard fingers were digging into the sides of her cheeks. His voice rasped in her ear as she saw him reach once again for his gun. "I'm going to take my hand away from your mouth. If you scream again, I'm going to shoot you. You got that?"

Merry nodded, trying to control a shaking fear sweeping through every cell of her body. He removed his hand, but his partner still held her hands behind her back.

"Where is it?" he said.

She shook her head. "I don't know."

He pressed the cold nose of the gun barrel against her temple. "Don't give me that. I said where is it?"

Merry heard the revolver click as he cocked it next to her ear. She tried to focus past the terror that was draining the blood from her face. Play for time, a little voice said.

"He has it," she said in a voice she did not recognize.

"Where is he?" he asked.

Merry shook her head. "I don't know. He was supposed to be here."

"Quit the stalling. We've searched the rest of the house. Nobody's here but you. I asked, where is he?"

Merry fought for the right words, but all she could do was shake her head. The blond man twisted her arm. Merry cried out uncontrollably at the sudden pain. "Why don't you let me try a few of my persuasions," he said.

Merry closed her eyes, trying to hang on as her heart thumped like the drum beat from a heavy-metal rock band. Wherever Simon had gone, he was obviously not on hand to help her this time. She was on her own, and she knew she could not tell them what she did not know. When they found that out, her usefulness to them would be at an end. They would kill her.

She heard someone else come into the room and a faint, familiar odor drifted toward her. Confused, she tried to place that smell. Then a new voice reached her ears, and she flashed her eyes open in surprise and encouragement.

"So, Ms. Anders. I suppose these two men are those abductors you've been so adamant about?"

He was standing right in front of her, impeccably groomed as always, his gun drawn and ready.

For one brief moment, relief swept over her. "Sergeant Calder! I'm so glad to see you!"

As soon as she said the words, however, she realized something was wrong. She was still being held. And Sergeant Calder's gun was pointed directly at her.

"Are you glad, Ms. Anders? I can't think why," Sergeant Calder said.

He's in on it. The words sloshed around in her numbed brain. And then bits and pieces of the policeman's perplexing past behavior began to mold themselves into a new meaning. Calder refusing to believe her story of how she had been pursued. His failure to have the bits of skin under her nails tested, or offer her mug books from which she might try to identify her abductors. His insisting on knowing where she would be. And then she realized she was not going to be saved. This man had come to seal her death!

His words stabbed at her like hard, sharp knives. "I guarantee you you'll tell me about your mysterious stranger now, Ms. Anders. Where is Simon Temple?"

Merry studied his face. Despite the fear licking through every nerve of her body, she told herself she must be brave for Simon's sake. They obviously knew who he was now. They would kill her, but she must not give them any information that would help them find him. When she summoned her voice to respond, however, she was dismayed to find it was only a croak.

"How can he possibly matter to you? You know neither of us had anything to do with Skabos's death."

"What is she talking about, John?" the blond man asked.

Calder waved away his question. "She's just stalling. But she won't for long. I'll find out about Temple if I have to beat it out of her."

Merry's thoughts raced. Had Sergeant Calder just been called John?

"Look, John, you're wasting time," the short one said. "We don't need to know anything about the guy, just where the diamond's stashed. I think she's the one with it."

Merry's mind reeled. At that moment her thoughts scrambled to gather several scattered facts. The first was Calder coming so immediately upon the scene of Skabos's death at the Smithsonian's Gem Room with a broken tie chain. Had it been broken in his struggle with Skabos? And what had Calder said about having assumed his duties as a policeman nine years before, exactly the same time that Skabos's partner, the handsome, well-dressed, suave seducer of wealthy women, had been released from prison?

If so, his connections with organized crime must have been excellent to have fabricated a past and an identity good enough to qualify him for law enforcement. It seemed incredible but inescapable. Mike Calder was John Kahr!

Her racing thoughts were interrupted by Calder's argument with the shorter man.

"Look, I tell you he's the one who saw me run down Richfield, the guy who described my green-and-gray Subaru in that anonymous letter to the department."

"You weren't sure before," the short man said. "You told us you only got a quick glimpse of his Porsche and the Georgia license plate."

Calder's voice sounded more and more angry. "He drives a black Porsche. I got his name from the Georgia registration on the license number—a *Georgia* license. We found this place by matching Temple's last name with last name of the guy who was checking all those garages to see if a green-and-gray Subaru had been brought in for repairs. Theodore Temple has got to be a relative. What the hell more do you want? I tell you Simon Temple can put me behind bars. I've got to get him."

"No, John," the dark-haired man said. "We've got to get the Fire Diamond. And we'd better or your tail will be on the line. This job was your idea from the first and from the first, things have been going wrong."

"Oh, I think things have gone pretty well considering," John Kahr, alias Mike Calder, said.

The thug's raspy tone dripped sarcasm. "Oh, sure. Considering the Richfield guy wouldn't let the damn thing out of his hands long enough for us to make the switch. The grieving widow decided to donate the diamond to the Smithsonian overnight, almost getting us caught putting the duplicate in place. And then this broad kills Skabos and pockets the real jewel before we have a chance to get it back. Yeah, everything's gone real well."

"Oh, lighten up," John Kahr said. "We've got her now. And she'll tell us everything, including where the Fire Diamond is before she dies."

Neither the dark-haired man's expression nor tone gave any indication John Kahr's words had placated him. "Yes, but if you hadn't insisted on being the only one to deal with Skabos, we'd have the jewel now. We could have watched him every minute and picked up this babe as soon as she materialized. As it is, we have no idea where she came from. Truth is, this damn scam has been nothing but a pain in the neck."

John Kahr almost smiled. "Don't you mean pain in the leg?" he said as he gave his accomplice's leg a small knock with the side of his shoe.

Merry heard the other man groan. "Damn it, John! If you don't stop poking me in my shot leg, I'm going to smash your face!"

Merry heard Kahr's unconcerned laughter as he turned back to her, his gun raising to her chest. The blond man still held her arms behind her back. She was no match for the three men facing her. Not physically, anyway. But she had learned a great deal in the last few minutes' conversation between them. They couldn't bind her mind, and that's where her strength lay.

She faced Kahr, fear shaking her voice, making it surprisingly convincing. "I won't let you double-cross me like you've double-crossed everyone else."

"Double-cross?" the short man echoed the words. "I thought you told me she only knew you as Mike Calder? What's this all about?"

Kahr's expression flashed a moment of startled fear. He laughed uneasily. "Don't be a fool. She's trying to pull a fast one."

"No, he's the one," Merry said. "He's the one pulling a fast one. He's the one with the diamond."

She was coming to that unmistakable conclusion at the moment she was saying the words. Merry saw the heads of the two men beside her turn in the direction of John Kahr.

The handsome man tried to smile nonchalantly. "You're a lousy liar, honey. Everybody knows you were Skabos's squeeze, not mine. You double-crossed him."

Merry knew she had to remain on the attack. She stared at the man before her. "Skabos wasn't the one who charmed the ladies, John. That was always your role."

Kahr snickered, but Merry could see the sweat that glistened on his upper lip. "You don't know anything about me, honey. Look, I'll leave you guys to the questioning. I have to get back to the office. Call me when she tells you where the diamond is."

The tall man gathered Merry's arms together so he could hold on to her with just his right hand. He spun her around as he faced Kahr, pressing his large left hand on the man's chest in a restraining motion.

"What's your hurry, John? A moment ago you were so hot to know where Temple was you didn't even seem to care about the diamond. Some reason for that? Like you already know where it is maybe?"

Perspiration sprouted on Kahr's forehead as the short man also got to his feet. Merry thought she detected the light of suspicion gathering in his eyes.

Kahr's voice was a little less than even. "Don't talk nonsense. Of course I want to find out where the diamond is and what's happened to Temple. But I just remembered that the Richfield woman might be out looking for this one. I've got to be on hand to direct the investigation away from here. You guys know I've got to maintain my cover on the force."

"You mean you've just decided you've got to leave town with the Fire Diamond, don't you, John?" Merry said.

She had their full attention now. The tall man jerked her around to face him. She winced as his strong fingers dug into her flesh.

"Okay, spill it. I'm only going to ask once. What's this all about?"

Merry knew what she was about to say was the truth. She stood as tall as she could in her bare feet, her shoulders back, her voice clear and unwavering, just as it had been for the pleading of a hundred court cases. "It's about John Kahr's clever plot to kill off his old partner, Ian Skabos, and steal the Fire Diamond for himself."

"She's lying! Let me at her. I'll get the truth!" Kahr said as he lunged at Merry, trying to silence her. But before he could reach her, the short thug put out a restraining arm and blocked his path.

"Maybe she's lying, maybe not. I want to hear what she's got to say. Plenty of time later to apply other persuasions. Sit down, John."

Kahr stood his ground a moment more, giving Merry an evil, murderous look, the look of the attic portrait she had suspected existed all along. The malevolent spirit that dwelt behind it caused a nervous shiver.

"I said, sit down, John," the dark-haired man repeated.

Kahr reluctantly stepped back two paces and half sat against the edge of the room's pale blue sofa. The shorter man seemed satisfied enough and turned to Merry.

"All right. You've got a chance to talk. Spit it out."

Merry's mind raced, trying to place the facts she had learned over the last several minutes into their logical order. The thoughts formed as she spoke the words.

"John Kahr killed Ian Skabos in the Gem Room of the Museum of Natural History last Saturday, breaking his tie chain in the brief struggle. He did it so he could steal the Fire Diamond for himself."

The dark-haired man frowned at her. "What proof do you have he killed Skabos?"

Merry knew Kahr had to be guilty, but at the moment proof was something she couldn't offer. She inhaled and tried to imbue her words with her conviction. "It's the only logical conclusion from the facts."

He wasn't convinced. "We're not novices. From the moment Skabos insisted he needed the real jewel to make a flawless copy of the Fire Diamond, we've watched both him and John constantly. Skabos had the diamond Saturday morning. When we found John at the entry to the Gem Room, saying you had killed Skabos, you can bet we searched him to make sure he didn't have the jewel. He didn't. That just left you. And that is the logical conclusion from the facts."

Merry knew she had to speak up quickly. "Except there is an additional fact," she said.

"Oh, yeah? What?" the tall thug asked.

The fear was forming heavy and sick in her stomach. She couldn't let it incapacitate her. She had to try to think through why John Kahr did not have the jewel on him when he left the Gem Room. He had to have been the one who took it. Where had it gone?

"Tell me something," she said to the dark-haired man. "Skabos made a flawed copy of the jewel and he made a flawless one. Did he create both using Sara Jones's photographs?"

He shook his head. "He used the photographs to create the flawed copy. But he said he had to make a better one for it to pass a collector's eye and give us all time to disappear. That's why we put the flawed copy in place of the real Fire Diamond while Skabos worked on the second fake."

Merry was beginning to understand. "So you made a second switch, putting the flawless copy in place of the imperfect one while the diamond was still in the possession of Richfield?"

"Yeah," the dark-haired man said. "That's when Skabos told John we were going to have to pay him more to get the original back. He had gotten greedy. John agreed to meet him at the Gem Room and pay him off. We were waiting outside to take care of him for good just as soon as we got the Fire Diamond back. We didn't figure on you getting to him first."

"And what happened to the copy with the flaw?" Merry asked as she began to adjust the pieces into a better fit.

He waved his gun impatiently. "What's with all these questions. You trying to stall for time?"

Merry's voice pressed for an answer. "What happened to it?"

He shrugged. "John has it. Now you better start explaining what this 'fact' is or I'm going to . . ."

It had been the answer she was expecting. Suddenly all the pieces meshed into an indisputable whole.

"That's the missing fact I was looking for!" she said. "That explains why you didn't find the Fire Diamond on either Skabos or John Kahr. John Kahr used the real Fire Diamond to choke Skabos to death!"

The dark-haired man's face puckered into a disbelieving frown. "What are you talking about? Skabos was choked to death with a woman's scarf," he said.

Merry shook her head. "No. If Kahr told you that, he was lying again. Skabos was choked to death when someone shoved a large red-centered diamond down his throat. All this time I thought it was the flawed replica of the Fire Diamond because that's what the Smithsonian gemologist found when he examined the rock taken from Skabos's throat. But now I realize Kahr made another switch. Skabos was killed with the real Fire Diamond."

"The real Fire Diamond?" the tall man said.

Merry was nodding eagerly. "It all makes sense now. Kahr saw his opportunity to steal it when Skabos was holding out for more money. When he went to the Gem Room Saturday, he did it knowing he would take the Fire Diamond and kill his ex-partner."

Merry's conviction clouded the men's faces with confusion. She didn't give them time to find other explanations.

"Think! You both searched Skabos's body while it lay on top of me. Did you see a woman's scarf about his neck?"

Neither answered, but the confusion seemed to mount on their faces as they searched their memories.

"Don't you see?" Merry said. "The plan was perfect. As the sergeant from Homicide on the case, Kahr probably just walked in afterward and substituted the flawed copy for the real diamond before the authenticity of the jewel could be verified. He might have done it in the evidence room or even right after the autopsy. All he needed was a second to handle the jewel and for someone to turn his back."

The tall man's voice sounded suspicious. "How do we know what you're saying is true?"

"You can verify it. The police report contains the information about the diamond-shaped stone being found in Skabos's throat. Check it out through a source other than Kahr. Or better yet, why don't you search Kahr now?"

The men turned to Kahr, but it was too late. They had been so intent on watching Merry that they had failed to observe the third man in the room. John Kahr stood with gun drawn, an ugly smile on his handsome face.

"That won't be necessary. This is what you're looking for," Kahr said as he held the sparking diamond in his left hand. "Beautiful, isn't it?"

The Fire Diamond caught the light, boldly splashing red sparks in all directions, mesmerizing its onlookers. Merry tried to step back as Kahr leveled the gun more pointedly in the direction of the short man, whose weapon was half raised in his hand.

"Drop it," Kahr said. "Nice and slow."

The man set the gun down very reluctantly.

Kahr smiled. "I'm afraid the lady attorney has argued her case a little too well. She's managed to sign both of your death warrants, as well as her own."

His intent was only too plain, and the two men who faced him knew what their fate was to be. As though of one mind, they rushed the gun. Kahr got the dark-haired thug on the deafening first shot. He fell with a heavy thud to the floor. By the time Kahr had rotated the gun to point in the other man's direction, he had thrown himself on top of Kahr and was wrestling with him for the weapon.

Merry began to run just as the gun went off a second time, piercing her already deafened ear drums. Out of the corner of her eye, she saw the blond man slump to the floor in front of Kahr, his hands still gripping Kahr's leg. Kahr shot again, this time directly into the thug's face.

Merry turned away in terror as she ran for the front door, knowing in her heart that the next bullet would reach her before she could escape.

But as she ran into the hallway, she felt a strong pair of arms tackling her legs and pushing her to the floor. She landed hard on her side, the wooden planks effectively knocking the breath out of her. A fourth deafening roar pounded somewhere above her, seeming to block out stimulus from all her other senses. She closed her eyes tightly, confused as to what had happened. The next thing she knew, Simon's clean scent reached her nose. She opened her startled eyes wide to see the dark outline of his profile lying next to her face.

Before she had thought to speak, he whispered desperately in her ear. "Lie still. I've got to circle around. Draw him off."

"But, Simon . . ."

Before she was able to form the words, he had noiselessly moved away from behind the couch where they had fallen, somewhere to her right. She fought with a moment of indecision as she tried to decide whether to heed his words or try to help. The room was dark, save for the light from the fireplace. Still, Kahr had to have seen where they had fallen. Wouldn't he be moving toward her now with gun drawn?

Just as the thought had formed, Merry heard a noise on the other side of the room and the quick, deafening blast of the gun. Her horror over the last few minutes seemed to magnify at the sudden, horrible thought that Simon might have been shot. She lay where she was in frozen dread until she heard a scuffle and the upsetting of a table lamp. She jumped to her feet, finding she could stay still no longer.

What she saw brought her heart to her throat. The two men were locked in a desperate struggle for the gun, silhouetted against the blaze of the fireplace, like two fearsome shadow characters in some grotesque play. Who would win?

Simon was taller and broader than Kahr, but Kahr had his hands on the gun and he was fighting desperately to aim it at Simon. His finger was on the trigger. If he could manage to point the barrel anywhere at Simon, he could get off a shot and wound him. It was obviously what he was trying to do. Merry found herself wincing at the thought.

Then she heard Kahr utter a foul oath as Simon dodged a heavy kick aimed for his shin, and the two men went down in a heap on the carpet.

Kahr landed on top, his red, straining face lit in an evil grin as he stared down at Simon. When Merry heard the final deafening blast of the gun, she felt her body recoil in dread. Simon had been shot! She grasped the edge of the couch as her knees gave out, but she found she could not avert her eyes from the two forms before her, despite the terror that drove ice into her veins.

Then Kahr suddenly fell over onto the rug, motionless. For several seconds Merry just stared at him, not believing that it was he who had been shot. But then Simon began to crawl to his feet and life seemed to return to Merry's body. She flew across the room to his side and threw her arms around him.

"Oh, God, Simon. I thought it was you."

He was still breathing hard, but he managed a slight smile as he circled his arm around her.

"It's all right. It's all over. The police will be here soon," he said.

Merry leaned back out of his arms. "The police?"

Simon nodded. "Yes, Merry. I had just left the house to turn myself in when I saw these three break through a front window. I hurried back and climbed up the fire escape and quietly entered through an open window upstairs. I called the police from there and started to make my way down here. That's when I heard the shots and thought I might be too late...."

He hugged her to him then, fiercely and possessively. Merry felt the breath squeezed out of her, but she didn't mind. At that moment all she wanted to do was to feel him warm and alive next to her.

But it wasn't to last. With a sudden loud bang the door burst open and three uniformed policemen rushed into the room with weapons drawn. Merry just stared at them, but Simon gently pushed her from him and raised his hands. He addressed them calmly.

"I'm Simon Temple," he said. "I'm the one who called you."

She watched their startled eyes as they looked around the room at the three bodies lying on the floor. In mounting fear, she realized one of the policemen kept his weapon aimed at them as a second approached her suspiciously. He pulled her away from Simon's side as the third officer proceeded to stretch Simon over the fireplace mantle and search him. Merry stood by in horror. Then the policeman handcuffed Simon and began to read him his rights.

As they took him away, she called out to him, but it was no use. He did not answer her call. He did not look back.

## Chapter Seventeen

"Merry, you won the case! Karen's letter says you've won the case! Justice Stone will be writing the majority opinion. Oh, Joseph, what a great wedding present!" Laura said as she turned to her new husband, throwing her arms about his neck, unashamedly enthusiastic as she waved the letter in her hand.

Merry watched her partner embracing Freedman, still wondering how she could have been so blind to their blossoming romance during the last year and secret marriage, planned while she went to the nation's capital to argue his case. She now understood that Laura's lies about Freedman's whereabouts were all to keep their impending marriage a secret. Laura had been extremely sensitive about Joseph being almost nine years younger and was hesitant to let the relationship become known.

But marriage seemed to have changed the cautious Laura Osbourne. One month had passed since Merry's return from the capital. During that time, she had seen her partner bloom under the warmth of her husband's quiet affection. And as Merry watched the light in Joseph's eyes as he looked at his wife, her own new-found loneliness seemed to grow.

The sadness that was never far gripped at her heart as she pushed herself out of her chair and came over to embrace her partner.

Joseph also shyly gave her a hug. "I've sent Ms. Richfield the papers proving I owned the Fire Diamond. I'm sorry I had to keep my acquisition of the stone a secret, but I thought that if the De Beers Company had found out I was securing diamonds from another source, they might have refused to sell me any more, and that would have been the end of my supply and my company. I hope Ms. Richfield can understand that was the only reason I asked her father to keep the sale in confidence?''

"Yes, Mr. Freedman, I mean Joseph," Merry said. "I have explained it all to Karen, but I know she'll be happy for the papers nonetheless. I suppose this is a time for celebration. Shall I open a bottle of champagne?"

"Absolutely not!" Laura said. "Bubbling champagne should never be opened by someone with such a flat voice. Besides, it's almost eleven. I made that appointment for you with that new client I mentioned earlier. He's waiting in your office. You wouldn't want him to get the wrong impression of our firm by smelling alcohol on your breath?"

Merry shook her head. "No, Laura. But I don't feel ready yet to take on a client. I wish you hadn't—"

"Look, you've been moping around here for a month, and enough's enough! Ever since this man Simon sent you word through his lawyer that he didn't want to see you again, you act as though the world has come to an end. It hasn't. The man didn't want you waiting around for a jailbird. He was right. That would have been no life for you, Merry. He did the right thing. For both your sakes."

"Laura, please don't—"

"Don't what, tell you the truth? You barely talk. You keep postponing court appearances. Your cases are collecting dust. You've got to snap out of it, Merry. This is your employer speaking."

Merry grimaced at the truth in Laura's words, although she felt some surprise at her partner's candor. Still, she was letting everyone down and she couldn't deny it. It was just that without hope of seeing Simon again, nothing else seemed to matter anymore. Laura shook Merry's arm lightly, her voice a bit more gentle.

"Look, Merry. We've been giving you time to feel better, but you're not making any progress. Trust me. Work can be a great healer."

Merry's sigh was heavy. "Yes, of course. You say the client's waiting in my office?"

"Yes. A most interesting case. I know you'll enjoy it."

Merry got up, knowing no case held an interest for her anymore, but also realizing she must try to make a show of carrying on, no matter how dead she felt inside. As she approached her office door, she could see the silhouette of a man's head through the glass. She straightened her shoulders and took a deep breath as she swung open the door and walked in.

"Meredith Anders. How may I help you?"

The man, whose back was to the door, rose and turned to face her, holding out his hand. "Simon Temple," his familiar voice said. "And I can think of several ways in which you could help me, Ms. Anders."

Merry stood stock still as she stared at his wonderful, smiling face. She could feel the blood drain from her face as her voice came out in a croak.

"Simon! I don't believe it. You're in jail. How can you be here?"

He stepped forward and took hold of her hands, urging her toward the office couch. "Don't worry, I'm not an escapee, Merry. Damn it, I didn't mean to startle you this way. Sit down. There's a lot I want to tell you. I know I should have called first, but I—I thought it might be better if I said these things to you in person."

Merry went willingly to the couch, trying to keep herself from being too excited by his presence, trying to remind herself of his cool dismissal of her after his arrest, trying to impress on herself his all too clear rejection of her. But still her silly heart skipped inside her chest.

She took a deep breath, controlling her voice as carefully as she could, extricating her hands from his. "I'm all right now, Simon. It was just the shock of seeing you so unexpectedly. Please go on with what you have to say."

He felt her withdrawal and lost much of the hope the first look in her eyes had given him. He had had no time to speak of the depth of his feelings nor to ascertain hers during their incredible adventures of the month before. Could it be he had assumed too much?

"A lot has happened. I hardly know where to begin," Simon said.

Merry heard the distant, cool formality of his tone, like ice water on her revived feelings. She fought more and more for the control that would enable her to deal with Simon in a professional manner and be able to forget all that they had shared, but the disappointment swallowed her heart, turning it into a painful lump inside her breast.

She found her voice. "Perhaps you can tell me about what the police have determined in Daniel Richfield's death."

Simon nodded. "Daniel Richfield was deliberately set up to be killed. I wasn't the only one who had called to meet him on the day of his death. His servants testified he had received a call from an unidentified man about an hour before asking Richfield to meet him outside his security gate to receive information concerning another red-centered diamond being offered for sale. The man who called, the one we now know to be John Kahr, planned and executed his death."

"But why kill Richfield? Why not just steal the Fire Diamond from him?"

"Well, it seems Richfield had begun to suspect something was wrong with his diamond. Once the thugs had replaced it with the fake, Richfield claimed the diamond no longer had the warm feel it did before. He was carrying it around with him while waiting for a gemologist to come to examine it. Your abductors didn't have an opportunity to switch it with the real one so the gemologist would be satisfied and give them the time they needed. That's when John Kahr decided Richfield had to die."

"But when the police arrested you that night in your brother's home, they thought you were the killer?" Merry asked.

Simon shook his head. "No. Unbeknownst to me, there was another witness to the hit-and-run. A woman neighbor was walking her dog and saw the whole thing. She told the police about the green-and-gray Subaru hitting Richfield and then my car and then about my getting out with a doctor's bag and trying to help the struck down man. She had run back to her house to call an ambulance before Richfield's security guard had come on the scene and began yelling his accusations."

Simon's words pricked Merry's memory. "He died even though a doctor was there right on the scene," she said.

"What?" Simon asked.

"Remember the statement contained in that tabloid article on Richfield's death?" Merry asked. "Remember it said something about how a doctor had been there?"

Simon nodded. "Oh, yes. Funny, I didn't even wonder how it got there at the time you told me. The only way that tabloid reporter would have known I tried to medically administer to Richfield was if he had spoken to the woman neighbor or got wind of her testimony somehow. That should have given me a clue that someone else had seen the accident. I guess my guilt at what I was keeping from you overshadowed my ability to evaluate everything you were saying."

Merry tried not to enjoy his small smile so much. She looked down at her hands. "Then you've been cleared?"

Simon shrugged. "There were some uncomfortable moments there when charges of obstructing a police investigation and removing evidence from the scene of a crime were being thrown around. The police were pretty embarrassed to learn they had a convicted felon as one of their homicide detectives. It made them rather . . . testy. I think the only two things that saved my bacon was the fact that I wrote the letter describing what I saw and that I kept intact the dented fender of the Porsche. I led them to it and it helped to establish Calder's green-and-gray Subaru as the murder weapon."

"Did they ever find out where he had his fender fixed?" Merry asked.

Simon shook his head. "No. He had had it fixed right after the accident by a private garage, just as I did mine. However, a forensics workup on the paint and blood taken from the Porsche's fender along with my testimony and that of the neighbor were sufficient to get him arraigned on Richfield's murder, as well as several other counts of murder."

Merry didn't think she had heard right. "He's not dead? You didn't shoot him?"

Simon nodded. "Just a flesh wound. Still, I very much doubt he'll live to stand trial."

"Just a flesh wound? He won't live? Simon, I don't understand any of this."

Simon nodded. "Of course, you wouldn't. I keep forgetting that you can't know what's been going on. You see, the district attorney has been keeping the whole business out of the press intentionally."

"Why? Aren't such proceedings within the public domain?"

"Ordinarily, yes. But the events surrounding the recovery of the Fire Diamond have proved anything but ordinary. Although the police cleared me pretty early on in respect to Richfield's murder and only held me in protective custody until I could testify against Kahr, I've been kept pretty busy most of the time attending to John Kahr. It seems the man is suffering from radiation sickness."

Merry couldn't help hearing the lightness in Simon's tone. She read the gleam in his eyes. "Simon, you found the black box?"

He smiled at her, encouraged by the excitement in her tone, not able to contain his startling news any longer.

"Yes, Merry, but it's just an ordinary shiny black box. As a matter of fact, David Carmichael used it to carry around loose tobacco before he found the Fire Diamond. It's harmless."

"But if the box is harmless, then what is causing the radiation sickness?" Merry asked.

He smiled at her eagerness. "The culprit is none other than our fabulous Fire Diamond."

Merry leaned back against the couch. "I can't believe it."

"It took me a while to get used to it, also. But what I found is that beautiful red heart of our fabulous Fire Diamond contains a highly charged, two-element combination of polonium and beryllium. Such a compound produces a neutron-type of radiation—ten times more damaging than gamma, X-ray or beta radiation. Anyone in close proximity to it for a lengthy period of time would receive a lethal overdose. It's what got Carmichael, Mabunda, the gem cutters, the auctioneer, Daniel Richfield and finally, John Kahr."

Merry sat back, feeling stunned. "It's unbelievable, Simon. You once called the Fire Diamond, Bloodstone. Now I can see how accurate a description that was. How did you find this out?"

"Well, it's like I told you before. People don't transmit radioactivity. Things do. And the only thing other than the black box that tied in Carmichael, Mabunda, the dead gem cutters and the auctioneer was constant—close and long exposure to the Fire Diamond. I had the stone taken out of the police evidence room and examined by a nuclear physicist from the Nuclear Regulatory Commission. I can tell you what he found caused quite a stir in several scientific circles."

"This polonium-beryllium compound?" Merry said.

Simon nodded. "And the possibilities its formation in the diamond represented from a geological point of view. You see, the half life from this neutron-emitting compound is around one hundred years. The physicists who have examined the diamond say the compounds have not reached their half life. That means the diamond was formed sometime within the last hundred years."

"I thought diamonds were supposed to be older than that?" Merry said.

Simon nodded. "That's what is setting the geological community on its ear. Until the Fire Diamond discovery, all gem-quality diamonds were thought to date from Precambrian times. Now Carmichael's discovery has added another dimension for study with this red beauty that defies all the rules."

Merry heard the satisfaction in Simon's voice and thought she detected the reason for it. "You said Carmichael's discovery. Will he get credit for it?"

Simon nodded, his expression relieved and unburdened. "Absolutely. I've seen to it. It was his dying request, after all. I only wish he could have lived to see what a truly remarkable geological find he had made."

Merry looked away from the sudden sad look in Simon's face, trying not to feel so easily moved by his emotions.

"What will happen to the Fire Diamond?" she asked.

"Eventually it will be returned to the Smithsonian for viewing by the public. But it will be encased behind a thick plastic shield with a molecular structure sufficient to absorb the harmful neutrons."

Merry worked hard at asking her next question with an even tone. "I suppose all this means that the CDC is accepting you back with open arms?"

She felt Simon watching her averted face as he answered. "Yes, they've wiped the slate clean. Discovering the Fire Diamond's radiation hazard has made me the fair-haired boy in Atlanta."

Merry sighed, knowing she had no more questions to ask and convinced now his future lay with his job. She still felt his eyes on her and was becoming uncomfortable at his continued scrutiny since she knew she could not feign her false disinterest much longer.

"I'm happy for you," she said as she got to her feet. "Thank you for coming by to tell me. It was most considerate." She extended her hand.

He rose to his feet then and reached out for her hand, grasping it in both of his. "I didn't come out of consideration, Merry. I came because... Merry, don't you care for me anymore?"

Merry looked up, surprised at Simon's question and the inquiring tone in his voice. His very blue eyes stared down at her, full of warmth and worry. They made her heart hurt.

"Of course I care, Simon. But you sent me away. You told me you didn't want to see me again."

Simon shook his head as he gently folded his arms about her. "I did tell my lawyer that, it's true. But I only said it because I didn't know if I was going to be charged and jailed for Richfield's murder. All I could remember was seeing the look on your face when they searched and cuffed me that night in Georgetown. I couldn't sleep for many nights following because I kept hearing your sad and anguished call of my name when they led me away. Darling, at first I thought I had years of jail ahead of me. I couldn't allow you to be a part of that kind of life."

Merry looked up into his anguished face, raising her hand to touch the frown on his brow. "But, Simon, I wanted to be there for you. You've been there for me when I've needed—"

Simon crushed her to him then fiercely. His voice was a hoarse whisper near her ear.

"Merry, I love you. I need you. I want to marry you. That's the real reason I've come here today. Those are all the things I couldn't say over a telephone. Give me time to prove them to you, darling. Please, give me time."

With his words the sadness was lifted from Merry's heart and the pain and loneliness of her last month became nothing but a distant memory. She leaned back in his arms, a happy smile on her face.

"We've got the rest of our lives, starting right this second. But you've got nothing to prove to me, Simon. I know the man you are. Your actions have spoken loudly for you since that first day in the Smithsonian's Gem Room when you risked yourself to save me. You're the man I love and want to marry."

He held her to him then, gently, lovingly, content just to feel her close. But Merry was never quiet for long, particularly not when a champagne-type bubbling had begun within her heart. She was bursting over with happiness.

"To be married to you sounds wonderful. But when shall it be? Where shall we live? There's so much to think about."

Simon looked at her a little guiltily. "Actually, I've already done a bit of thinking about it already. I've leased the vacant offices down the hall to set up my private practice here on Bainbridge Island."

Merry looked at him in surprise. "You're not going back to Atlanta? You're going to practice here . . . in this building?"

Simon shrugged. "I've had enough traveling with the CDC. I want to be near my home, near my wife and, hopefully one day soon, near my children, our children, Merry. Besides, I didn't know how quickly I could win you. I thought I'd best be set up close by for a long siege, just in case. I hope you're not angry?"

Merry shook her head and found herself smiling. "Oh, Simon, I couldn't be happier. You're going to love Washington State."

"How could I help it with you here?" As he leaned down to kiss her, Merry wrapped her arms around him, happier than she had ever been in the warmth of his love. When he finally leaned back, he was smiling contentedly.

"I have the marriage license all ready. We can have the ceremony performed whenever you say, although I must tell you that the justice of the peace is waiting and Laura and Joseph are standing by to be witnesses. But of course, there's no rush. I could tell them all to have lunch first."

Merry shook her head, trying unsuccessfully not to smile. "Humph. What was all this stuff about your needing time to win me over?"

Simon was grinning happily. "I was preparing for all contingencies, knowing I was dealing with a sharp lawyer. However, I have left the site of the honeymoon open. What would you say to the nation's capital? You might even get to do some sightseeing this time."

Merry looked into the handsome face she loved so well. "Wouldn't we be tempting fate just a bit, considering what happened to us there the last time? Or is it that adventurous spirit of yours? Are you trying to get us to live up to what Shakespeare wrote in *As You Like It*, 'We that are true lovers run into strange capers'?"

Simon laughed his warm, happy laugh and leaned over to gather Merry more fully in his arms. "Frankly I hope our strange capers are behind us, darling. I'm more interested in concentrating my energies on the true-love part of that quote."

And in proof of his words, he kissed her then, long, deep, giving kisses full of the promise of an exciting love that was only just beginning.

# Have You Ever Wondered If You Could Write A Harlequin Novel?

Here's great news—Harlequin is offering a series of cassette tapes to help you do just that. Written by Harlequin editors, these tapes give practical advice on how to make your characters—and your story—come alive. There's a tape for each contemporary romance series Harlequin publishes.

**Mail order only**

**All sales final**

## Harlequin Superromance®

**A June title
not to be missed....**

Superromance author Judith Duncan has created her
most powerfully emotional novel yet, a book about
love too strong to forget and hate too painful to
remember....

Risen from the ashes of her past like a phoenix,
Sydney Foster knew too well the price of wisdom,
especially that gained in the underbelly of the city.
She'd sworn she'd never go back, but in order to
embrace a future with the man she loved, she had to
return to the streets...and settle an old score.

Once in a long while, you read a book that affects you
so strongly, you're never the same again. Harlequin is
proud to present such a book, STREETS OF FIRE by
Judith Duncan (Superromance #407). Her book merits
Harlequin's AWARD OF EXCELLENCE for June 1990,
conferred each month to one specially selected title.

S407-1